The Phantom Glare of Day

three novellas

The Phantom Glare of Day

M. Laszlo

SPARKPRESS

Published by SparkPress, a BookSparks imprint,
A division of SparkPoint Studio, LLC
Phoenix, Arizona, USA, 85007
www.gosparkpress.com

Published 2022
Printed in the United States of America

Print ISBN: 978-1-68463-175-9
E-ISBN: 978-1-68463-176-6
Library of Congress Control Number: LCCN: 2022912629

Interior design by Katherine Lloyd, The DESK

To R.G.C.

And they are as my soul that wings its way
Out of the starlit dimness into morn:
And they are as my tremulous being—born
To know but this, the phantom glare of day.

SIEGFRIED SASSOON
"Butterflies"

CONTENTS

book one

The Ghost of Sin

I.

CHAPTER ONE

London, 29 September 1917.

Sophie paused beside a stock-brick building and listened for the unnerving rumble of an airship's engine car. *How long has it been since the last bombardment?* Sometime before, as she had stood in this very spot, she had heard the Zeppelin clearly enough.

At that point, a Royal-Navy carbide flare had streaked heavenward. Then, from the neighboring rooftops, fifty or more pom-pom guns had opened fire–and the night air had filled with the odor of something like petroleum coke.

Yes, I remember. Now she braced herself for a salvo of fire.

No deafening tumult rang out. Neither did any sickening, stenchful fumes envelope her person.

No, it's just my nerves. She glanced at the sky, and she whispered a simple prayer of thanksgiving.

From around the corner, an omnibus approached. She climbed aboard and rode the way to Mayfair Tearoom.

The establishment had never looked so inviting as it did that night. By now, the proprietress had decorated the tables with Michaelmas daisies the color of amethyst, and she had adorned the china cabinet with ornamental cabbage. Moreover, how appetizing the scent of the fresh Eccles cakes.

The tearoom had attracted quite a crowd, too, the young ladies all decked out in silken gowns.

I wonder why. Sophie removed her coat, and she suddenly felt underdressed—for she had not worn anything too fancy that evening, just a puffed blouse and a fluted skirt. At once, she sat down at one of the last available dinette tables.

An eclipse of moths fluttered through the transom, meanwhile, and even *they* looked better than she did. What beauty the creatures' wings—a fine royal purple.

Don't look at them. Alas, when she turned her attention to the doorsill, a dull ache radiated up and down her left arm. Not a moment later, a tall, gaunt lad, his eyes a shade of whiskey brown, entered the tearoom.

For a time, he glared at the patrons—as if, at any moment, he might remove a musketoon from beneath his frock coat and shoot everyone. Slowly, the menacing figure continued over to the last available table—one standing not three feet away from Sophie's.

When they exchanged looks, he grimaced some—as if for no other reason than to bare his dead tooth.

In vain, she sought to feign indifference to his presence.

The young gentleman removed his frock coat. How bony he looked in his shirtsleeves—how sickly and how frail.

She brushed some tea leaves off the tabletop. When she felt his steady gaze upon her yet, she turned her thoughts to the bill of fare. Her last time here, she had enjoyed the cream tea. *And the raspberry jam, with a wee bit of . . .*

The peculiar youth glared at her.

She could not help but feel self-conscious. Soon, a bead of sweat trickled down the nape of her neck.

Oddly, the proprietress did not even trouble herself to take Sophie's order. Instead, the woman walked right past Sophie's table and sat down beside the ominous fellow. And now the proprietress whispered something into his ear.

Finally, he grinned and nodded some.

At that point, the proprietress climbed atop a wooden soapbox standing before all the little tables. Three times, she snapped her fingers. "Well then, why don't we get along with our evening of poetry? Please, everyone, let's welcome back to our humble hideaway the one and only Jarvis Ripley."

As everyone applauded, the mysterious youth climbed atop the soapbox and bowed the incorrect way—with his neck as opposed to his back.

He's a poet?

As the young gentleman stood there waiting for the applause to die down, he looked more like a nervous thief standing in an identity parade.

Now it was Sophie's turn to glare at him. *Have I ever noticed him here before?* She sat back. *Maybe.*

He scrunched up his pug nose, and like any foolish youth, absent-mindedly scratched at some of the crimson boils about his chin. "I well appreciate why you've come here tonight," he spoke up in a sleepy voice. "You know I mean to recite a poem on good and evil, the lawful and the unlawful, crime and punishment, what to proscribe and what to reprove and reproach as some great trespass, aye, and what to consider a just claim. Well then, I'll give you what you yearn to hear."

He proceeded to recite from memory the most sensual prose poem—a tale of vampirism, a vision involving a fiendish creature that lords it over a helpless young lady by sucking up her soul from the depths of her warm, wild heart.

As the young gentleman spoke, Sophie fathomed every allusion—and he did make several references to a Gothic opera, *Der Vampyr*. Did the insolent youth think that no one knew enough German to grasp the instances of plagiarism? She caught each one, for over the years, she had practically taught herself the German tongue by reading various libretti.

When the peculiar youth concluded the poem and everyone applauded anew, the proprietress introduced several other performers.

One young lady climbed atop the soapbox and draped herself

with a white sheet painted a bright, glistening crimson here and there. Then she proceeded to recite from memory a poem all about an imaginary mob pelting her to death with stones.

In the end, the young lady drooped over and held herself perfectly still—and almost everyone in the tearoom gasped at the unspeakable abomination of it all.

The theatrics failed to impress Sophie. *What a to-do*. Impulsively, she eyed the young gentleman from before. *Jarvis*.

Once the very last of the poets had performed, the intimidating youth walked over to her table. A butter knife in his hand, he poked her elbow. "You stopped by here tonight for a good reason," he told her. "Just from looking at you sitting here all alone like this, I know you're no sentimental hairpin. The precise opposite, you'd be. Right, you'd be a bluestocking. And that's why you rolled in here tonight. I know it. You were hoping to learn something about all those willing to turn their hand to wickedness and avenge whatever the reproof."

"No, I didn't even know there'd be any poetry this evening," she told him. "It's just that what with all the broadsides and bombardments of late, I thought I ought to step out and have a drink and make merry and—"

"That's a fib. I'd say the grave conditions what face England, all them bloody German volleys of late, they got you thinking about the big issues, the perils of—"

She held up her hand. "How old would you be? *Seventeen?* Listen, you've got no business trifling with a woman of my station. Furthermore, you can't just invite yourself to sit down at someone's table and—"

"No, love. Your own bloody misery betrays all. Deep down, you well appreciate the fact that things like vengeance and—"

"What gives you the right to impugn my integrity? You know nothing about me, and you have no idea just why I'd happen to—"

"Go on with your empty words." For a time, the young

gentleman hummed the tune to what sounded like the overture to the Italian opera *Turandot.*

At last, she smiled. "I know you nicked much of your poem from that German fantasy opera, the one about the vampire that has to sacrifice the three virgin brides before—"

"You know what I think? You're much too bookish. That's your trouble." Quickly, the menacing youth collected his frock coat and ducked out the back door.

Five minutes later, once Sophie had settled the bill, she departed the tearoom. When she reached the bus stop, she paused beside a rusty fingerpost and looked to the sky. The clouds shone bright silver, and one had even assumed the shape of a pillory. She thought of the youthful poet. *What a maniacal fellow.*

Riderless, a horse-drawn carriage rolled by. As she watched it vanish around the corner, she wondered if a walk might do her some good.

From down the street, the howl of a carbide flare rang out. Had the Royal Navy spotted an airship looming in the clouds? She braced herself for the burst of drumfire sure to commence.

Nothing of the kind happened, and the light of the flare bled into darkness. Perhaps the whole incident would prove to be yet another false alarm.

Like so many times before, she studied the clouds—and like so many times before, she strained to hear the rumble of a Zeppelin's engine car. When she finally looked down, she continued along. One block ahead, not far from a derelict, jasmine-yellow townhouse, a band of youths darted off behind a broken-down, electric hackney carriage.

A moment later, a lone figure appeared beneath the lamppost—and the powerful glare bathed his eyes and face in a metallic glow.

She soon recognized him as Jarvis Ripley. *Of course.* Slowly, she advanced.

The insolent youth curled his lip. "What's wrong with you then?" he asked her. "Got a case of trench fever, have you?"

"Why would you be mucking about at this hour?" she asked, a cold bead of sweat dripping down her left sideburn. "Don't you fear the Zeppelins?"

Another unsettling, high-pitched howl rent the night: yet another bright, blinding carbide flare streaking across the sky.

Jarvis drew close and sniffed at her throat. "I don't care a blue damn what the Germans do to this city. In fact, I admire their vengeful ways. Did you know them Huns got the best intelligencers? They come and go stealthily, and they do whatever they'd do in such a way that no one should ever pin nothing on them."

Over to the left, the band of youths from before emerged from behind the broken-down, electric hackney carriage.

Jarvis turned and pointed at them. "Look there. Each one of me best mates wears a velvet waistcoat as ornate as anything a vampire of the Victorian age might've worn." When he turned back, he studied her face. "You got Oriental eyes," he told her. "Just like one of them snuff-and-butter maidens, a girl from Azerbaijan or someplace abutting." At that point, Jarvis reached out his hand and removed something from her jawline—a tea leaf.

How could such a young chap act all so presumptuously toward a woman of twenty-one years? The more boldly he behaved, the more frigid and bitter and repressed she felt.

Jarvis peered deep into her eyes. "Do you know what makes them German intelligencers so deadly? The very best of them would be whores. They call upon some bloody hapless gent, an officer or whatever, and then she gives the bastard a taste of the juice in exchange for the jelly, and anywise, she learns just what he's got to say. All them German whores, they probably got themselves gilded bollocks."

From behind the hackney carriage, one last figure emerged—someone all decked out in a preposterous bat disguise. And now the personage leaped about, all the time flapping his large, rubbery bat wings.

Sophie laughed nervously, and then she turned back to Jarvis. "Why do you and your mates obsess about vampirism? I find it all terribly sinister and—"

"You fancy staying up until all hours? If so, come waltzing with us. Have you ever visited a proper dance hall? I prefer the Bessarabia Ballroom, just off Regent Street. Have you heard of it? Everyone dances in the height of Gothic fashion there, just like the bloodsuckers of old."

The last of the carbide flares fell from the sky, and the clouds returned to darkness.

Jarvis tapped Sophie's wrist. "Join me at the Bessarabia. They got a Yankee-style cocktail bar there, and I'm sure you'd be quite pleasant over a pint."

She continued walking. "I wish to sleep," she told him, over her shoulder.

Jarvis followed her all the way back to her place of residence. Then, as she approached the door, he read aloud the words painted over the architrave: "Chelsea Court Hotel."

She let out a sigh. "Nag off already." When he failed to answer, she turned around to chide him—but he had already slipped away, into the shadows.

CHAPTER TWO

London, 18 October.

When Sophie awoke that morning, she sat up and studied the side jamb to the left of the window. All throughout the night, she had heard a series of uncanny cries and soft murmurs seemingly resounding from within that very part of the wall.

Whatever it had been, the vocalizations had sounded bestial— perhaps, even diabolical.

She walked out into the sitting room and paced back and forth awhile. Several times over, she arranged and rearranged the floor mirror. Before long, she turned to her Victorian press-back chair and pictured Jarvis sitting there. Ever since she had encountered the youth some two and a half weeks before, she had felt anxious. Until that evening, she had never spoken to anyone so obsessed with the idea of vengeance. *Jarvis.*

Someone knocked upon the door now.

For a moment or two, Sophie held her breath. Then, when the chambermaid continued inside, Sophie exhaled.

The servant drew close. "Has something gone wrong?" she asked. "Beset by problems, are you? Do your stockings want darning?"

Sophie guided the chambermaid into the bedchamber. With the tip of her finger, she tapped the casing. "I'm not alone," she whispered. Then she placed the palm of her hand flush against the side jamb. "I do believe I've got some kind of hobgoblin buzzing about the studs and wiring."

The chambermaid made a face, and then she departed.

Sophie returned into the sitting room, sat down at her writing table, and studied the lump of dead skin protruding from the side of her finger—the very place where her pencil had always rubbed up against the tender flesh. There could be no avoiding the unsightly injury, for she had recently begun to pen a journal:

The Days and Nights of Miss Sophie Shreve: a London Diary

She had always longed to succeed as an authoress. In all likelihood, she had inherited the inclination from her late father. Years ago, he had distinguished himself as a most urbane social critic. Still, given his knowledge of just how decadent modern times could be, he had sheltered her overcautiously. With regard to her schooling, she had enjoyed private instruction. Then, not two weeks before his death, he had arranged for a trust fund to provide her with a flat here at the hotel. What a pity, though. Because of how thoroughly her doting father had shielded her from the world, she had nothing to write *about*. If only she had something profound to inspire her—the kinds of struggles that informed her favorite novels.

From back inside her bedchamber, the chorus of peculiar cries and gentle murmurs recommenced.

What could that be?

At midday, she rode the lift downstairs and asked after both the hotel detective and the maintenance man—but according to the manageress, neither one of the dependable chaps had reported for duty just yet.

After waiting awhile, Sophie walked off into the hotel café. Much to her dismay, she could not muster an appetite—even after the hostess had served her the house specialty: roasted rack of lamb.

Little by little, a pall darkened the hotel café's picture window.

Finally, a hard, fast, cacophonous, autumn rain began falling.

Sophie's thoughts turned back to Jarvis. Might the vengeful, young gentleman be capable of committing some grisly crime?

Perhaps it was only her dread regarding the somber, mercurial youth that had her hearing things.

As the downpour abated, both the hotel detective and the maintenance man walked into the hotel café.

When they stopped at her table, she blushed. By now, she felt half certain that she had hallucinated the whole commotion back in her room. With greatest reluctance, she guided the party upstairs. Once everyone had gathered beside the window, she pointed to the side jamb and shrugged nervously.

Without a word, the maintenance man guided her out onto the balcony. There, he proceeded to work all the rusty nails loose from the shutter.

When the hotel detective came along, the maintenance man laid the panel at his feet to reveal a brown bat bundled up in its wings—the harmless creature clinging to one of the louvers, where it had been facing the siding.

"Glory be," the hotel detective declared. "That's all it was. Nothing but a flittermouse purring away there."

"Of all things," she whispered. "So, we'd better put everything back before the little one wakes up and—"

"I'll show you how to handle vermin," the maintenance man interrupted. Quickly then, he grabbed a hammer and a nail from out of a pocket in his leather apron and promptly pounded the point into the bat's heart.

Despite the horror of it all, she could not turn away. As the helpless creature twitched this way and that, she gazed into its blinded eyes and felt its anguish. Soon, she even twirled her left forearm around—the same pitiful way in which the bat's left forelimb whirled about.

The hotel detective turned to her and cleared his throat. "What's the trouble? You're looking all abroad."

She did not respond. Instead, she turned to the maintenance man. "Why did you kill this innocent, little c-c-creature?"

He laughed. "Why'd I kill it? Because it'd be a bloody louse, right? Its life ain't worth a continental note, don't you know? Hell's bells, since when do high-society girls cotton up to a no-good pest like this one here?"

The bat's left forelimb grew still.

She pulled the nail from the animal's body then and dropped the warm, bloodied spike into an empty, clay flowerpot.

And now the bat's left forelimb drooped to the side, lifeless.

She caressed the creature's wing membrane, only to find that it felt *human*—not unlike the soft, pink webbing between her own thumb and first finger.

From the direction of the sitting room, the dumbwaiter resounded—and soon the scent of charred mutton drifted out through the balcony doors.

"Have a whiff of that," the maintenance man announced. "Smells just like shark's fin soup. Makes me think of Japan. All them fishermen there, they got sliced fins lying here and there, and all about the waterfront. Meantime, just imagine all them sharks finned alive and then cast back into the sea, all them daft beasties powerless to swim straight, while they're bleeding to death." The maintenance man burst into laughter the way the heartless do.

With the lifeless bat cradled in her hand, Sophie walked into the sitting room. With her free hand, she opened the little mahogany door in the wall and checked the dumbwaiter table: the hostess had sent up the lamb. Sophie left it where it was, and she walked over to her father's wooden footlocker.

For the first time in four years, she opened the chest and removed his spade bayonet.

Twenty minutes later, she walked into the gardens at Chelsea Square and continued along the tapestry-brick footpath through the beech trees. When she reached the glade where she often came to read the papers, she knelt amid a patch of plume thistle. With the spade bayonet, she carved out a shallow grave fit for a small animal.

Once she had placed the bat down inside, she pulled upon its wings and hind legs so that the poor creature might look as dignified as possible.

No sooner had she filled the plot than a ray of sunlight shone down upon the spade bayonet's crosspiece—and it flashed a blinding silver.

The trick of the light awoke a memory of that time she visited her cousin, Augie, at his public school. Midafternoon, she had followed him into the crowded fencing hall, where the instructor had arranged a trial for all the lads hoping to join the team.

At first, most of the youths and prefects had sat about—each one cleaning his silver foil with a leaf of glass paper.

Later, when the sullen, old instructor came along, everyone grabbed a mask and a set of gloves from the trolley table and commenced action—their fine sabers and competition *épées* clattering against one another. What a shrill din, the swordplay.

"You mean to stick me in the gut?" one of the youths had asked his mate. "Well then, let's have ourselves a barney. Prepare to feel the wrath of my blade. En garde."

Moments later, once Cousin Augie had demonstrated a series of feints and thrusts, the instructor had pointed to the door: she had already rejected him and all so disdainfully, too.

Augie had flashed a sheepish smile, and then the humble lad had dropped his ornate *épée* into a fluted urn standing in for a rubbish bin. Afterward, without a word, he had departed.

Left alone there, Sophie had approached the rubbish bin. Gingerly, she had taken his weapon by the pommel and had wrapped her hand around the finely swept, serpentine hilt.

For her part, the plainly indifferent instructor had already hobbled over to one of the youths who had apparently secured her approbation.

Together, they had laughed it up awhile.

Then the youth had lunged back and forth a few times, as if to run through some adversary.

Sophie had observed the second lad closely, hoping that he might prove himself to be manifestly superior to Augie. If so, then why doubt the instructor's judgment?

Much to Sophie's surprise, the second youth had not demonstrated an especially impressive technique at all.

In the end, she had dropped Augie's *épée* to the pressed-wood floor. "How sinister the process of selection," she had whispered then.

At that point, she should have approached the old woman. "How could you be so *random* in banishing people from your midst?" she should have asked. "Haven't you any sense of right and wrong? Haven't you any decency? There's no reason to be so cruel and . . ."

Back at Chelsea Square, the trick of the light altered some—and now the spade bayonet's crosspiece flashed a dazzling, metallic gold.

Like my diary, its gilt-edged pages.

Her thoughts turned back to Jarvis. *What if he stood here just now?*

He would flash a crooked smile. "You fretting about me then?" he would ask. "Do you fear I'll kill some bloody bastard? Aye, but how should a chap like me manage something so foul as all that? I'm no vampire. No, no. A poet, I'd be. Nothing more. I channel all my scars, all my alienation into my work."

"What scars?" she would ask. "What alienation?"

"What do you mean?" he would ask in turn. "Have you never attended no bloody heartless public school?"

"No, but you ought to be thankful you get to live a life filled with trying experiences and such."

"How's that?" he would ask. "You think I ought to be grateful for the opportunity to debase myself in front of all the bullies and bashers and bloody contemptuous schoolmasters and the like?"

"Maybe. What better way to learn about the self than public humiliation? By testing the very limits of nonconformity, perhaps you'll learn something about how the malevolent and the insecure feed on the anomalous. Not unlike a vampire feeding on some helpless girl."

Displeased, he would walk off then.

She returned to the hotel. Back in her sitting room, she stood before her writing table and gazed upon the pencil caddy. *It's too quiet.* She returned to the side jamb.

If only another bat might come along, its cries and murmurs reverberating softly through the wall. No such visitor came calling, though.

Even in the night, whenever she checked and listened very closely, neither any cries nor any rhythmic purring greeted her.

The next day, the telephone rang: Jarvis Ripley calling to trifle with her and to confabulate in his way. No matter his impudence, she felt thankful that the young gentleman had reached out. For one thing, she well discerned his loneliness. Second, she could recognize a cry for help when she heard it. On and on, they spoke of this and that and whatever else.

In the end, he must have grown weary of her: just like that, the line went dead.

She returned to the side jamb, and she placed her ear against the casing—and now the silence put her to shame.

CHAPTER THREE

London, 13 November.

At dusk, Sophie resolved to visit the Bessarabia Ballroom. All day long, she had been toying with the idea. Indeed, for the past week or so, she had been debating whether she ought to make Jarvis Ripley and his friends the focus of her diary. What could be more marketable than an exciting exposé about the burgeoning, Gothic youth culture?

As the last glow of twilight died out, she dressed herself in the only gown that she owned—a wilted crepe in faded, violet blue. Given its age and unfashionable style, the habitués of a place like the Bessarabia Ballroom would probably approve. Even if she had a gown with a classic silhouette, why wear something conventional?

Late that night, a taxicab brought her to the ballroom. Left alone on Regent Street, she paused beside a lamppost. *What if Jarvis doesn't even show up?* She felt like a fool, and now she doubted all her designs. Given how troubled Jarvis was, why would he permit her to write some scandalous book about him? Even if she promised to change the names of this person and that, he would never place his trust in her. *All told, we're practically strangers.*

When she finally continued into the ballroom, she found the establishment much too dimly lit. Still, how to deny its charm and opulence?

The ceiling loomed higher than a cathedral vault and boasted a hundred or more dark-rust chandeliers, each one of the fixtures flashing its eerie light down onto a dance floor that shone as white as Tasmanian oak.

She stood beside one of the windows, where the light of a lamppost glowed through the drapes. *Come along, Jarvis.*

The ballroom filled with revelers: Gothic youths in velvet suits and Gothic girls in long, rippling sable gowns.

She scanned the crowd. *Jarvis, are you here?*

As the numbers grew, countless fragrances swirled through the air—lilac water, and sweet peppers, *Eau de Cologne Impériale*, myrtle, and nutmeg, too.

In short order, the fumes intoxicated her—almost to the point of delirium.

A figure approached from the side, tapped upon her shoulder, and clicked his heels.

She turned to find herself face to face with an androgynous youth wearing much too much greasepaint and a Madame-Pompadour wig.

Without a word, the stranger removed a spike of ghost-white asphodel from beneath his cape and pinned the flowers to Sophie's corset bodice.

Had the stranger mistaken her for someone else? Even if he had, nevertheless, she found herself powerless to refuse the offering, or to spurn the peculiar fellow's advances. Before long, she averted her gaze and studied the chain of faux-diamond pendants dangling from the copper *fleur-de-lys* clasp at his throat.

At last, she permitted herself to look into the stranger's orange-brown eyes. As they sparkled so, she felt as if she were gazing upon a reflection of her own soul.

The stranger whispered a poem about the Asphodel Meadows, and then he grinned.

Could this be love? She hoped not, for whoever the youthful gentleman was, he could not have been much older than Jarvis. As such, the chap would be too young for her. Ashamed of herself, she stepped back. "Leave me be," she told him. "Go on."

The stranger reached into his cummerbund, removed a coin purse containing a mascara brush, and proceeded to touch up his eyelashes.

Now she felt uncertain of herself. Just as she had felt underdressed that night at the tearoom, again, she felt much too drab. If only she had unraveled her French braid. With her long, auburn hair hanging down, she would have looked better. At the very least, she might have plucked her eyebrows, or else applied some soft, purple eye shadow. As it so happened, she had not even thought to powder her nose. *Rats.*

On the stage at the far end of the ballroom, a pallid young lady in a gown of puckered cloth emerged from behind a section of the proscenium—and now she sat down at a large reed organ.

In that moment, the stranger offered his hand to Sophie.

Taken aback, she winced and shuffled her feet. "I can't dance with you just now. I'm waiting on a friend." Sweating profusely, she sniffed at her armpits and decided that she smelled like a cross between a handful of dried flowers and a bowl of warm, day-old clotted cream. *Good gracious.* She stepped back a bit more, only to bump into a steam radiator.

On the stage, meanwhile, the girl commenced playing the reed organ.

As everyone danced a slow, methodical *sarabande*, the overpowering fumes swirled through the air even more—and over to Sophie's side, several lively moths began darting about in a solitary ray of light.

Oh my. Until that moment, she had presumed that the last moths of summer had died out weeks before. *I must be hallucinating.*

Sure enough, the winged creatures dematerialized now—as if they had never even been there.

With the tip of his finger, the stranger tapped her wrist. Then, with the tip of the very same finger, he traced the contours of her face.

She felt too infirmed to protest, so she studied the uncanny youth's Victorian-Gothic mourning ring. "Have you got any image inside it?" she asked him. "Or did you inscribe the name of the deceased upon a gemstone? Tell me, why do you care for such morbid things?"

Without answering, the stranger took her arm and guided her out onto the dance floor.

Despite her growing sense of intoxication, she did her best to keep up. *What a disgrace it'd be to do otherwise.*

Faster and faster, the dimly lit ballroom reeled.

Soon, someone bounding all about in a preposterous bat disguise approached through the crowd and flapped his freakish bat wings. "God save the House of Lords," he shouted.

She recognized the figure from the night in Mayfair, so she broke free from the stranger and pointed at the bat personage. "Please, let's stop that fellow in the bat clobber and ask him if he knows where Jarvis might be."

The stranger chased down the other fellow and wrestled him to the floor, at which point the figure in the bat disguise feigned the most spirited, tragicomic death.

As he did, Sophie fell to her knees: by now, the potent perfume fragrances had her feeling bloodless.

The stranger returned, and he knelt beside her. "What's all this?" he asked in a Cockney accent much too affected to be genuine. And now he recited a bit of verse:

> "*Young love lies drowsing*
> *Away to poppied death;*
> *Cool shadows deepen*
> *Across the sleeping face:*
> *So fails the summer*

With warm, delicious breath;
And what hath autumn
To give us in its place?"

Three times over, the stranger wiggled his eyebrows. "So, do you approve of my wee little poem?" he asked in the same accent from before. "I wrote it only last week, when—"

"I'm sorry to spoil all the merriment," she interrupted. "I'm quite sure I must be suffering from some kind of fragrance sensitivity. Enough to make me dizzy." Too unsteady to stand, she attempted to crawl away.

The stranger took her into his arms, carried her over to the cocktail bar on the far side of the ballroom, and placed her down into a chair at one of the little tables. Then he turned to the barmaid. "Bring us a bottle of your finest Grande-Champagne Cognac."

Sophie grabbed at the stranger's neckcloth. "What do you look like beneath all that greasepaint and blush?"

"You don't want to know," he answered. "I'm loathsome of visage, I am." He employed the most exquisite sleight of hand then, and he suddenly produced a cigarette box fashioned from what looked to be bronzed pewter. And now he opened the lid to reveal a bundle of newspaper clippings, which he dumped out onto the table lace.

Silently, she leaned forward and unfolded one.

The text spoke of the technology that went into a Zeppelin's brand of radio navigation, the latest version of something called *'der Telefunken Kompass Sender.'*

She sat back, studying the stranger's face all the while. "I already know all about those awful dirigibles. Maybe you should recite another lovely poem, or . . ."

He turned the clipping over to the other side, and he tapped it with the tip of his ring finger. Then, in that same highly-affected

Cockney accent, he whispered, "On wrongs swift vengeance waits."

She leaned forward yet again and read the headline's large, bold typeface: *'Vampire-Obsessed Lad Drives Stake Through Bully's Heart.'*

Almost immediately, she thought of Jarvis and could not help but shudder.

The stranger cracked his knuckles. "Think of it. Gothic youths driving pickets through their tormentors' left breasts, the way vampire hunters dispatch the undead. The basher staked right through his malevolent heart. Aye, it's happening all over. Giggleswick Grammar School, they got maybe thirty or so vampire youths. You'll find us at Magdalen College, Oxford as well, and one of them charity schools up in Leeds. Saint Edmundsbury, too. Here and there and damn near everywhere, we aim to put an end to the stony-hearted bastards what bash us and—"

The barmaid returned with a rounded, flattened cognac bottle, and the customary shot glasses.

When she walked off, the stranger drummed upon the table. "One fine day, I'll best all vampire blokes everywhere," he continued in the highly-affected accent. "Someday, I'll square accounts with the footballer always taking the mickey out of me, and I'm not letting on, neither, dear. No, no. Consider me words an oath of vengeance. I'll bloody well box his ears."

"But *why*? It never profits anyone to exact retribution. I'd say it's better to strive for—"

"What's all this?" the stranger asked. Plainly cross, he bared a dead tooth not unlike the one Jarvis had. "You doubt the bloody yob deserves his due? Well, I don't care a louse what you think because I know damn well when the aggrieved present the wicked with his comeuppance, the aggrieved tastes *victory*. And in the hereafter, the wicked one must be the avenger's eternal reward. A slave everlasting."

"That's preposterous."

"No. A slave everlasting. That's the prize. Not one brass farthing less. I bloody well read it in that gothic novel, *Die Elixiere des Teufels*."

Having heard enough, Sophie stood up from the table. "Listen here, I've g-g-got to locate my friend Jarvis, and when I do, maybe he'd be willing to talk some sense into you. Haven't you ever heard of Jarvis Ripley?"

"Get knotted, why don't you? What makes Jarvis Ripley so great? He thinks pumpkins of you, does he? Maybe he only wants to have it off with you."

In an instant, Sophie attempted to slap the stranger—but before she could, he grabbed her wrist. She sought to break free but could not do so. With her free hand, though, she did manage to remove the asphodel and to cast the corsage at a table on the other side of the cocktail bar.

As the flowers landed amid a jumble of champagne flutes and crystal stemware, the stranger let go of her arm.

"How bloody glorious it'd be to command the infernal power of a vampire," he announced in an oddly familiar voice. "If I held that glorious kind of power like what a vampire possesses, I'd make myself a nemesis to anybody what wronged me. And time and again, I'd bring all so much intrigue into my worst adversary's life. One bloody exquisite reprisal after the next. As like as not, he'd soon go buggy."

"That sounds like fascism and vigilantism and—"

"No. I'd be *godlike*. I'd hold the power to avenge any trespass. And what could my rival do? Whatever course of action the bastard might attempt, it'd prove to be futile. For I'd be like a ghost, something fluttering through the shadows, *invisible*." Without another word, the sardonic youth removed his Madame-Pompadour wig—and then, with his left sleeve placket, he mopped up some of the greasepaint.

Sophie almost shrieked. Even in the dim light of the cock-tail bar's gas lamps, there could be no mistaking him any longer. "*J-J-Jarvis.*" And now she collapsed to the floor, and she buried her face in the palms of her hands—not unlike a little girl undone by inhibition.

CHAPTER FOUR

Marlborough College, Eighty Miles West of London,
14 December.

Having borrowed Cousin Augie's new touring car, Sophie pulled into Jarvis Ripley's boarding-school campus and parked behind the fencing hall. *So, here I am.*

Two days before, a bully by the name of Liam Asquith, together with two burly mates from the rugby club, had doused Jarvis with a water pump—at which point a whole crowd had stood there, reveling in his debasement.

According to the regulars at the Bessarabia Ballroom, the episode had shaken Jarvis to his core.

Now she climbed out from behind the wheel, and she closed the car door behind her. As she looked upon the fencing hall, the whole of her body grew warm. Suddenly, she realized just why she had come here. Had she not come to *betray* Jarvis? Given the dramatic turn of events, she had to lay bare all his obsessions and vengeful schemes before he did something awful.

When she reached the headmaster's residence, she dug her hands into the pockets of her winter coat. For a time, she studied the streak-free Georgian windows. Then she looked to the symmetrical pairs of chimneys standing on either side of the rooftop.

How immaculate everything appeared: despite the wintry breeze, not even one fallen elm leaf tumbled about the property.

She hunched her shoulders and drew a deep breath. *How to trust anyone so seemingly perfect?* She drew a little bit closer to the door, only to realize that someone had nailed a hag stone to the heart of the cross rails. *Curiouser and curiouser.* Twice, she knocked.

Moments later, when a tall, redheaded woman answered, Sophie bowed some and did her best to smile. "Good morning, I wish to speak with Headmaster Ravenscroft regarding a pupil, a chap by the name of Jarvis Ripley."

"What's the little blighter done?" the redheaded woman asked, her breath reeking of milk stout.

"He hasn't done anything. At least, not yet. It's more what I *fear* he'll do."

"*Fear?*"

"Well, yes. Have you heard of all the grisly murders? Apparently, not a few vampirism-obsessed youths have begun driving stakes through their tormentors' hearts."

"Yes, that's right. I'd say it comes down to all the shilling shockers the lads read these days."

"You think so?"

"I *know* so. Some well-heeled, self-satisfied authoress pens an immoral novelette, and her writing leaves the reader scarred for life."

"Yes, well, *I'd* say the trouble follows from the way certain students bash and bully the others. That kind of thing, it's not easy to forget. And the endless memories of the abuse tend to gnaw away at poor Jarvis. And that's why I fear the day's fast approaching when he'll explode in a fit of rage. And that's why I'm so concerned about the incident that happened just the other day when Liam Asquith went and—"

"Yes, I heard all about it," the redheaded woman interrupted. "The whole row happened over in the physics laboratory. Anyway, I'll speak with the headmaster and ask that he declaim against that kind of hooliganism. How's that then?"

"I don't know. Do you think it'd suffice?"

"Yes, tonight at vespers, I'll have the headmaster deliver a sermonette, and he'll conclude with a stern vow to reprimand—"

"*Please.* How should some contrived sermonette resolve anything?"

"Don't worry your fat. The fine young lads here at Marlborough, they'll listen to their beloved headmaster." Without another word, the woman closed the door.

Alone on the doorstep, Sophie felt both numb and mystified. Slowly, she turned to consider the campus.

How dreamlike the way the chapel gleamed in the afternoon light. Had the medieval masons fashioned the structure out of quartz-bearing sandstone?

She walked past a few withered trees, and then she stopped. *How could I betray a friend the way I just did?* Before long, she walked back to Cousin Augie's touring car—but she could not bring herself to drive away. Good manners obliged her to speak with Jarvis.

In the evening, as a procession of housemasters, schoolmasters, and students marched their way into the chapel, she finally located him.

At first, Jarvis looked quite surprised. For a moment, he fussed with a button on his overcoat. "What're you doing here?" he asked, a suspicious look in his eyes. "Why didn't you get me on the blower? If I knew you was coming, I could've . . ."

A snowfall commenced, and she pointed to the door. "Let's go inside."

Once they had taken their places in the pews, she felt unbearably guilty. For the longest time, she gazed upon the chancel, where a row of tall, baby-powder white Advent candles shone their light upon the altar. "Don't you find old-time religion inspiring?"

He only laughed and shook his head. "What brings you out here?" he asked. "Could it be you heard about what happened the other day?"

She turned to the window, watched an array of snowflakes

falling all over a barren hemlock tree, and then turned back. "Do you know what I like about the various religions of the world?" she asked. "They entreat the wronged party to *forgive*."

The chapel continued to grow gradually more crowded—until every pew had filled, along with the balcony.

Eventually, a dramatic hush fell over the house of worship.

His head held high; the choirmaster walked past the altar. Looking disdainful, he gestured to the elderly woman sitting at the pipe organ and then turned to face everyone. "Let's take up our hymnals," he announced.

The congregation proceeded to belt out a carol: "Good Christian Men Rejoice."

Afterward, as the reverend father commenced the homily, Sophie turned back to the window. The storm having grown intense, she felt cold and sick. How she longed to be home in the warmth of her hotel suite. There, she would make a long entry into her diary. Subsequently, she would climb into bed and seek to forget all her troubles.

The reverend father concluded his homily with a prayer for "all the fine lads down there in Étaples," and then he grew quiet.

Her intuition told her that it would not be long before the headmaster commenced his sermonette.

Sure enough, the reverend father gestured toward him.

A smirk on his face, the headmaster climbed to the dais. As he did, the communion rail creaked, too—for what a powerful frame he had. "One last point of order," he spoke up, as he fussed with the last few strands of ginger-blond hair falling over his scalp.

From the corner of her eye, Sophie glanced at Jarvis. When he returned her gaze, she turned back to the hemlock tree.

"I must insist there be no more gamboling about with the water pumps," the headmaster continued. "The Goodwife Ravenscroft says she witnessed quite a row the other day, over in the physics laboratory."

From here and there, several students and prefects laughed maliciously.

The headmaster's ears turned red. "Let me remind you all, we require those water pumps should some fiery calamity befall us." As several more heartless students and prefects snickered, the headmaster pulled a face. "Listen here, I say. Come next semester, any tomfool who dares to make mischief with a fire-suppression device, he'll get himself a right good birching. No giggles and doubts about it."

As the headmaster continued to speak, Sophie trembled all over. *How could he miss the point of his own sermonette?* She bit her nails. *How could anyone be so prideful and indifferent as to care more about the water pumps than the degradation of a living soul?*

In one of the pews up ahead, someone turned back to point at Jarvis.

What a terrible place. Confounded, she raced outside. *Get on home and—*

The wintry wind rattled a pair of half-frozen blackthorn trees to the right.

Despite all her zeal, she stopped in her tracks. Given how bad the storm had grown, she realized that she would not get far in these perilous conditions. As she turned back, she tripped over the remains of what looked to be a burnt Catherine wheel lying in the walkway.

No sooner had she regained her footing than a vast, earthen mound caught her eye. She had heard of the formation: the medievalists had always believed it to be the final resting place of the legendary Merlin.

Intrigued, she trudged off through the freshly-fallen snow and climbed the spiral path that provided access to the summit.

Despite the ongoing storm, the earthen mound afforded a commanding view of the windswept hills, deep gullies, and turbulent chalk streams of the downland.

She fixed her gaze upon the quarry where the historical, true-to-life Merlin would have harvested the bluestone pillars that form the monument at Stonehenge.

Beneath her feet, a clamor commenced—a sound as of someone tapping upon a rock.

Am I hearing things? Perhaps she had heard Merlin's ghost; if the ancients had buried him with his golden sickle, maybe he had begun to drum against his tomb.

She eyed a patch of dying yarrow, and she listened very carefully.

There it was again: a steady, unmistakable thumping.

She looked to the sky, and she went lost in reverie.

How good it would be if Merlin's golden sickle existed. If I were to hold it in my hand, at once, I'd possess the wisdom required to temper justice with mercy—and I'd possess the wisdom necessary to stand sentinel against any and all kinds of injustice.

A fierce current kicked up and tore through the boughs of a solitary gray willow standing to the side.

Some ten minutes later, a voice resounded on the current— what sounded like Jarvis calling out her name.

Evidently, the vespers service had already concluded. Much too ashamed to face him just now, she dug her hands into the pockets of her winter coat and stood still.

A second time, Jarvis called out her name—his voice growing faint.

After a long while, she continued back down the spiral path. Anxious, she stopped beside a snow-covered sundial and looked back in the direction of the chapel.

There, within the darkness of a lancet archway illumined by a string of electric fairy lights, stood a dozen or so shadowy figures. Soon enough, each one of them emerged from the passage—and then they stopped before a building overgrown with dying ivy, wilting toadflax, and browning snapdragon.

She recognized the party as a band of lofty students along with a tall, balding, broad-shouldered gentleman—Headmaster Ravenscroft himself. *Yes.*

Their voices growing louder, the party began to debate the question of just which one of the lads had the strongest, flattest belly.

No matter the cold weather, one youth even removed his overcoat and unbuttoned his dress shirt to exhibit his abdominal muscles.

At that point, the headmaster looked him over pridefully—not unlike the way a racehorse breeder might delight in a champion thoroughbred.

She felt sick. Could it be that Headmaster Ravenscroft permitted the footballers to bully whoever they felt like only because he himself once delighted in taunting other children out in the schoolyard?

When the party moved along, she turned back in the direction of Cousin Augie's touring car. *Shall I take refuge there?*

The night would be much too bleak.

Careful not to slip, she continued over to the building to her left. Thankfully, when she pulled upon the brass knob, the door opened into a warm foyer. *Hello.* She walked the length of the corridor, until she reached an office boasting a chesterfield that reeked of tobacco.

The wind whistling and the windows rattling, she lay down on the sofa and went lost in dreams of the good life—memories of how ideal and how uplifting it had been to learn at home by reading reputable books and asking herself questions, a little girl wholly sheltered from the everyday barbarism of academe.

CHAPTER FIVE

London, 13 February.

Early that morning, Sophie followed Jarvis into Madame Tussaud's. "So, what're we doing here?"

Jarvis did not answer. He paid the cashier, took Sophie's hand, and then shot a glance over toward the lost-property room. "Won't it be good fun to knock about awhile?" he asked her then. "If nothing else, it ought to make for a gay episode in your diary."

Immediately, she hiccuped—three times over. And as she did, her mouth filled with the taste of the honey-pear tea that she had downed at breakfast. Already, she regretted her decision to meet with Jarvis today. *What was I thinking?* She revisited the dread that had afflicted her for the last month or so—all her misgivings regarding his propensity for violence. Indeed, her fears had grown so severe that she had begun absent-mindedly tugging at her French braid—a habit that never failed to uproot a clump of hair.

Boldly now, Jarvis guided her into the period-rooms gallery—where five young ladies from the Bessarabia presently stood near the House-of-Tudor exhibition.

"What're *they* doing here?" she asked. "What's this all about?"

"They're here to spread the toils," Jarvis whispered, drawing her along past several more galleries and into a candlelit chamber. "We're here," he announced then, pointing with his free hand to a sign stenciled with a most curious designation: *Vampyre Hall.*

Looking positively giddy, Jarvis rubbed his hands together.

"Stay here, love. If a guard happens by, it's down to you to delay the bloody bastard." With that, Jarvis darted off into the gloomy chamber and onward through a vast maze of vampire exhibits.

Eventually, he stopped before an archer with a suede quiver slung over his shoulder and took the crossbow from the wax figure's hands. And now he grabbed all the bolts, too.

"For pity's sake," she protested as soon as he returned to her. "Don't you want to stay out of the dock? Put the plunder back."

"Don't be a vain little shrew," he told her. "Do you realize what I've got here? I've just nicked Van Helsing's crossbow. *Van Helsing*. Ace of vampire hunters. Aye, and I pinched his quarrels as well."

She pulled upon her braid, until several hairs came loose and attached themselves to a fold in her fluted skirt. Already, she intuited just what Jarvis intended to do: someday soon, he would slay one of his tormentors, perhaps Liam Asquith, the lout who had doused him with the water pump.

As another strand of Sophie's hair floated to the floor, Jarvis wrapped his left hand around the crossbow's cocking stirrup.

She let out a deep sigh. "Don't you realize what's bound to happen to you once you murder someone? It's off to Wormwood Scrubs with you then."

"I don't care a brass farthing what you say," he told her.

"No?" She attempted to grab the weapon and to wrest it away—and in the ensuing scuffle, she fell onto her bottom.

"Steady on, love. If you don't play along, I swear I'll load up this bloody spring and shoot you dead here and now."

Not five feet away, a museum guard stopped to check his timepiece.

She could not bring herself to say anything, so she let Jarvis huddle close—at which point he concealed the crossbow beneath his cape.

Looking serene and quite composed, Jarvis guided her back to the House-of-Tudor exhibition—where each one of the vampire girls now stood motionless, everyone striking obscene poses as if pretending to be wax figures themselves.

And now the vampire girls hurried forward and raced all about the grand lobby, as if to create a distraction.

Given all the sudden commotion, neither the guards nor the cashier even seemed to notice as Jarvis escorted Sophie through the doors and out onto the walkway.

For an hour or more, they traipsed about the city—and as they did, she pleaded with him to return the purloined weapon.

Finally, as they walked along Carnaby Street, Jarvis ducked into an antiquarian book shop.

For a time, Sophie paced along the walkway. Then she contented herself to study some of the chancery-hand manuscripts on display in the window.

At last, she realized that Jarvis must have slipped out the back door. *What a scoundrel.*

Several blocks on, she sat down before a boarded-up pub and debated whether she ought to track him. Most likely, he would be hiding out with one of the Bessarabia regulars. If so, how trying could it be to find him? One fellow had a place off Gracechurch Street, and another lived off Holland Park Avenue. She had also heard that three girls shared a flat on Thrawl Street, and another rented a room in the Borough of Hackney. Sophie sighed, for she realized that she had no hope. *Everyone's all of a scatter.*

She closed her eyes. *How long before Jarvis kills somebody?* As yet another bout of hiccups commenced, she envisioned the murder inquiry. *Oh God.*

Eventually, a police constable down at Scotland Yard would wish to look through her diary—and no matter how vigorously she might bridle at the suggestion, the authorities would accuse her of having served as an accomplice, or at least, the enabler.

In the end, she would have no choice but to turn king's evidence.

Her eyes shut yet, she pictured herself at the courthouse. If a trial judge called her up into the witness box, just what would she tell him? As tempting as it would be to dissemble the truth, she felt certain that any wise, dependable magistrate would expose any fib that she might cobble together—and then she would pay dearly for her deceit.

The winter breeze grew very strong now, and a piece of paper brushed up against her ankle. When she opened her eyes and looked down, she discovered the refuse to be a fragment from the *Sunday Times*—an editorial all about how to survive a Zeppelin raid.

Just like that, she looked to the sky and smirked. *Three cheers.*

Late in the night, powerless to sleep, she dressed herself in a simple blouse and a long, boiled-wool skirt—and then she took a taxicab to the Bessarabia. If Jarvis happened to be there, she would demand that he relinquish the crossbow.

When she entered the ballroom, she checked the dance floor.

What a desolate scene as the pallid young lady sitting at the reed organ performed a slow, doleful waltz, and a despondent-looking girl in a sable-brocade corset gown danced with a girl in black satin.

Sophie walked over to the steam radiator, where a sickly-looking girl with an oval-shaped face smoked a cigarette. "Do you know if Jarvis might be around?"

When the girl shook her head, Sophie resolved to check the cocktail bar on the other side of the ballroom.

She found it deserted but for three girls standing around the wine cabinet.

After a while, Sophie sat down. All the time brooding, she studied her faint reflection in the red-elm tabletop. *Where could Jarvis be?*

The barmaid walked over. "Shall I bring you something?"

Sophie looked up. "Have you noticed Jarvis Ripley out and about?"

The barmaid fussed with her black-ribbon bow tie. "I'm sure he ought to be around somewhere."

As the barmaid walked off, Sophie returned to her feet and sought to eavesdrop on the trio standing near the wine cabinet.

"Don't you grasp what he means to do?" the first brunette asked now.

"No, I don't," the other brunette answered. "A proper vampire kills his prey by sucking up the doomed soul's blood, no?"

"Yes, many a time and oft," the third girl spoke up now. "Ah, but our boy aims to best everyone by going about things in a right, bloody *ironic* way. Yes, indeed, because he grasps the art of *insolence*."

Sophie felt certain that the young ladies must be talking about Jarvis—his scheme to slay his tormentor with Van Helsing's crossbow. Before long, she snapped her fingers. "Pardon my intrusion, but might you girls be talking about Jarvis Ripley, the chap from—"

The first brunette held up her hand. "We wasn't talking to you, right?"

The other one giggled then, until she blew a bit of snot through her nose.

At that point, the third girl turned to Sophie and frowned. "Don't pother about our business none, governess."

Before Sophie could respond, something like the tip of a gloved hand tapped upon her elbow. Certain that Jarvis himself must be standing at her back, she spun around. What a surprise: no one stood there at all. In truth, a fragment of Acadia-white tulle had drifted in from the back door. As the fragment of silk netting settled at her feet, her intuition told her to walk over to the doorstep—and then she continued forward.

Outside, a brass lantern dangling from the wall shone down a faint light. To the left, someone had nailed a tattered gown up against a moldy linen press—the whole thing looking like something an archer might arrange for the purpose of target practice.

Jarvis. Immediately, she turned to the other end of the alley.

Sure enough, he and his mates stood there with the crossbow.

She raised her hand. "Give me that bloody weapon, *forthwith.*"

He turned toward her, grinned, and recited a German-language poem.

She folded her arms across her chest and waited for him to finish the piece.

When he did, he held the crossbow against the cobblestone. Then, before she could say anything, he placed his foot into the stirrup—and then he grabbed one of the bolts standing up against the drainage pipe to his right.

"Stop," she cried out. "Goodness knows I didn't come here to view some pointless archery exhibition, nor did I come here to—"

"Look at this arrow's right fine sinew and jagged point," he announced, turning the bolt this way and that. Then he extended his leg in order to draw the bowstring back, and he arranged the bolt into the flight groove along the length of the tiller.

Silently, insidiously, Jarvis proceeded to take aim.

No sooner had he squeezed the tickler than the bolt sailed past her temple—so close that the draft stirred her left sideburn. And now the bolt found its mark within a section of the gown mounted to the linen press.

She pulled upon her braid—forcefully enough to tug loose several strands of hair.

Once they had fallen to her feet, she marched forward. "Give me that goddamn thing before you kill someone."

Laughing excitedly, Jarvis held fast the stock—at which point they grappled while struggling for control of the crossbow.

In the end, he proved too strong for her. Upon cursing her several times, he and his friends darted off down the alley—and everyone vanished into the marsh-brown fog.

Off to the side, in the shadows of the doorway built into the brick wall, someone stood up from a wooden crate.

"Who's there?" she asked.

"It's only me." Slowly, the figure emerged into the light. He proved to be a tall, fair, slender young gentleman dressed in a Turkish-blue greatcoat open just enough to reveal his white, pleated dress shirt and cravat. "Ludovic Ozols, at your service."

"Have we met?" she asked, a curious, unsettling sensation nagging at her.

"In a way," he told her. Then he reached into his pocket, and he offered her a liqueur chocolate. "Please accept this token of my esteem."

Reluctantly, she took the offering into her hand. "Ludovic Ozols. No, I'm sure I don't know the name. And I don't recognize your face."

He shrugged, as if he did not care. Then he reached back into the shadows to collect an overnight bag, at which point he walked off.

She considered the suitcase in his hand: something dark and rubbery protruded from a hole near the handle.

Might the object be some kind of giant, hideous bat wing?

At last, she realized that this Ludovic Ozols must be the chap who always dressed up in the preposterous bat disguise. Might *he* know just where Jarvis intended to secure the purloined crossbow? Five times over, she stomped her foot. "Come back here."

The peculiar youth continued on his way, turned to the left, and disappeared from view.

Yet another bout of hiccups commenced, and once more, she found herself alone. *Oh yes, all alone.*

CHAPTER SIX

Marlborough College, 80 Miles West of London, 18 March.

Having borrowed Cousin Augie's touring car for the second time, Sophie had only just reached Jarvis Ripley's boarding-school campus when she espied a ghastly heap lying in the street.

The object proved to be the bloodied carcass of a doe. What a harrowing spectacle: the fallen beast's anguished expression and contorted body, its cracked ribs, and the labored rise and fall of its belly.

She gripped the wheel tighter all the time. *What to do about the poor thing?* She looked into the animal's eyes. *How long before it expires?* Before, she had never had to ask herself such a question: whenever she had passed by whatever the roadkill, she could always take comfort in the fact that the creature had already breathed its last.

All so poignantly now, the doe scraped one of its hooved feet against the gravel.

I can't look any longer. She slipped the touring car back into gear, and she continued along.

When she reached the fencing hall, she sought to forget all that she had witnessed. A boundless sorrow gripped her, however. To be sure, the foregoing scene did not augur well for the day's crucial agenda.

Despite all, she turned her thoughts to the task at hand and climbed out from behind the wheel. *Find the crossbow.*

When she reached the residence hall where Jarvis lived, she

gagged. The whole place reeked of steam coal. Still, when a game, young lad happened along, she dropped a Victorian gold sovereign into his hand. "Kindly show me to Jarvis Ripley's room."

Once the chap had pocketed the gold piece, he guided her to the partitioned cubicle in question. "It'd be this one here," he told her.

Without a second thought, she passed through the pleated drape that served as the door.

How austere the space. As if to keep his vampire fetish a secret, Jarvis had not affixed any peculiar sketches or oils to the antique-cream walls. Atop a heap of books, though, he had arranged a marble idol—an Assyrian sphinx just like the one that Oscar Wilde once kept on his writing table.

She walked over to the twin bed and checked beneath the box springs. Alas, she found nothing more than a fork-tip knife. When she returned to her feet, she opened the bin cupboard and rifled through the young man's personal effects. *No crossbow.*

In the end, she discovered nothing more suspect than an erotic photograph: a half-naked woman posing beside a scimitar-horned oryx, the two incongruous figures standing in terrain looking to be the Spanish Sahara.

Crestfallen, Sophie walked over to the window. There, she rested her brow against the side jamb and sobbed. *Now what?*

A few gnats began buzzing about the windowsill, where Jarvis had left a dish of spotted dick with custard.

Repulsed, she exited the residence hall.

At dusk, she walked over to the refectory. *Why not confront Jarvis?* In full view of the whole school, she would demand that he tell her just where he had concealed the weapon.

When she entered the dining hall, she looked all about but could not locate him.

In a cold sweat, she finally turned toward the high table.

Among the prefects and students sitting there, everyone

demonstrating proper social grace, Headmaster Ravenscroft passed around a silver platter filled with boiled stew and herb dumplings.

At his side sat the flaxen-haired Liam Asquith, the bold, perfect sporting youth.

For a time, she thought back to an article that she had read in the *Daily Sketch*—a lurid account describing the Battle of Nueve Chapelle. How long before Liam Asquith served, and how long until all of England celebrated him as the very embodiment of heroism?

Like so many times before, she could not help but pity Jarvis—yet here she was, scheming to deprive him of his oh-so-precious prize. *What a terrible betrayal.*

Eventually, she returned outside. *Why not drive back to London?* Safe and warm in the hotel café, she would treat herself to supper—either a blood sausage or a pork pie. Later, in her suite, she would sit down at her writing table and pour all her sorrows into her diary.

When she reached Cousin Augie's touring car, she paused to think. Might there be any route she could take to avoid driving past the fallen doe? For a moment or two, she went lost in a poignant memory of childhood—a remembrance of that evening she had espied a lone, helpless fawn cowering in Cousin Augie's tomato garden.

Had some incorrigible lout killed the young deer's mother?

From the other side of the motorcar park, an elderly woman holding a candle lantern approached—and now the elderly woman studied Sophie's face. "Would you be that game gal from Tintinhull College of Arts and Technology?" the old lady asked. "*Gilda*, wouldn't that be your name?"

As disconsolate as Sophie felt, she welcomed the idea of being someone else—so she nodded her head. "Yes, I'm Gilda."

"Well then, I'm Professor Lycett. Come along. But before you do, you ought to collect something warm to wear. It's still a bit raw out there in the forest."

At that point, Sophie noted the elderly woman's attire. She had dressed herself in a polo shirt, a pair of white riding breeches, and a heavy, blue dressage coat. *Has a pony gone lost in the woodland?* Whatever had gone wrong, Sophie turned to Cousin Augie's touring car and opened the boot—and now she cursed herself, for she had not brought along anything more substantial than her windcheater.

Once Sophie had slipped into her coat, Professor Lycett guided her past the reverend minister's elegant manse. Before long, they reached a well-trodden footpath winding past a coaltax post. From there, the two women continued all the way up to the gates of the forest.

Once the professor had unlocked the wicket, the two women followed along the bank of a millstream.

The further they walked, the darker the forest grew.

Down by a little crack willow, the professor stopped. "Don't you find it dreadfully sad how quiet the brush? It feels a wee bit like Christmas Day in the workhouse around here. Still, if either you or Flossie Talbot come to help us in the summertime, the forest should be ringing with the rattle of bush crickets. I promise."

As the two women continued further along the winding path, Sophie could not help but wonder just what it was that she, or rather *Gilda*, had volunteered to do out here.

When the two women reached the glade, Professor Lycett grinned and pointed toward an adjacent cavern. "That there's our bat grotto."

The cavern resembled the clamshell shape of the lips surrounding the passageway into a lady's womb; moreover, a tangle of vines and brambles had grown so wildly all about the rock above that the whole effect served to suggest a tuft of crotch hair.

Sophie gasped. *The whole thing, it looks like a Lady Jane.* Powerless to suppress the urge, she laughed—albeit ashamedly.

The professor looked into Sophie's eyes then. "You must be keen as mustard to get inside."

A second time, Sophie gasped. *Inside?* The whole of her body cringed, and she retreated a few steps.

At the same time, a clamor echoed through the forest—what sounded like a dozen or so bicyclists rolling across a wooden bridge.

"That'd be Marlborough Bat-Society," Professor Lycett explained. "When they get here, we'll form a queue."

The bat-society ladies rolled up into the glade, and when they climbed down from their bicycles, the professor introduced Sophie as Gilda. Afterward, one by one, the bat-society ladies illumined their lanterns and then crawled into the grotto.

In time, Sophie found herself alone again with Professor Lycett—but before Sophie had even had a chance to reveal her identity and to express her reluctance to participate, the elderly woman knelt to the earth and crawled into the cavern.

A second time, Sophie studied the passageway. *How obscene.* She placed her hand between her legs, poked herself, and quietly cursed all her frigidity.

The professor peeked outside. "Come now, Miss Gilda."

On her hands and knees, Sophie made her way forward.

Inside the grotto, the air felt cool and exhilarating. Even better, a freshwater spring to the right emitted a soothing aroma as of modeling clay. Most remarkable of all, the limestone walls shone with semiprecious gemstones and peanut wood.

What a magical place. Despite all the mushy bat droppings, she crawled forward even further and followed the professor to a darkened alcove.

"Squeeze yourself into that nook there," Professor Lycett told her, handing her the candle lantern.

"What precisely do I do?"

"Just count all the pups."

"Oh? Count all the—"

"Yes, and hurry. We must be out of here before the mother bats return."

"As you wish." With the candle lantern's twine handle clenched between her teeth, Sophie crawled into the alcove.

Just like that, the light of the candle lantern filled the cramped space with a tender, creamy glow. *How lovely.* Despite the jagged pieces of alabaster littering the floor, she lay down upon her back and studied the eggshell-white dripstone above. *There.*

Unmistakably, two little vesper bats dangled in the dripstone's shadow—the pups' talons locked in place around a fragment of glorious, rose-colored quartz.

After a while, a hand reached into the alcove and tugged at her foot. "Chop-chop," the professor called out. "We haven't got much more time, Gilda. A few of the mother bats have already come back. No more gassing around. Have you got the number?"

"Yes, I've got the number," Sophie answered. "I count only two."

"Only two? Stone the crows. I do believe the running total has decreased. Yes, the cauldron must be dying out. I'd say it's all that arsenic the farmers throw about the fields. It's killing off all the wee, savory centipedes our hungry bats crave."

Sophie crawled out of the alcove, at which point no less than a dozen fully-grown bats fluttered by.

Moments later, as the bat-society ladies returned from deeper inside the cave, she followed everyone outside.

As the bat-society ladies rode off, one of them offered a ride to Professor Lycett who gladly accepted. She turned to Sophie then. "You'll find your way back, dear?"

"Yes, of course," Sophie answered, brushing some of the dust and debris from her coat and skirt.

Not long after all the bicyclists had departed, a familiar clamor rang out—the riders crossing what sounded like that same wooden bridge from before.

Then, from within a dense thicket of wayfaring trees, a young lady emerged—a candle lantern in her hand and a courier bag slung over her shoulder. "Have you already completed the count?" the stranger asked.

"Yes," Sophie told her. "For all the good it did."

"And Professor Lycett, she's already gone off?"

"Yes, she left not two minutes ago."

"Dash my buttons." Frowning, the young lady turned to look upon the grotto—the erotic passageway. "Tell me, did the professor happen to mention just when we're to begin protesting all those schools?"

"What schools?"

"The ones that use animals in their laboratory experiments."

"No, she made no mention of it to me. Sounds like a good idea, though. There's nothing so innocent as an animal, eh?"

Unresponsive, the young lady groaned very quietly and then turned around.

Feeling guilty, Sophie watched her walk away. *Was* that *the elusive Gilda?*

After a long while, Sophie looked to her feet—where a seemingly diseased, erratic, glow worm inched its way through a patch of reindeer moss. The feeling of guilt growing stronger all the time, she took the creature into her hand. *How do I stop Jarvis from killing someone?*

A moment or two later, she returned her hand to the earth and freed her captive.

CHAPTER SEVEN

London, 29 April.

After several weeks of meticulous planning, Sophie finally found herself poised to take possession of the crossbow. All night long, Jarvis had been walking about with a long, thin chest tucked beneath his arm—and she just knew that the case must contain the weapon. As soon as the opportunity presented itself, she would seize the crossbow and run away.

At eleven o'clock or thereabouts, she followed a drunken Jarvis, and some of his friends, to Regent's Park. When they reached Queen Mary's Gardens, the party sat down to rest.

A sensation of presentiment came over her person, and she turned to look upon the moon mirrored in the nearby fishpond.

By the time she turned back, a chap by the name of Nigel had taken the case into his hand—and now he opened the lid to reveal a jumble of equipment bundled up in haircloth.

The crossbow. Sophie breathed in, and then she quietly exhaled. *Here's my chance.*

Alas, a fragment of an old newspaper came tumbling by in the breeze, and the debris brushed up against her ankle. The clipping proved to be a column from the *Sunday Times*, another disconcerting article all about the Zeppelins.

While she found herself momentarily distracted, Nigel unwrapped the weapon.

As for Ludovic, the fellow all decked out in his customary bat disguise, he suddenly returned to his feet. "*Commencer les manœuvres,*" he announced.

With a gleam in his eye, Jarvis collected the crossbow. Then he extended his leg in order to draw the bowstring back, and he arranged one of the bolts within the flight groove.

"Don't you think it'd be rather foolish to muck about with a weapon like that?" Sophie asked him then, her sense of foreboding having grown much worse.

Ludovic flapped his wings, and he drew close enough to Jarvis to grab the drinking flask from his cummerbund.

"Give me back that satinette," Jarvis shouted.

"Bugger and blast," Ludovic shouted in turn, hopping up and down. "You think you'd be sporting enough to take back these precious spirits, do you? Well then, the best of Britannia to you. That said, no matter what you do, you'll never corner a freakish bat personage as full of beans as I'd be tonight." With that, Ludovic raced off through the moonlit fields.

"Go on," a drunken Nigel called out to Jarvis. "Trap that vile flittermouse. If you don't, he'll put the mockers on you. Yes, indeed. I know that reprobate only far too well, and that's just what he'll do."

"On that account, I'll show you all who pounds longest," Jarvis announced. "To the field of honor." The drunken youth patted the weapon's stock, and then he chased Ludovic around the fishpond. "I demand satisfaction," Jarvis shouted.

"Ah, you think it's the end of the bobbin for me then," Ludovic cried out. "Well, I'll be the judge of that." As he flapped his preposterous wings, he continued to race all about.

For a time, Sophie studied her hand. Oddly, the whole of her palm *ached*—as if she herself had only just fired off the crossbow and now felt the shock of the recoil. *Oh God.*

Finally, she willed herself to hurry after the others.

By now, Ludovic had already guided Jarvis up the better part of Primrose Hill—and now they reached the summit, and each fellow promptly turned from the other. Like duelists then, each one determined to restore his honor, Jarvis and Ludovic stood at one another's back.

Sophie ran harder through the wet spring grass. *I've got to stop all this.* As soon as she reached Primrose Hill, she kicked off her dancing shoes and commenced her ascent.

Up above, Jarvis proceeded to count off his steps—and now he and Ludovic marched off in opposite directions.

Just as Jarvis grew quiet, Sophie reached the top of the slope. At first, she paused to catch her breath. "That's quite enough," she blurted out then, her sense of presentiment having grown unbearable. "Jarvis, give me that bloody relic before something goes wrong."

Jarvis ignored her, and he turned to face Ludovic. "*Ego invictum,* belligerent bat personage. Prepare to pay your debt to nature."

"Cheese it," Ludovic countered. "As soon as I've conditioned me right, fine, trusty plagiopatagium, I'll swoop down on top of you and bite your nose off." Ludovic dropped the drinking flask at his side, and then he leaped up and down while flapping his bat wings. "You're well in Dutch now, young Dutchman."

Looking almost reverential, Jarvis fired off the bolt—and Ludovic fell to the earth.

Lost for words, Sophie walked forward. *Did the bolt pierce Ludovic's heart?* At the top of her voice, she let out an awkward, woeful shriek.

The ungraceful noise must have amused the drunken Jarvis, for he smirked. "Hell mend you then," he announced, pointing at the body.

Sophie knelt at Ludovic's side, and she sought to free the bolt by grasping the parchment that served as the cock feather.

Eventually, when Nigel reached the summit, he shoved her out of the way. Once he had, he endeavored to stop the bleeding by tearing asunder one of Ludovic's bat wings and applying it to his chest.

At last, Jarvis seemed to realize what he had done. "To be honest, I meant to hit one of them turkey oaks over there," he muttered, pointing toward a thicket of dwarf trees.

Nigel turned to look upon him. "Don't just stand there pale as ashes. Collect your bloody wits and go get help, you threepenny masher."

"Maybe there's a night watchman down at the London Zoo," Sophie added.

"That's right, go tell the chap down at the menagerie," Nigel cried out. When a plainly discombobulated Jarvis failed to respond, Nigel cursed him and then returned to his feet. "Very well then, I'll go."

Once the frantic youth had raced off, Sophie grabbed the bloodied bat wing and continued to apply pressure to Ludovic's chest. And now she managed to remove his absurd mask. "Be strong," she implored him. "It shan't be long before . . ."

Ludovic flashed a polite smile. "We was all full to the bung tonight. More's the pity." He coughed up a torrent of blood then. "I suppose I must've had me a touch too much of that right-splendid Bessarabia-Ballroom barley wine with its buttery, caramel aftertaste." Now he licked his upper lip, as if he believed the wine's frothy foam might still be there. "All them strong spirits clouded me judgment, obviously. Quite apart from the fact that . . ."

Sophie drew close enough to detect the lime water by which Ludovic had spiked his hair earlier that evening. Tenderly, she kissed the cleft at the tip of his nose.

"I hope you don't regard me as coming off a touch too blandiloquent," Ludovic whispered then. "It's just that I wouldn't want you to be blighted by nightmares."

"Don't fret about anything," she told him. "Soon, we'll get you to the hospital. And they'll get you into the operating theater, and then—"

"No, love. With a twinge in me heart, I must confess I'll not be strong enough to keep body and soul together."

"No, I'm sure you'll survive. You're so young and—"

"Never mind all the blood and guts," Ludovic interrupted. "Everything ought to come out in the wash." His eyes rolled back then, and he lay perfectly still.

For the first time, she noticed her bloodied hands—at which point she felt a sensation worse than numbness, as if her flesh must be dissolving into sand. Despite all, she placed her palm upon Ludovic's left shoulder and squeezed. "Please come back, friend."

The passage of time assumed an agonizingly slow pace, or so it seemed.

She looked to the sky. If only some godly portent might have presented itself in that moment—a sign to absolve her, a sign to suggest that fate itself had predetermined Ludovic's death. What about a shooting star streaking from east to west, the fireball shining marshmallow white tinged with baby blue? She glanced at Ludovic once more, and then she looked to the sky yet again.

No miraculous portent appeared.

She looked upon the darkest cloud that she could find and envisioned her own death and the subsequent process of her damnation—her soul bursting from out of her warm, vile heart and then sailing off into the ether, only to vanish into a parallel universe, a place where none of the other abominable penitents even cared whether she once possessed any semblance of character.

From across the park, a dissonant clamor rang out—a noise as of someone sounding a brass signal bell. Perhaps Nigel had located the night watchman, who had subsequently rung some hospital.

Sure enough, off to the north, a field ambulance appeared—the glare of the headlamps blinding her, just for a moment. As the vehicle continued its rapid approach, she closed Ludovic's eyelids.

When the field ambulance reached the summit, the signal bell ceased. Then the doors opened, and the unmistakable odor of copper sulfate invaded the night air.

A moment later, once they had removed several dressing tins from their cherry-wood medicine chest, the medics must have realized that there was nothing to do. They did not even trouble themselves to remove the bolt from Ludovic's heart.

In the end, she managed to slip the mask back over Ludovic's face. Wringing her hands then, she walked over toward Jarvis.

Looking profoundly ashamed, he slumped to the ground and crossed his legs. Then he began to rock back and forth—not unlike a child coming down from a fit.

The rest of the night passed by in a reeling, rueful, bemoaning blur.

In the morning, when the detective from Scotland Yard finally released her from the interrogation room, she wandered the streets. Time and again, various wind-driven fragments of newspapers tumbled by. Gently, they brushed up against this lamppost and that.

At a funeral pace, she walked up and down Borough High Street. If she had succeeded in taking the crossbow from Jarvis, perhaps she might have dumped it in a place just like this. Even better, she might have thrown the weapon off Westminster Bridge.

As it so happened, Scotland Yard had the crossbow now—and the courts were sure to put the weapon into evidence when Jarvis stood trial.

Early afternoon, Sophie stopped off in a pub and ordered a plowman's lunch. When the hostess brought everything over to the table, Sophie downed the onion slices. Afterward, she sat back and gazed upon the establishment's sole working light—a genuine Victorian police lantern, of all things.

How long before Scotland Yard asked after her writings? Before the day was done, she would have to destroy her diary. *Why not reduce it to ashes, the whole sordid account?* Heavy with grief, she felt for the box of matches in her coat pocket. *Yes, I'll do it.*

Someone walked past her table. Then several others passed by on their way to the next table over. And now the establishment began to fill up with a lively, felicitous crowd.

Soon, the barroom reverberated with talebearing, the news of the world, talk of inquiries, this scandal and that.

Unconsciously, she moved her hands—as if working a type-writer. All along, perhaps a part of her had always hoped that Jarvis might do something tragic. That way, she might have written a memoir worthy of publication.

The floorboards seemed to shudder violently beneath her feet, and her hands dropped to the table.

What a heartless young lady she had permitted herself to become—someone depraved enough as to conspire to profit from another person's blood. *Yes, that's right.* She closed her eyes, and she prayed for transformation.

II.

CHAPTER ONE

Weimar, 29 September 1919.

Early that morning, the very moment Sophie reached the campus of *das Bauhaus*, she bumped into a young lady brandishing a gas-operated crossbow.

And it looks like the one that killed Ludovic, just last year.

What a peculiar young lady, too. She did not look well: considering the way her pupils shook and spun, there could be no mistaking the madness that afflicted her. Moreover, she wore a dusty, crooked, much-too-large, Prinz-Heinrich hat. As if all that were not enough, the young lady had dressed herself in a wholly-inappropriate, silk-crepe gown—one with a scalloped hem no less.

It's a tea gown. Wistfully, Sophie thought back to Mayfair Tearoom—the little place where her initial, chance meeting with Jarvis had transpired. By the time she turned her attention back to her present surroundings, the young lady had walked off.

Had she ducked into the art school's industrial building?

Sophie pulled upon her fishtail braid such that three strands of hair came loose, one of them alighting upon her button-up and the others sticking to a fold in her skirt. Despite all her trepidation, she found herself greatly intrigued by the young lady. To be sure, there had to be a good reason for the fateful encounter. Sophie let go of her braid and paused to reflect for a moment. Ever since she had undergone hypnosis therapy to program her unconscious mind with a strong impulse toward moralism, she had yearned for the chance to make amends for what had happened back home. And now she wondered if she had stumbled upon the answer: if she were to befriend the troubled young lady, perhaps they could *learn* from one another—and might that kind of cultural exchange provide the fulcrum for redemption?

Over the course of the next hour, Sophie spoke with some of the school's faculty members and sought to gather as much information as possible.

Most of the instructors seemed reluctant to volunteer too many particulars, but each one told her not to worry.

At one point, Walter Gropius even sat her down in a folding chair. "Why did *you* come to *das Bauhaus*?" he asked. "Obviously, you traveled here to learn art and to feel the great sense of elation that comes with discovery. And that's why *all* students come here, even the more *exotic* ones."

Thankfully, as Sophie continued to ask around, some of the other students enrolled in the book-design program shared more details.

The person in question went by the name of Adolpha T. Unbekömmlich, though almost everyone believed it to be an alias. With regard to the crossbow, most of the students felt that she carried it around due to suicidal inclinations. Apparently, she longed to be ready to shoot herself in the heart whenever and wherever she chose to terminate her life. As a consequence, she could not bear to be without the weapon—nor could she bear to be without a bolt. In point of fact, she had attached the shaft to her left leg—or so the rumor went.

As the morning hours passed by, Sophie followed Adolpha through the campus and soon decided that the rumors must be true: as Adolpha walked along, she did indeed drag her left leg behind her. *What a tragic case.*

Late afternoon, Sophie walked outside and noticed the young lady sitting beneath a beech tree. *And there's the crossbow lying at her feet.*

For the longest time, Adolpha sat perfectly still. Then, as a dazzling ray of sunlight bathed the industrial building's gamboled roof, she narrowed her big, blue eyes and seemed to contemplate the glare bouncing off the orange-red shingles. Once the light had shifted ever so faintly, Adolpha turned to the building's electric-blue cupola. At that point, she adopted a blank expression—as if she hoped to grant the deepest recesses of her unconscious mind a moment to process whatever influences that the day's events had wielded.

Sophie smoothed out her skirt, and she picked a long strand of hair from her ruffled collar. Slowly then, she approached. *"Hallo."*

As if she had discerned Sophie's London accent, Adolpha looked up and greeted her in fairly good English.

No sooner had she spoken than a cacophony of industrial noises resounded from several blocks to the east.

Adolpha turned away and cocked an ear, as if it pleased her to contemplate the ongoing clamor. Only when the commotion died down did she turn back. "Are you the only student to come from England?"

"Probably."

"I am the only one from Europe, Switzerland. You know Europe, Switzerland? It's a peaceful republic with lofty mountains and winding rivers. When I was a little girl, I inspired there for my little handmade gifts, my pretty kidskin gloves, and my knitted accessories. Then my family relocated to Weimar." As if the behavior must be unconscious, Adolpha took a fragile, fallen twig into her hand and began tapping her left shinbone.

"So, what would you be studying here?" Sophie asked her.

"Why do you ask?"

"Just because."

"For now, I learn art. A favorite theme for me, anatomy. I love *legs*. Every little thing about them. And I am happy if people

love my paintings of beautiful legs and feet. *Ja.* All this inspires."
Adolpha let go of the twig and studied Sophie's left thigh. Then,
with something like hunger in the young lady's eyes, she wrapped
her hand around Sophie's left calf. "What an ideal body you
have. Like an art model." For a time, Adolpha dug the tips of her
thumbs into Sophie's left kneecap.

Heavens.

When she let go, Adolpha removed her hat and rolled around
in the grass—any number of weeds entangling themselves in her
curtained, flaxen hair.

With increasing apprehension, Sophie stepped back some.
"Why the fascination with legs?"

As if she had not even heard the question, Adolpha continued to roll around for three minutes or more. Then she sat up and
ogled Sophie's left leg anew, and the young lady's pupils shook
and spun—just as they had done earlier that same day.

Only when a columbine fluttered by did Adolpha turn to
watch. What a remarkable songbird, its feathers a pleasing shade
of antique white. When the winged creature finally continued
along, Sophie folded her arms across her bosom. "Tell me why
you're so obsessed with the human leg."

Adolpha pointed toward the walkway, and she muttered
something about the simple, logical design by which the archi-
tects had arranged the faded, ash-gray bricks. Then the young
lady collected her funny hat together with the crossbow. Afterward, she guided Sophie into the industrial building. "I'll show
you to my studio."

Powerless to suppress her sense of frustration, Sophie paused
by the door. "*Why* the fascination with legs? Answer my question."

Adolpha pointed to the electrical conduit on the wall. "A fine
woman from Maastricht designed that piece there." For the longest time, Adolpha studied the contours of Sophie's left leg. "The
shape of your ankle, it's perfect. As perfect as—"

"Somehow your fascination with legs feels all wrong," Sophie interrupted. "For some reason, the whole idea feels . . . *perverse*."

Adolpha did not respond. Instead, she turned to the futuristic flying staircase. "Look at that construction. A gentleman from Weißensee designed that flight of steps there. Or maybe it was Professor Euwe. No, maybe it was . . ."

When a dour-looking Adolpha continued up to the next floor, Sophie hesitated. For a time, she debated whether she even wanted to view Adolpha's work. Perhaps her studio space would be filled with legs—a jumble of limbs fashioned from a block of granite, the hammer and the chisel lying upon the floor. And there would be all so many peculiar images, too—a still life, an oil on board, an easel painting. And if the young lady had embraced modernism, why not several disturbing, experimental works involving either the art of photolithography or some newfangled variation on the copper-plate process? Whatever the medium might be, how shuddersome a roomful of legs would appear.

Adolpha glanced back over her shoulder. "Come, please. You won't regret it."

All the time pulling upon her fishtail braid, Sophie followed along. *Oh my, my.*

Upstairs, toward the very end of the corridor, she willed herself through the door.

The faculty had granted Adolpha an oblong, private studio with plenty of large casement windows and a profusion of light. Still, the studio had a disagreeable odor—something like melted plasticine. In addition, aside from a drafting table, a box of art supplies, and a lovely art nouveau work lamp, the space contained no work whatsoever.

Not even one leg. Sophie found herself confounded. "Where's all your output?"

Adolpha placed her crossbow alongside the easternmost skirting board. Obsessively, she arranged and rearranged the implements in her art-supply box—a glue brush, a colored pencil, a pair of deckle shears, and a line gauge. In time, she wandered about the room—until she stopped beneath the skylight. Then, looking up, she clenched her jaw—just like a pathological little girl fighting off a laughing fit. "*Meine werke*," she whispered.

Sophie thought of her long-lost diary. "Did you *destroy* your work? If so, what a pity."

Calmly and oh so languidly, Adolpha looked down from the skylight and stared at the crown of Sophie's left foot. And now Adolpha clenched her fist, as if she held an imaginary grip knife. "A long time ago, all the fools from *Die Kunstakademie Düsseldorf*, everyone there, how they laughed at me."

"Because you fetishize the human leg?"

"Yes, I suppose so," Adolpha whispered. "Still, *anything* should be art. Yes, *anything* may serve as an art piece."

"But why a leg?"

"Why *not*? I study my theme with precision arithmetical. Every aspect, every precious detail." The excitable young lady clenched the imaginary knife that much tighter in her hand, and she drummed her fist against her left leg—as if she longed to shatter her thigh bone and to leave it in a thousand pieces.

Sophie grabbed the young lady's forearms.

As if to drop the imaginary knife, Adolpha opened her hand.

Sophie let go. "*Bitte*. Let's be friends. I'll share with you whatever I know, and you'll share with me all your wisdom. Won't that be just great? Together, we'll walk the paths of *redemption*."

Over to the side, a songbird crashed into one of the casement windows—and now the creature fell to the earth.

Had the troubled young lady even noticed? Adolpha only looked heavenward, as if she espied something through the skylight—a reassuring, godlike glow, the ineffable promise of transfiguration, metamorphosis.

CHAPTER TWO

Weimar, 18 October.

Midmorning, as Sophie walked along through *der Goetheplatz*, she felt a sensation as of someone watching her. For a time, she looked this way and that—until she finally espied a sleek, black Mercedes-Benz Knight idling not twenty feet away.

What mystery the way the vehicle's opaque windows obscured the interior.

With all her might, she gazed deep into the darkness of the windscreen. Could it be some sick debauchee? She doubted it; back home, that kind of thing had never happened to her.

As she continued down the street, the motorcar slipped into gear and followed her.

Not a moment or two later, as soon as she paused between a couple of leafless plane trees, the Mercedes stopped.

By now, she had little doubt as to who must be sitting behind the wheel; the driver just had to be Adolpha's maniacal, vindictive, identical-twin sister, Friedel.

Only a few days earlier, Adolpha had told Sophie all about her.

Once, long ago, the twins had been very close. At times, the two sisters had made all kinds of mischief. When the one would go somewhere, she would claim to be the other one's doppelgänger. Often, too, the one might claim to *be* the other—as if the other possessed the magical power of bilocation.

By the age of twelve, the twins had begun to grow apart.

Apparently, the discord had commenced just after the family had emigrated from Switzerland. One morning in Jena, the twins had stopped to watch a pair of street performers—two identically disguised mime artists who so affrighted Friedel that she raced off to the constabulary, which in turn unjustly arrested the two buskers.

Later that day, Adolpha had done her best to defend the street performers—and from that moment on, Friedel had despised her.

An autumn rain commenced now, and Sophie took shelter beneath a pair of bare plum trees standing in the park.

If only the black Mercedes would continue on its way. Alas, the motorcar did no such thing.

On and on, Sophie felt Friedel's eyes upon her.

There could be little doubt that the intolerant young lady greatly objected to Sophie's presence in the city. Could it be that Friedel felt jealous? Perhaps Friedel feared any newfound friendship that Adolpha might develop. Could it be that Friedel feared that a bold confidant might encourage Adolpha to do something drastic with regard to her art?

Sophie rubbed her thigh—and as she did, she revisited Adolpha's obsession with the human leg. *How very odd.*

Twice now, the unseen Friedel gunned the engine.

What does she mean to accomplish by doing that? Sophie debated whether she ought to walk over to the driver-side window. *No, don't do it.*

If she were to walk over, perhaps Friedel would open the driver-side door—and then the frenzied young lady would attack her with a truncheon. At the very least, Friedel would smite her with a big pepper salami.

Determined to remain calm, Sophie eyed the bakery across the way and wondered if she might purchase a bag of honey-spice cookies once the rain had ceased.

Soon enough, the autumn rain died out—and as the sun returned, a resplendent double-rainbow appeared in the eastern sky.

Go. Sophie attempted to cross the street, at which point the motorcar pulled up and blocked her way.

For the longest time, she studied her reflection in the driver-side window. Given the darkness of the tinted glass, her face appeared all so dreamlike.

Inside the motorcar, Friedel killed the engine—and now the streets of Weimar grew perfectly quiet but for the breeze stirring the treetops here and there.

"I know who you are," Sophie announced, looking into the faint reflection of her own eyes. "Your twin has told me all about you."

The black Mercedes remained silent.

After a while, Sophie tapped upon the driver-side door. "You have no reason to fear me any," she continued. "As a matter of fact, you ought to be happy that I've grown friendly with your twin. Just a few days ago, Adolpha let me read some of your poetry, the verse you wrote when you were a little girl. Anyway . . ."

The motorcar remained silent.

Sophie shook her head. "Haven't you ever longed to release some of your work in print form?" she asked. "If so, I could help you. As a matter of fact, I've come to Weimar for no other reason than to learn book design. Yes, one of these days, I hope to found my own press. And I'd be quite willing to publish some of your work. Wouldn't that be good fun?"

If it truly were Friedel sitting behind the wheel, she did not respond.

Sophie took hold of the door handle but found it locked. "*Bitte komm da raus,*" she pleaded.

From down the street, a pair of thrush nightingales fluttered past—their tail feathers an exotic shade of Persian orange. Gracefully, the two songbirds proceeded to circle about a half-timbered manor house two blocks down.

At last, both songbirds came to alight upon one of the structure's second-floor window stools.

Sophie let go of the motorcar's door handle. "Why don't you work with me and help me design your debut? We'll plan everything. I'll let you look through my best lettering book, and you'll choose the font. Do you know what else? You'll choose what kind of clay-coated paper my printing press ought to employ. Would that please you?"

Not surprisingly, the black Mercedes remained silent.

Back at the manor house, the two thrush nightingales began tapping their bills against the window's lower sash. Had the songbirds grown alarmed by their own reflections, and if so, how long before the confounded creatures injured themselves?

The black Mercedes roared back to life, and the motorcar drove away.

In the evening, Sophie told Adolpha all about the encounter with Friedel.

Just like that, Adolpha turned up the whites of her eyes and staggered back.

Later, as if hoping to make amends, Adolpha took Sophie's hand and guided her into a poetry café on *die Schillerstraße*.

The coffee house proved to be a dimly lit hall with little to show other than a welter of oval tables with lyre-shaped legs. With regard to the modest number of patrons, each one seemed exceedingly glum—as if only the lonely would even think to visit such a somber establishment.

The hostess poked at one of the logs burning within the fire-box built into the cracked, bone-white wall to the left. Afterward, the poetry café returned to quietude, lifelessness.

Sophie sat down and asked the hostess for a slice of lemon poppy bread.

Adolpha placed the crossbow beneath her chair, and then she sat down on the other side of the table.

A moment or two later, as Adolpha proceeded to order a slice of butter cake, the roar of a motorcar's high-performance engine awoke from somewhere down the street.

Could it be Friedel? Feeling uneasy, Sophie turned to the oriel window.

Sure enough, the Mercedes-Benz Knight approached ever closer—until it came to idle some twenty yards away. Thankfully, Friedel dimmed the headlamps—at which point a subdued light returned to the poetry café.

When the hostess brought the cakes over, Sophie could not muster an appetite. Shivering uncontrollably, she warmed her hands over the tea-light. "What does your sister want?"

Adolpha shrugged in an almost robotic fashion. Then she lit a cigarette, puffed upon it, and blew a stream of smoke into the air—the scent of the tobacco slowly commingling with the aroma of Arabian coffee sailing over from one of the other tables.

With a frown, Sophie gazed out the window to the motorcar. She longed to run. Still, even if she had chosen to do so, any attempt at escape would have proven to be futile: her left foot had fallen asleep, and when she shook her head, it did little to boost her blood flow.

At last, she turned back and placed her hands upon her lap.

Adolpha put out her cigarette. She stood up then, made her way through the maze of tables, and exchanged words with the hostess. Afterward, Adolpha climbed atop a footstool that the poetry café apparently employed as a dais. With a blissful expression on her face, she removed a bundle of papers from her coat pocket and proceeded to read one of Friedel's works—a prose poem entitled "*Nachtlied.*"

The dreamlike verse related the tale of a phantasmal Mercedes forever wandering the streets of Weimar—both the vehicle's bonnet and dented roof glistening as radiantly as the shell of an Egyptian scarab beetle, "*eine ägyptische Skarabäus.*"

Sophie turned back to the window, and she gazed into the darkness of the motorcar's windscreen. *Friedel, why so vengeful?* With a sigh, Sophie turned back.

The prose poem continued, the work turning to the moment the black Mercedes pulls up to *das Hotel Ratskeller*. At which point the driver-side door opens to reveal a big rat personage sitting at the wheel. And now the hideous creature walks into the hotel, his pink, mangled tail protruding through the hole in the back of his *lederhosen*.

Outside, Friedel gunned the engine a few times over.

What does she aim to do? Sophie held her breath and glanced back. *What if Friedel means to crash through the damn window?*

Little by little, the headlamps shone blindingly bright.

The poem turned to that moment the rat personage grows transfixed by the sensuous *kabaret* dancers performing upon *das Hotel Ratskeller* stage. And now Adolpha recited the verses in which the rat personage lunges at one of the dancers and holds fast to her long, sinewy, left leg.

The poem finally concluded, and the patrons applauded.

A terrific explosion echoed all throughout the poetry café then: a piece of cordwood had popped within the firebox, the subsequent shower of orange sparks falling all about the stone hearth.

At that point, Friedel must have slipped her motorcar into reverse—for the Mercedes retreated two whole blocks before turning east into the Old-Town market square.

Twenty minutes later, outside in the street, Sophie stopped beneath a lamppost and turned to Adolpha. "What shall we do about your twin?"

"What do *you* think?" Adolpha asked in turn.

"How about I publish her work? Wouldn't she find that a gracious tribute? Given how surreal Friedel's poetry tends to be, we might even give the work an elegant, dreamlike name, something like *Traumnovelle*. Does that sound good to you, or what about something safe and traditional? How about *Buch der Traumgedichte?*"

Adolpha held the crossbow close to her bosom, and she looked down the street toward the theater where the Weimar Festival Ballet often performed. "Yes, of course, a book with a dreamlike name. *Ja, gut.* That inspires."

From the end of a narrow lane to the right, the hum of a powerful automotive engine resounded. A moment or two later, the black Mercedes drew close—and now it stopped. Sophie felt puzzled. In that moment, she almost expected the driver-side window to roll down to reveal the rat sitting at the wheel.

For a time, he would glare at her. "*Was warten sie noch?*" the personage would ask then, ogling her leg. "*Kommen sie mit.*"

Slowly, the black Mercedes drove off.

Befuddled yet, Sophie chased after it—until she found herself lost amid a haze of neon-gas light and dark, silvery mist—the unforgiving night.

CHAPTER THREE

Weimar, 13 November.

Late that morning, when Sophie reached the student center and checked her mailbox, she found a telegram from London. What an opening line, too:

> *Bad news stop Jarvis Ripley has died stop committed suicide stop*

The message went on to tell the tale: having secured a furlough from his remand home, he had obtained an illicit firearm, then later, on Guy Fawkes Night, while polite society celebrated in Parliament Square by burning the customary effigy, Jarvis had made his way into an abandoned brewhouse on the edge of the city. There, sitting on the kiln floor, he had dug the pistol's barrel into his left breast—the subsequent, contact-range gunshot shattering his heart and killing him instantaneously.

For a time, Sophie teetered back and forth. "*Gott im Himmel,*" she whispered several times over.

A songbird, either a robin or a sparrow, streaked past the student center's post-office window.

With a heavy sigh, she folded up the telegram and placed it inside her coat pocket. Then, as she exited the building, she debated whether she had dreamed everything. Just like that, she felt for the telegram—and there it was. *No, it's no dream.*

When she reached her studio, she looked all about. *Has someone been here?*

Everything lay about in complete disarray—her galley shears, her graphite paper, her slide rule. Beneath the worktable lay her try square and some pasteboard, her type gauge, too.

She sat down in the corner. As she picked a dull strand of auburn hair from her blouse, she thought of Jarvis. *What if his ghost were to appear before me here?*

First, the ghost would flash a grin. "Don't feel so bad," he might tell her then. "Had to bowl off, I did. They had me bang to rights. The bloody fool solicitor and the goddamn bloody law office in Roundhay, they can't never do me no good. I buzzed poor Ludovic that night, and no matter how much I might buck down all humbled and repentant-like, I'm not getting out of the basket. Bloody hell, if the Old Bailey could, he'd probably send me off to some goddamn penal colony."

A strong autumn breeze sailed into the room, stirring to life a newspaper clipping that had been lying perfectly still on the floor.

Intrigued, she crawled over and took the leaf of paper into her hand.

The clipping proved to be a story all about a gothic picture show just now entering post-production in Berlin—*Das Cabinet des Dr. Caligari.*

Whoever had disturbed her worktable must have left the article behind.

She placed the clipping inside her coat pocket, just there beside the telegram.

An hour passed by, and suddenly it was time for her book-design seminar. What a strain the lesson promised to be; the instructor, Professor Eitelkeit, had a habit of calling upon her and asking her the most pointed questions. Overcome by the news out of London, Sophie felt much too fragile to attend. *I've got to stay put and restore myself.*

In time, she resolved to enter into a brisk round of self-hypnosis. *That should do.* She would simply revisit the bed-sit days back at the hotel and lose herself in soothing memories of that time in her life *before* she had ever even heard of the Mayfair Tearoom—that time in her life *before* she had ever even heard Jarvis perform one of his macabre poems.

As the day progressed, self-hypnosis failed. Each time she endeavored to go lost in the past, her thoughts returned to Ludovic's tragic death—every awful, lurid detail.

More than once, she revisited the tense moment when the custody sergeant had forced her to tell him where Jarvis had obtained the crossbow.

At three o'clock, she went lost in a memory of the inquest—which bled into a memory of that dismal day when she had learned the news that Scotland Yard would indeed prefer charges against Jarvis.

Finally, she recalled the day Judge Lord Thomsett issued his writ—the summons obliging her to appear before him. *How to forget that morning down at Courthouse Square?* After a long delay, a detective sergeant had guided her into the judge's chambers.

"You might as well turn copper," His Honor had told her. "Why should some unwitting accomplice like you have to go off to the nick? You'll be our crown witness, and you'll lay bare the whole scheme. So, come forward. Otherwise, we'll have ourselves a weekslong trial, the lot of them Bessarabia-Ballroom hooligans signing confessions to this and that, only to recant the next day and . . ."

The studio door opened, and Adolpha continued inside—the crossbow in her hand, of course. She had dressed herself in the same old silk-crepe tea gown, and by now, the scalloped hem looked badly frayed. Very much favoring her left leg, she paced awhile.

When she finally stopped in the opposite corner, she removed her Prinz-Heinrich hat and sat down upon the floor. Then she reached up beneath her tea gown, and in so doing, revealed a perilous bolt nestled within a drop-leg sheath.

Sophie pulled upon her fishtail braid. "Did you come around here last night? Have you got something on your mind?"

Looking disoriented, Adolpha took the bolt into her hand and tapped the shaft against the floor—not unlike a magistrate tapping his hardwood gavel in order to disband the jury.

Sophie's thoughts turned back to Jarvis. If self-hypnosis would not help her, might there be some other way to come to terms? Given all her torment, she would have to do something extraordinary.

On the other side of the room, Adolpha burst into laughter and snorted—and now she placed her hand over her nose, as if to demonstrate that she had never before committed such a shameful, unladylike indiscretion.

Sophie looked deep into Adolpha's eyes—her spinning pupils. "I know you've got something of paramount importance to say, so why not tell me already? Let's talk it over."

Adolpha refused to speak up, her left leg slowly kicking back and forth; she only caressed her thigh.

Sophie crawled over to the wooden crate filled with all her book-design supplies, and without a moment's hesitation, removed a box of charcoal pencils. Then she took into her hands one of the leather-bound books that she had brought from London, a template by which to model her own work—*The Posthumous Papers of the Pickwick Club*, a pristinely-preserved first edition that she had found in Surrey. Having sat down again, she flipped through the novel and stopped on page thirty-three. Then, guided by her stream of unconscious, and nothing more, she jotted down any number of words and phrases across the top margin:

Must perform this mournful rite and call upon my anguish to conjure revelation.
Must make books filled with beauty. Perfect, precise conceits.
Must make atonement and taste redemption.

Just as she had done before, Adolpha tapped the bolt against the floor. "What are you doing with that book there?" she asked in the most solemn tone. "What a pity. The way you endeavor to destroy your lovely book, it's something like what a spoiled brat might do, yes, a sinful, selfish girl who smashes all her toys."

Sophie dropped the charcoal pencil from her hand. For a moment, she studied the once-pristine, Victorian novel. *Already, I've gone and ruined it.*

Taking its time, a strand of hair drifted down to her lap.

Adolpha crawled toward her and stopped not three feet away. "Today I wish to confide in you my secret desire . . . my most implacable obsession."

Involuntarily, Sophie's left leg kicked—and then her left hip joint swiveled just so. "Yes, go on. Tell me everything."

"No, maybe not. At present, I can't help but notice that you appear to be under great duress. As if a ruthless spirit terrorizes you."

Emphatically, Sophie shook her head. "Never mind my little quirks. Take me into your confidence. Ever since the day we first spoke, I've always wanted to know just why you fixate on—"

"Yes, you look unwell. As if you suffer great torment. Maybe even sleep deprivation, like a prisoner of war."

Once more, Sophie's leg kicked uncontrollably. "Tell me about your obsession," she insisted.

"But maybe you'll find it . . . *übernatürlich*. Oh, yes. And then you'll act reproachfully and accuse me of perversion."

By now, Sophie's left leg throbbed—the ongoing ache streaming down from her thigh and onward along her shinbone. At the same time, she felt short of breath. "Trust me when I tell you that I'll not do you any harm," she promised, gasping some. "Confide in me. *Please.*"

Adolpha reached for Sophie's color wheel, where it lay near the skirting board. Then she drew her hand back. "All my life, I've never felt . . ."

"*Whole?* Like you require something to make you feel complete?"

"No, the *opposite*. Ever since I was a little girl living in Europe, Switzerland, I've always felt like my body was too much."

"What do you mean?"

"It's my accursed left leg," Adolpha whispered. "All my life, this would be my sacred obsession. I never wanted the left one. Always, always, always, I hoped to remove it."

"*Remove* your left leg?"

"Yes," Adolpha almost shouted. "Can't you hear? Ever since I was a little girl, I've felt that I should have only *one* leg. Yes, *one* leg." Very quietly now, Adolpha crawled back to the crossbow. And now she loaded the bolt, only to decock the weapon.

Sophie's left leg kicked yet again, so she rubbed her tender thigh. "Do you hope to find someone to help you do away with the unwanted leg?" she asked.

"Yes. For the last year, the alienist, he's interviewed me many times. That's how they practice medicine here in Europe, Weimar. No hospital honors any amputation request unless a reputable *doktor* approves of the procedure."

"And *has* the physician approved your request to remove your left leg?"

"Who knows? Maybe someday soon, the alienist should decide. What a big day of reckoning it should be. I'll learn if he'll permit the amputation or proscribe all treatment."

Sophie continued to rub her aching left thigh, and then she looked up. "I think some kind of magical transference exists between us."

"No, that's impossible. *Sei nicht hysterisch.* In time, it should pass. I promise."

"Oh, you promise, do you?" Several times over, Sophie sought to pick herself up but could not manage.

Adolpha folded her arms. "How terribly vain that you should

imagine feeling anguish in your leg at this time, as if you must feel what I feel only because we would be friends. How very petty. You make me think of a selfish girl who comes to school, and when she notices a homely girl wearing the same gown, so the selfish girl comes to despise the other."

Feeling insulted, Sophie returned to her feet. Then, dumbfounded yet resolute, she staggered off into the drafty corridor. *Whither?*

CHAPTER FOUR

Weimar, 18 December.

As Adolpha's appointment with her alienist dragged on, Sophie began to regret her decision to accompany the young lady. Before long, Sophie left the waiting room and stepped outside. A storm of isabelline-white snowflakes falling all around, she buttoned up her winter coat and looked to the pavement. *What if the alienist consents to Adolpha's request?*

If and when he did, Friedel would learn of his decision soon enough—and she would be furious, of course.

Sophie looked up from the pavement and turned east—just in time to catch a glimpse of a familiar-looking motorcar turning onto *der Doppelkristallstraße.*

The black Mercedes-Benz Knight slipped into gear and drew close. When it stopped to idle alongside the curb, the motorcar's exhaust filled the air with an odor as strong as blasting-grade fuel oil.

Sophie sought to glare at Friedel, but the opaque windscreen, together with the tinted driver-side window, precluded all. Before long, Sophie turned back to the alienist's door.

Adolpha stepped outside, the young lady beaming with exultation. "I inspire for the whole world to hear the good news," she announced, apparently having failed to notice the motorcar's presence. "Doktor Schwindel, he's approved my humble request."

The revelation struck Sophie hard, and a burning sensation immediately awoke up and down her left leg. When she nearly lost her footing, she reached for the alienist's door and inadvertently knocked the Christmas wreath to the pavement.

Adolpha must have noticed the Mercedes just then, for the crossbow very nearly fell from her hand. Once she had secured the weapon, she marched over to the motorcar and touched the spare tire mounted upon the running board.

A few times over, Friedel revved the engine.

As if to prove herself undaunted, Adolpha studied her reflection in the driver-side window. At the same time, she turned this way and that—in such a way as to suggest that she must be admiring her double-breasted overcoat's stylish sewing pattern.

Moments later, as Adolpha continued down the walkway, Sophie followed along.

Not surprisingly, Friedel released the clutch and kept pace with them. What did the maniacal scold hope to accomplish?

Adolpha stopped beside a lamppost and looked directly across the street to a Lutheran church, where a band of children stood in line to audition for the upcoming Christmas play. For a moment or two, she laughed like a little girl. "Who shall be angels and who shall be mortals, the wondrous women of Weimar must decide."

The black Mercedes stopped alongside the curb.

As a swathe of malodorous smoke emanated from the motorcar's exhaust pipe, Sophie looked into Adolpha's eyes. "Don't go through with the amputation. Think of the locals, why don't you? When they learn what you've done, won't they find the whole idea obscene?"

Adolpha's leg kicked back and forth a few times. "*Verdammt.*" Once she had grown calm, she continued along two and a half more blocks—until she stopped to look directly across the street to *das Liszthaus*.

A moment or two later, Sophie followed along to the place where Adolpha stood—and then the motorcar rolled forward.

Adolpha turned to Sophie and flashed a smile. "Let's visit *das Liszthaus*. We'll sit in the museum café. It's lovely there. They've adorned it with Christmas candles and holly leaves and pine garlands and . . ."

An icy breeze played through Sophie's hair as she looked to the sky. "Don't dispose of your leg. *No*. Perish the thought."

Adolpha poked Sophie's shoulder with the end of the crossbow. "Let's go," Adolpha told her. "Inside *das Liszthaus*, we'll inspire for the book of songs you'll make, that beautiful, little book of Swiss-German prose poems. Friedel's song."

Sophie turned to a lamppost. Twice, she tapped her brow against the pole—as much to nettle Adolpha as to express a sense of growing frustration. "Don't listen to what the alienist says," Sophie told her. "If you do away with your leg, I'm sure that Friedel should grow as vengeful and as vindictive as—"

"Who cares? Let's challenge Friedel. Let's defy the hand of ascendancy. *Ja*. We'll champion the cause of liberty." Without another word, Adolpha walked out into the street.

The motorcar lurched forward, and the front bumper almost slammed into her shin.

Adolpha gazed into the darkened windscreen. "Doktor Schwindel has approved my request," she shouted. "*Komm damit klar, Liebling*."

As Adolpha kicked the number plate, the unseen Friedel gunned the engine.

Calmly then, Adolpha placed the crossbow onto the bonnet and lit a cigarette.

Several passersby gathered on both sides of the street, meanwhile, everyone watching the ongoing stand-off.

And now the traffic began to back up. What a fine host of vehicles, too: a lovely, sea-green *Phänomen*, a sky-blue *Doppel-Phaeton*, and a dozen other elegant passenger cars.

When a policeman finally came along to intervene, Sophie's heart raced—and now she retreated into the alleyway.

Later, when she returned to the boarding house where she had rented a modest room, a paroxysm awoke deep within her left leg. For a time, she stood in the foyer and sought to assure herself that the condition must be stress-induced and nothing more. Still, she wobbled so badly that she soon collided with the console table. *Good God, am I dying?*

At last, she took hold of the banister and made her way upstairs.

Inside her darkened room, her left leg ached even more. As she struggled to maintain her balance, she knocked a few of her typography books from the shelf. Then she bumped into her writing table, toppling her best lettering set.

Deep down, she grasped the source of her agony: the sensation followed from guilt, for she knew that Adolpha was right. *There's no good reason why someone must be able-bodied.*

Another sharp paroxysm awoke all along Sophie's leg, and the meat of her thigh burned and throbbed as never before. Soon, it felt as if some godly force had chosen to slice the thigh bone in half.

Now she reeled about the room, and she knocked over her urn lamp. Then she stubbed a toe against her *chiffonier*. When she fell to the hardwood floor, she could not muster the strength to crawl over to her bed. *Just sleep here.* Bundled up in the warmth of her winter coat, she closed her eyes and nodded off.

At length, a terrible dream presented itself.

And she walks out into the street, where the glistening, black Mercedes awaits her.

And now the ghoulish, fantastical rat personage rolls down the window, and he waves her over. "Herkommen."

She draws near, peers in at him, and admires his ingenuity—for he sits upon a wooden crate arranged atop the driver's seat, a stilt attached to each of his four limbs that he might steer the wheel and work both the treadle and clutch.

He gestures back toward the boot. "Go. Collect your Christmas gift."

Reluctantly, she walks back to the boot and opens it to find a glittery Christmas stocking.

Charmed, if not wholly entranced, she eventually slips the stocking over her left foot and ankle and shin, at which point the black Mercedes proceeds to roll back such that the automobile severs her left leg and . . .

She awoke in a terrible fright. Having fallen asleep on the floorboards, she had managed to cut off the circulation to what felt like the whole of her left side. Indeed, the whole of her left leg felt lifeless—as though it would never function again. In absolute desperation, she reeled all about the floor—as if to do so might encourage her bloodstream to flow as it should.

The commotion must have awoken the manageress of the boarding house; the elderly woman, Frau Schmerz, called out from downstairs.

As her circulation improved, Sophie crawled to the door and continued down the corridor before collapsing upon the needlepoint runner.

When the manageress found her there, the woman patted Sophie's shoulder. "You feel a little bit ill, yes? So, maybe I bring you powdered milk. No, maybe I bring you a glass of spring water from Bad Liebenstein."

Once Frau Schmerz had walked off, Sophie sought to pick herself up. Alas, she only managed to lurch forward some—and now she tumbled down the staircase, all the way to the bottommost step.

Frau Schmerz returned with a pilsner glass, and she placed it to the side of the newel post. Then she felt up and down Sophie's spine. Afterward, the elderly woman collected the pilsner glass and let Sophie drink.

The water reeked of poppy-seed oil, but even so, Sophie swallowed a mouthful. Then, even if the sensation followed from some kind of placebo effect, she soon decided that she did indeed feel at least a little bit better.

Frau Schmerz switched on the console-table light. "Everything good? Do you have double vision?"

Sophie studied the doormat's wild, intricately embroidered design—a series of highly stylized vines surrounding a grand *cartouche* medallion. Then, when she turned away, she studied the floral-white foyer wall. "*Mir geht es gut,*" she answered.

"*Ja?* So, maybe I prepare you a plate of potato noodles. Or maybe a spoonful of cinnamon sugar."

Sophie shook her head. "*Nein, danke.*"

Looking confounded, Frau Schmerz sat down at the foot of the stair. "We must find a good *doktor* to look at you."

"*Nein.*" With that, Sophie returned to her feet. Then she made her way outside, where a pristine sheet of snow presently blanketed the hushed city.

On and on, Frau Schmerz pleaded with her to return inside.

Sophie walked all the way back to *der Doppelkristallstraße*. There, she stopped before the alienist's office window.

A creamy, white glow radiated from behind the curtain lace— as if he must be hard at work yet, the dedicated physician looking through his patients' files.

She knocked upon the windowpane, and she called out.

The alienist's silhouette passed by the curtain lace. How gently the figure glided along, too—like an aged saint, someone in possession of great wisdom. He did not respond, though.

Did the alienist fear that she disapproved of his recent accession to Adolpha's demands?

Sophie felt guilty, for she had no right to second-guess an experienced physician. *Even if his therapy might seem unconventional, so what?*

The wintry current growing colder and colder, she knelt to the walkway.

Alongside the curb, a puddle of water had flowed out from the drainage pipe and had turned to ice—and a solitary, discernible wave had frozen in such a way as to retain the shape of a hollow curl.

She touched the unmoving wave, and she gasped—for what a shock to witness the elements' dominion over something so poignant, something longing to be free.

CHAPTER FIVE

Weimar, 13 February.

Early that morning, Sophie visited Adolpha's design studio. *Where could she be?* At present, Sophie knew very little; Adolpha had traveled off to Stuttgart, where an operating theater had agreed to perform the controversial amputation. Other than that, Sophie had no idea just what had become of her. *Did she really go through with it?*

Downstairs, the door opened and closed with a heavy thud. After a long pause, someone commenced to climb the flying staircase—and it sounded as if the person must be hobbling on crutches.

That's Adolpha, obviously. Sophie bumped into the drafting table and knocked a box of charcoal crayons to the floor. At the same time, a powerful, ill-boding sunbeam shone through the skylight, only to bounce off the brass work lamp—and now the glare left her blinded, for a moment anyway.

On crutches, Adolpha hobbled through the studio door. The remarkable young lady had only one leg, her right.

The oddity of it all confounded Sophie, and she trembled all over. Her hand trailing along the length of the drafting table, she absent-mindedly knocked a jumble of rollers and mechanical pencils onto the floor. Then she glowered at Adolpha. How to think of her as anything more than a conniver, the worst kind of intriguer? Suddenly, there could be no doubt that Adolpha had only ever longed to lose a leg so that she might command others' sympathy.

What kind of insipid sob story would she relate in order to

augment her act? Perhaps she would claim that she had lost her left leg to a childhood poliovirus.

Adolpha adjusted the left crutch, where it pressed up against her topmost rib. By now, she must have noticed Sophie's great displeasure.

After a while, Adolpha looked into Sophie's eyes and sighed. "I've freed myself, and that inspires. You should be happy for me. Truly, you have no reason to take exception."

The steady radiance pouring through the skylight shifted, and now the glare served to illumine a long, shimmery grip knife lying upon the floor next to a set of wooden print racks.

With the end of her crutch, Adolpha pointed at the sharp implement. "If you wish, I'll take *your* left leg now. That way you may feel the same good, free sensation that I feel."

"That's not funny," Sophie told her. With that, Sophie grabbed the grip knife. Five times over, she tapped the cheek of the blade against a section of her thigh. Then she marched over to the cupboard, and she placed the perilous implement behind a box of rubber type.

When she turned back, she pulled upon her braid several times—until three strands of hair drifted down to the hem of her skirt. Anxious, she checked herself—and much to her dismay, she realized that several more strands had attached themselves to her cardigan.

With her left hand, Adolpha reached down to the space where her left leg should have been and scratched here and there—as if she felt some insidious itch up and down her phantom limb. Before long, she hobbled back to the door. "Next week, on Ash Wednesday, shall we go to church together?" she asked, over her shoulder. "The priest, he'll imprint the sign of the cross on our foreheads."

"But we're not even *Christian*," Sophie shouted. Her leg hopping some, she slumped into a futuristic-looking chromium chair. "Bloody hell, there's no limit to your vanity."

"Maybe after the worship service, we'll go to a picture-show premiere," Adolpha continued, fussing with her left crutch yet again. "*Das Cabinet des Dr. Caligari.* This feature promises to be great. All the newspapers say so."

Without another word, Adolpha departed the studio.

Sophie returned to her feet and paced awhile. How good it would be to convince herself that she must be dreaming, sleep-walking. When she awoke, she would find that the displeasing encounter with Adolpha had never happened. Even better, she would learn that Adolpha had never gone through with the amputation.

Ah, but she did.

As the day passed by, Sophie consulted several different sources and learned the most extraordinary rumors regarding Adolpha's severed leg. Apparently, while recuperating from the surgical procedure, Adolpha had read a detailed biography of Sarah Bernhardt and had learned that an arthritic condition had compelled the famed stage actress to have her right leg removed above the knee.

And that was not all.

A while later, P. T. Barnum himself had sought to purchase the severed limb so that he might exhibit it in a dime museum— and though Sarah Bernhardt had refused to sell her leg for such an ignoble purpose, Adolpha had decided to embrace the whole idea: by all accounts, she intended to exhibit *her* severed leg in the campus art gallery.

Several faculty members confirmed the rumor. One of the highest-ranking architectural-design instructors heard that Adolpha had contacted an Austrian *Privatdozent der Philosophie*, who had in turn contacted Walter Gropius so as to urge him to permit the experimental project to go forward. Another instructor heard that Adolpha had contacted Wassily Kandinsky, who had in turn wired *das Bauhaus* with his approval of the scheme. The latter rumor seemed plausible, for how could Herr Gropius ignore *him*? To be sure, Herr Gropius had always wanted Kandinsky to leave Mother Russia and to take a tenured post here.

Early afternoon, Sophie sought to locate Adolpha. Alas, the peculiar young lady eluded her to the point where Sophie wondered if it must be willful. *Adolpha, she's avoiding me.*

At three o'clock, Sophie returned to the beech tree where she and Adolpha had spoken for the very first time several months before.

From somewhere in the heart of the city, the deafening cacophony of what sounded like a newfangled industrial machine reverberated—and now the air filled with the malodorous traces of smelting ores.

Sophie recalled some of the books in the opulent *Bauhaus* library—all those illustrations of the big, strong foundry workers who had forged the gates of Potsdam. Without a doubt, such strait-laced workfolk would not look favorably on Adolpha's scheme to exhibit her severed leg in an art gallery. Even now, Sophie envisioned the endless protests—the socially conservative populace, the irate crowds descending upon the campus in order to decry the decadence.

Late afternoon, Sophie returned to her studio and revisited the notion that she might someday publish a collection of Friedel's prose poems. Might a volume like that help to appease a skeptical public? Sophie could always include a proem, and in praising Friedel's rat-personage character and his obsession with legs, the text could, in a way, serve as a subtle-yet-fairly-robust defense for Adolpha's questionable exhibition.

In addition, Sophie could present a copy of the book to some of the more prominent figures in Weimar society—and she could design a series of flattering, personalized bookplates for each one of the dignitaries. Even if Sophie's efforts failed to placate everyone, much of the public would at least note just how much alike

Friedel and Adolpha had once been—and as a consequence, the vast majority of the more influential people might very well come to concede how hypocritical it would be to tolerate the one but not the other.

By the end of the day, as the light of dusk shone brightest orange, Sophie had designed much of Friedel's book. With great care, Sophie had chosen the proper typesetting—a traditional style sure to please. She had even reedited Friedel's most ambitious work, entitling the opening sequence *"Die Ouvertüre"* and the concluding sequence *"Epilog."*

As the light of dusk turned to the darkness of night, Sophie reread several sections of the work and shuddered; even if everyone in Weimar marveled at her book design, nevertheless, the citizenry would be sure to look harshly on the content.

One reader might find the verse too simple, the work of a poetaster—and at the same time, a dim-witted reader might accuse Friedel of obscurantism. Some other glib critic might find her poetry vulgar and too fantastical, a rather callow brand of surrealism—and that critic's own associate might regard the work as a touch bland, the stuff of social realism. At some point, some muddled critic somewhere would be sure to contradict himself by arguing at least three wholly *dissimilar* views at once. Worst of all, how to stop the malevolent kind? Surely, all throughout the world, there existed countless, self-appointed experts who feel compelled to denounce just about *any*thing—even a well-intentioned, little book.

At seven o'clock, Sophie walked outside. *Where could Adolpha be?*

With no better option, Sophie made her way back to the beech tree.

From the direction of the dining hall, the scents of herb-roasted pork and potato dumplings drifted by. Sophie did not feel at all hungry, so she turned in the opposite direction—toward the art gallery.

By a twist of fate, Adolpha stood before the doors.

A bundle of nerves, Sophie approached very slowly.

Adolpha reached into her coat and produced an object of some kind.

It's a pair of cloth-paper shears. And now Sophie looked a little bit closer: oddly, something had become trapped within the hinge. *Oh yes, a pretty, little feather.*

What a glorious plume: due to the shimmery light emanating from the art gallery's foyer, the feather shone the vivid purple red of magenta dye.

"Have you heard what I intend to do with my leg?" Adolpha asked.

"Don't do it. The whole idea, it's all so *undignified.* You can't be so depraved as to think to exhibit your own . . ."

Adolpha looked to the shears in her hand, the feather. "I must honor what inspires. How to ignore the creative impulse? Think of the beautiful, sublime Swiss Plateau. At times, the she-wolf steps into some iron trap. So, what does the she-wolf do to be free? She gnaws the trapped leg from her body. Anything to be *free.*"

"Maybe it's true what you say," Sophie conceded. "Still, no animal dishonors itself by *flaunting* the lost limb."

"No, but maybe the prideful hunter does. Maybe he comes along, and he discovers the wolf's severed leg. So, what does he do? He brings it home. As if the leg were a prize."

Sophie drew a deep breath. "Tell me something. How do you aim to preserve a leg made of flesh and bone? Did you put it inside an ice cabinet? Do you mean to treat the limb with some kind of embalming elixir, some kind of grave wax? What about Walpurgis oil?"

Adolpha did not trouble herself to answer. As she gazed upon the feather, she acquired the most blissful expression. Plainly, a sense of jubilation had seized hold of her—one of those fleeting sensations of ecstasy that comes upon the psyche every now and then, one of those uncanny instances when everything feels right with the world.

The whole display made Sophie feel doubtful and miserable—as if she had no hope of dissuading anyone from looking askance at the impending exhibition.

At last, she stepped back. "I know it's wrong for me to play the would-be savior. We're not in England, nor do we study at Marlborough College or someplace like that. German society, it's none of my affair. No, I'm only a guest here at *das Bauhaus*. But even so . . ."

Adolpha removed the feather from the shears' hinge and let the bright plume drift this way and that before alighting upon the cracked asphalt. And now her expression grew into a blank stare.

CHAPTER SIX

Weimar, 18 March.

The date of Adolpha's exhibition had arrived.

Midmorning, Sophie sat brooding in her room back at the boarding house. She felt the urge to ruin the affair. *I've got to hatch a plot, but what?*

Twenty minutes later, the answer came to her: as soon as the art gallery opened that evening, she would purloin the leg.

At midday, she sat down at her sewing table—and with utmost dispatch, she proceeded to cobble together a disguise consisting of a Basque-style evening coat, a wig of ginger-dyed wool, and a lovely *charmeuse* gown emblazoned with sequins.

If anyone at the art gallery happened to ask for a name, she would remain calm and introduce herself as Frau Dagmar von Fischblut from *das Institut für Sexualmedizin*. What a perfect scheme: unrecognizable and unsuspected, she would bide her time and then collect the leg as soon as the opportunity arose.

At two o'clock, she designed a *second* disguise. Then she brought it to her studio back on the campus, and she concealed the alternate getup inside a pine-wood cello case. Later that night, once she had returned with the purloined leg, she would slip out of the first disguise and into the second. Afterward, once she had concealed the leg inside a big bundle of graph paper, she would arrange the plunder inside the cello case. Then, acting perfectly innocent, she would saunter off through campus—and if anyone were to catch her unawares, she would claim to be a musician from Bologna.

In the evening, Sophie capped off her two disguises by borrowing two different pairs of spectacles from Frau Schmerz. At that point, Sophie drew a deep breath and then made her way back onto campus. Nervous, she paused between two plum trees. *Courage.* She had to remember that tonight she was Frau Dagmar von Fischblut and that nothing could dismay a scholar of her renown. *Stay in character.*

The art gallery proved to be very crowded. In the public lobby, a catering service passed out butterscotch schnapps and smoked carp. From every direction, meanwhile, the sharp scent of organic perfumes lingered in the air—pungent black rose, grapefruit, and a dozen other dizzying fragrances.

As she made her way through the throngs of people, she pinched her nose shut and breathed in. *Go easy.* Various students and faculty coming and going, she feigned interest in some of the exhibits hanging on the south wall—a mundane cloudscape, a silk tapestry, and a dozen or more intricate *a-la-poupée* prints depicting the townhouse where Frau von Stein once entertained Goethe.

An adjutant professor turned from a woodblock-print landscape, and he seemed to study the shape of Sophie's nose. Did he recognize her?

Quickly, she made her way into the north gallery.

And there it stood: beneath a ray of Alice-blue light falling from the wall sconce, the oblong reliquary awaited. Inside the glass box, Adolpha's severed leg seemed to hover within a glow of immaculate phosphorescence—an effect that made the limb look otherworldly, the flesh ablaze yet undying.

Startled, Sophie shuffled from side to side and studied the exhibit from a variety of angles.

How had Adolpha achieved the feat of levitation? Had she concealed a network of magnetic lodestones?

Sophie breathed in, and she detected a repulsive stench: the severed limb reeked of coal-tar pitch and mildewy cereal malt.

Momentarily overcome, she stumbled forward and bumped her brow against the reliquary frame's intricate beading. *Damn.*

Thankfully, it did not seem as if anyone had witnessed the infraction. Just by chance, though, the crowd suddenly quieted down.

Sophie felt muddled. *What's all this?*

In unison now, the silent crowd parted.

Dressed in a silk evening gown studded with rhinestones, Adolpha hobbled forward on her crutches. Seemingly unimpressed by her surroundings, she turned to gaze upon something in the west wing.

At last, she turned back and continued forward. Only when she reached the reliquary did the crowd resume with all their repartee and laughter.

Adolpha turned to Sophie then. "*Hat das bein sorgen?*" the young lady asked, as if she feared that Sophie found the exhibit objectionable.

Sophie rejoiced, for she felt certain that the disguise had worked. Still, she did not know how to answer the question. Would an erotic, almost even obscene, severed leg like this trouble a scholar such as Frau Dagmar von Fischblut? Perhaps it would, for no matter how exquisitely the limb graced the gallery, how should any properly-educated soul tolerate the objectification of a woman's body?

With a loud sigh, Adolpha adjusted her crutches and shuffled to the side. "*Es tut mir leid,*" she continued then. "*Ich nehme an, das bein tut . . .*"

Sophie grinned, for her ongoing silence had plainly wounded Adolpha.

When the young lady finally hobbled off, Sophie turned back to the leg. With all her might, she pushed the reliquary off the table.

No sooner had the metallic frame crashed to the floor than she grabbed the moist, sticky, chemically-treated leg. "*Keine pornografie mehr!*" she cried out in a disguised voice. Then, as everyone stood there aghast, she hurried off down the west wing.

The route proved to be unideal: as if they had prepared themselves for the commission of the crime, two gypsum-plaster figures loomed up ahead. One looked like *der Friedensengel,* and the second looked to be a likeness of Marie Antoinette— the queen consort all decked out in the most luxuriant *robe à la Polonaise.*

Sophie turned to her right and gasped.

A life-size swan maiden stood there, the sculpture standing stalwart in her long gown of magnolia-white feathers. What a high, elongated neck she had, too. Most extraordinary of all, the sculptor had gifted the swan maiden with dazzling eyes: in the subdued light of the wall sconce, one iris shone as brightly as strawberry quartz and the other something like rainbow pearl.

As Sophie marveled at the jewels, one of the school's trustees approached from behind and grabbed hold of the plunder. "*Was ist der sinn dieser empörung?*" the gentleman asked, drawing upon the leg with great force.

As hard as she could, Sophie pulled the other way. In the ensuing struggle, she fell back into the swan maiden and knocked the figure down from its matte-black pedestal.

As quickly as she could, she returned to her feet and fixed her tousled wig.

Meanwhile, what looked to be almost everyone from all throughout the gallery hurried over.

Soon enough, Adolpha herself hobbled forward—the panicked young lady sobbing and rambling on and on in her distinctive, Swiss-German dialect.

At that point, a long-haired *dachshund* broke away from its master—and now the dog raced forward, its leash dragging behind it. All the time howling and growling and hissing, the animal took Marie Antoinette's gown into its jaws and pulled such that the likeness fell against the sculpture resembling *der Friedensengel*, which immediately fell to the floor.

As more and more irate students and faculty members crowded about, Sophie let go of the leg and collected the swan maiden. With no better option, Sophie brandished the figure the way a brute might hold a battering ram—and now she jabbed at one of her own instructors with the swan maiden's sharp, pointed toenails.

When someone finally managed to grab the other end of the sculpture, Sophie let go and raced out the west-wing door.

As soon as she reached her darkened studio, she changed into her second disguise. Then, with the help of her pocket mirror, she checked herself. *Do I even resemble an Italian cellist?*

If anything, the cheap wig, and tattered coat made her look like a destitute widow driven into a life of prostitution.

At last, Sophie turned to consider the empty cello case. *I failed to purloin the accursed leg.* Instantly, she melted into tears of rage.

Ten minutes later, once she had collected herself, she continued through the campus as patiently as she could. Even with the second disguise, if she did not act casual, who could say whether someone might stop her?

Slowly, someone came up from behind—the crunch of broken glass resounding from beneath the sole of the person's shoe.

Sophie glanced over her shoulder. *Adolpha, damn.*

The maniacal, red-faced, young lady held the crossbow—the weapon fully loaded. And now she called out in Swiss German.

Sophie's heart pounded. *My goodness, Adolpha thinks I'm Friedel.* As quickly as she could, Sophie raced along down the street. Then, the cello case having grown burdensome, she ducked into an alleyway and dropped the pointless prop beside a broken carpet loom.

From what sounded like no more than half a block away, a plainly-excited Adolpha called out a second time—again, in perfect Swiss German.

Sophie shook her head. *Damn.* Breathing heavily, she raced past a Lutheran church embellished with gilded-egg wreaths and other fanciful Easter decorations.

A bolt streaked through the sky and landed some ten feet to the right.

Oh my. Sophie continued along—past a transit shelter and onward through the deserted trolley station. *Keep going.*

In the shadow of a plane tree, she tripped over what looked to be a ragpicker's basket left forgotten on the walkway. Her left knee aching badly, she no longer had the power to run. Nor could she walk without a pronounced limp. *I'm cursed.*

She made her way forward the best that she could. Not two blocks from the boarding house, though, she very nearly swooned: up ahead, someone had parked a familiar-looking, black Mercedes-Benz Knight alongside the curbstone.

The motorcar just had to belong to Friedel. How to mistake the distinctive, tinted-glass windscreen?

Sophie studied the neighboring half-timbered townhouses. What a funny feeling to realize that Friedel lived so close by.

A second bolt streaked through the sky and landed some ten feet to Sophie's left.

She should have taken cover. As confounded as she felt, though, she could not even decide if the bolt was real. *God help me.*

From out of the shadows, a figure holding a hand over half her face approached slowly and guardedly.

Despite the woman's hand, Sophie recognized her as Adolpha's twin.

Friedel studied her, and then the young lady smirked—for *she* had plainly recognized *her*, despite the disguise. "Well then, what's your review?" Friedel asked. "Have you great praise for my twin sister's grand premiere? Do you adjudge her art experimentation not a little bit ahead of its time? But of course, you do. I imagine you regard her leg so timeless and enduring as to be something sublime, something paramount, a work of true genius."

"No, I prefer *your* work. Prose poetry. Tell me, though. Why the rat personage? How did you ever dream up such a vile character?"

All so mercurial, Friedel refused to answer. She only turned away and vanished back into the gloom of night.

And now a third bolt streaked through the sky.

At last, Sophie raced along. *Head for the hills.*

CHAPTER SEVEN

Weimar, 29 April.

Late afternoon, as Sophie's last lecture of the day concluded, the riots commenced.

By now, the whole city knew about Adolpha's leg—and everyone disapproved. As such, more than a thousand impassioned people participated in the melee.

At one point, someone from the mob fired off what appeared to be a newfangled rifle grenade. The spring breeze blowing wildly, several buildings soon caught fire—including the art gallery. Almost immediately, a pall of smoke suffused the whole of the campus.

When the fire brigades arrived, the overzealous rioters cast stones at them—and then several protesters overturned one of the hand-pull hose wagons. Not to be undone, five or so hooligans pelted one of the gas-engine motor trucks.

Like so many others, Sophie exited the industrial building's back door and took shelter among the elm trees standing on the far side of the school grounds.

For a time, Walter Gropius and some of the other instructors debated just why and how the leg had affected the populace in such a visceral way.

Several instructors wondered if the people of the city had misinterpreted the leg as some kind of Bolshevik symbol. Most of the faculty theorized that the people considered the leg to be an emblem of decadence, the amorality of modern art—a wildly grotesque indulgence intended to undermine all of German society.

Looking delirious, a girl from the architectural-design program began to weep. Did she fear that the public backlash might force *das Bauhaus* to move to some other city?

As the flames consumed the industrial building, Sophie mourned all the work that she stood to lose—especially the book that she had designed all so diligently, that ornate volume housing Friedel's verse.

The galley proof had turned out well. Determined to impress, Sophie had included not only a detailed preface but a proper afterword—not to mention an austere flyleaf to follow the endnote. Even the dust wrapper had come to look all so ideal—the title and such centered amid a seamless, geometric pattern. Had the galley proof included a solitary imperfection? Even if the design had, what could the flaw possibly matter? Sophie had never intended to create something immaculate. Like any other humble printer or copyeditor, she had preferred the notion that there might be mistakes here and there. With all that in mind, she had even made a point of designing the most wondrous and clever colophon: a smoky-white shape resembling a feather inclusion, the kind of minor defect that an exacting jeweler might espy within an otherwise exquisite diamond.

From the other side of the campus, the sounds of mayhem continued to ring out: officers shouting orders, the mob shouting insults, and the fire brigades' dissonant alarm bells pealing all the while. What a pungent odor, too. By now the smoky fumes reeked of asphyxiant gas. There could be little doubt as to why: in as much as the raging fire had consumed an art school, several gallons of toxic oil paint had surely seeped into the air.

In short order, almost everyone staggered off.

No matter how badly Sophie coughed, she could not bring herself to depart. *How to leave my book?* She stood firm. In time, she looked up through the smoke and fixed her gaze upon the one place where the April sky shone a soft blue. "Please, let my work survive," she prayed.

In the end, she sat down upon the roots of an elm tree.

Thankfully, just at dusk, a soothing rain commenced.

Little by little, some of the fumes lost their power.

Gradually, nightfall descended upon a weary city. Then the night grew quiet, as if the riot had abated.

She checked her timepiece. *Nine o'clock.* She returned into the industrial building, only to find the place gutted. Even if she wanted to check her studio, she could do no such thing; the flames had reduced the flying staircase to ash.

Holding herself close, she exited through the remains of the front door.

A thick haze of smoke streaked with bright, silver-chalice flourishes lingered in almost every direction.

Off toward the east side of the campus, a pair of German-Army field wagons lay in ruin—billows of smoke the color of Spanish gray drifting through the wreckage.

As for the art gallery, the mob had left the building thoroughly battered—every window smashed.

So, what's become of Adolpha's leg? Sophie just had to know, so she climbed through the gaping hole where the art gallery's doors once stood.

Inside, what a stench—something like burnt toast.

A solitary wall sconce flickering on and off, she continued forward through the endless debris. *What a shambles.*

In the place where the reliquary should have stood, an array of broken glass lay strewn across the floor. Not surprisingly, though, there was no sign of Adolpha's leg.

How would the excitable young lady respond to the devastating news?

Sophie thought for a moment. How long had it been since

they had even spoken? A week before, they had gone to *das Licht-spielhaus* to view that frightful, new, gothic film, *Das Cabinet des Dr. Caligari*. Afterward, they had sat together in the lobby—each one profoundly affected by the revolutionary picture show.

Adolpha had appeared dumbstruck—something like an artist witnessing every shape and color in nature as the fulcrum for yet another canvas or momentous design, or what about a mad composer who hears every sound as yet another leitmotif to some intricate opus?

As for Sophie, the night at the cinema house had been just as much a revelation. Because she had delighted in some elements of the film and had disliked others, she had come to fathom the pointlessness of passing any kind of judgment on anything. In a world where every person, place, or thing would be subject to relativity, why praise or denounce or compare whatever the phenomena? The only way to relate to the nature of reality would be to content oneself to seek to comprehend the *meaning* of things— and to eschew any impulse to cloud the analysis with either glib opinions or personal projections.

The wall sconce flickered a touch more slowly now—as if at any moment the light must go dark altogether.

From out of the shadows, a noise as that of a person walking with crutches resounded.

Adolpha.

The whole of her body bathed in sweat, she hobbled up to Sophie's side. Like a star-struck fool longing to say something to some celebrity, Adolpha moved her lips but could not manage to utter a single word. Even if she could have spoken in that moment, what might she have said?

Adolpha's eyes all aglow in the subdued light, at last, she let out the most heartrending shriek—and in an instant, the echo bounced off the wall and returned to her lips.

Sophie remained silent. *What do I say?* There was nothing

to say. No kaiser had ever invested her with some kind of critical authority over the German people. *So, let it go.*

For her part, Adolpha sobbed. In a frenzy, she snorted. Then she fell to the floor, as if in the throes of an epileptic seizure.

"Come to your senses," Sophie implored her. "Try to be strong. Maybe someday—"

"They're burning my leg," Adolpha blurted out, reaching with both of her hands to feel at the space where her left thigh should have been. "Yes, I feel my flesh melting away."

Sophie nudged Adolpha's right flank. "You don't feel anything at all. It's just a figment of your imagination. Come tomorrow morning, you'll regain your strength and—"

"Yes, I feel the heat of the flames," Adolpha whispered. "Yes, it's as if my left leg must still be attached to my body." At once, the young lady writhed all about. Then she kicked at the crutch where it lay on the floor.

Finally, she seemed to fix upon some spectral presence hovering above her.

Sophie almost laughed. "Settle down already. There's nothing there. *Nichts.*"

Adolpha reached out to the illusory being. "How do you do?" she asked in a raspy whisper. "I am Adolpha T. Unbekömmlich from Europe, Switzerland. A beautiful republic with big mountains and strong rivers. This would be the place where once I inspired for my art pieces and handmade crafts. Oh, but the best theme for my work would be the human leg. That inspires me. So, come to my design studio. And if you travel to Europe, Switzerland, do come visit my grandmother's shop for knitted-wool accessories."

A moment later, Adolpha lay still. Inexplicably then, the whole of her body acquired a sweet scent something like *die knödel.*

Sophie smacked her lips. "Adolpha?"

Slowly, the young lady's eyes rolled back.

Adolpha's dead. Sophie could not bring herself either to shriek or to hurry off. In a state of shock, she reached for the wall in order to maintain her balance. Not a moment later, she fell to the floor. Gasping for breath, she studied Adolpha's face.

How blissful the young lady's expression—as if in dying she had attained deliverance, salvation.

Through the flickering light, yet another figure appeared—a person with the frame of a strong, healthful gentleman.

It's Walter Gropius.

Looking cold and undemonstrative, he knelt beside Adolpha's body. Then, as if to check for a pulse, he felt at her throat.

"How could it be?" Sophie asked.

"*Sie bezahlte das lösegeld,*" Herr Gropius muttered, a wrinkle appearing between his eyes. "Adolpha has paid the ransom."

"Adolpha has paid the ransom?"

"Yes, that's right," he answered.

"I don't follow, *mein herr.* How do you mean precisely?"

"She *redeemed* herself, and having done so, she knew that there was no longer any good reason to continue. Suddenly, it was time to die."

"No," Sophie countered. "I'd say it was trauma, the jolt she felt when she realized the leg was gone."

"No. She knew it was time to go free."

"*Free?* Free from what, *mein herr?*"

"From her*self,* her burdens, her obligations."

"But are you sure that's redemption, *mein herr?*"

"Yes. Until this night, the unhappy girl could not let go of life. Tonight, though, she realized she finally could, for her master-piece, her severed leg, had become the stuff of legend, the stuff of dreams." With that, Herr Gropius placed his silken handkerchief beneath Adolpha's chin, and in the most reverent, loving, fatherly manner, pushed very gently in order to close her mouth. "*Schlafen sie gut,*" he whispered.

Sophie's thoughts turned to her book, and she envisioned herself working in a newly-refurbished campus. Why *not* redo the project? If she gave the next design marbled endpapers, might the alternate version be better than the first? At the very least, she might create a better, more whimsical colophon. *Why not a woman's long, curved leg?* Calmly, she rocked back and forth. *Yes, what a good idea for an imprint.* Her left knee trembled. *Yes, of course, a woman's leg all ablaze.*

Herr Gropius returned the handkerchief into his coat pocket, and he began to hum an opera tune. Did it come from that gothic opera, *Der Vampyr*?

Sophie's thoughts turned to Jarvis, and she cringed. Obsessed with mere revenge, just what had *he* achieved in life? She had to strive to be something better than him that she might eventually register the taste of true redemption. And there was only one way: someday, she would have to complete her work. Until she did, she would remain a slave to vanity.

book two

Mouvements
Perpétuels

I.

CHAPTER ONE

London, 29 September 1917.

Early that morning at the Chelsea Court Hotel, Cäcilia finally realized that last month's assignation with her ice-skating instructor had left her pregnant. For the longest time, she paced about her suite and debated the question of what might be the best way to tell him. Whatever she said, Herr Wechseljahr would be galled. The old man would almost certainly accuse her of being marriage-minded, and he would insist that she had planned everything all along. At some point, too, he would be sure to lament her upcoming debut.

"For so long, I've been choreographing that glorious ice ballet," he would tell her. "And you treat me like this?"

At nine o'clock, when Cäcilia reached Empress Avenue Ice Arena, she continued into the grand antechamber but then stopped. *How do I tell him the bad news?*

In time, the wintry air of the electric skating palace made her teeth chatter. Worse still, the aroma of the snack bar's freshly-brewed, Cadbury drinking chocolate happened to be very strong that day—strong enough to make her retch.

The ice arena's various loudspeakers crackled to life, and as she continued to convulse, a warped recording of Édouard Lalo's *"Ballade à la lune"* commenced.

As the music played, several diminutive schoolgirls laced up and ventured off into the imponderable beauty of the oval rink.

Cäcilia climbed into the hard-oak terrace and watched the most winsome of the children perform a fan spiral.

The Lalo recording concluded, and the vast skating palace grew as quiet as the ruins of the Colosseum.

Cäcilia's thoughts turned to Knightsbridge Casino. One week earlier, she had lost a considerable amount at the baccarat table. As such, she did not have sufficient funds to hire someone to tend to a newborn baby. Before long, she turned to one of the loudspeakers.

If only another recording would begin—and disrupt the quietude, the solemnity.

From the direction of the snack bar, the aroma of Cadbury drinking chocolate grew even more sickly-sweet. Worse yet, the scent of the pungent cocoa essence had begun commingling with the smoldering lampblack odor of the rubber tiles surrounding the boards.

Down on the ice, the little girl from before, the one who had performed the fan spiral, commenced a series of intricate step sequences.

And now the door to the grand antechamber opened, and Herr Wechseljahr made his entrance. When he reached the terrace, he flashed a proud, fatherly smile and greeted Cäcilia with his customary Roman salute.

With a fluttery feeling in the pit of her stomach, she descended the steps and drew near.

Before she could say anything, he touched the mole to the left of her nose and caressed the little white strand of hair that had always reached out from between the pillars of her upper lip.

"Why are you not skating, *mein lieber schatz*?" the old man asked, his breath reeking of peppermint schnapps.

Her legs twitching, she turned to the boards. *What do I say?* Gently, she placed her ice skates upon the top plate.

A moment later, as she traced the tip of her thumb across one of her skating shoe's toe-picks, César Franck's "*Prélude, Fugue et Variation*" poured out from the loudspeakers.

As the piece continued to play, three shapely French maids emerged from the changing room and proceeded to lace up—and when they ventured out across the rink, Herr Wechseljahr grinned and tipped his hat to the tallest one.

Several times over, Cäcilia pulled at her woolen jumper. Then she fussed with one of the pleats in her skating trousers. As she did, she thought of the ice ballet—the regal character that she was to play, a princess living in one of the moon's icebound craters.

At last, she turned back to the young French ladies. Did they not hail from some war-torn locale? If so, she could not blame them for seeking refuge here. Still, she despised them so. If she were to prove unfit to skate the coveted role of the moon princess, then Herr Wechseljahr would surely cast one of the foreigners and let *her* have the part.

Boldly, one of the young French ladies glided by.

Cäcilia felt sick. *I can't permit anyone to usurp me.*

Looking free and easy, Herr Wechseljahr removed a silken handkerchief from his houndstooth coat and then turned away to blow his nose. When the old man turned back, he studied Cäcilia—as if he intuited all her troubles.

She felt too ashamed to say anything, so she gazed into his hazel-flecked eyes for a moment and then looked to her feet.

The old man folded up the dirty handkerchief very slowly, and then he returned it into his coat pocket. "I know what vexes you."

From the way he spoke, she felt certain that he would immediately complete his train of thought. Instead, a pregnant pause lingered in the air.

Herr Wechseljahr reached into another coat pocket and removed his snuff box. In his own good time, he inhaled several pinches of powdered tobacco.

"What vexes me then?" she finally asked him.

"Could it be our little tryst from the other night?"

"*Yes.*" For a time, she revisited the night they had slept together. At some point, one of his associates had stopped by to tell them a terrible rumor: Whitehall felt certain that sometime before dawn, yet another fiery Zeppelin bombardment would terrorize the city.

How to forget the feeling of dread as she had walked back from the old man's flat? Three blocks from the hotel, a powerful, Royal-Navy searchlight had illumined the clouds. Not a moment later, she had stopped beside a terraced house and had looked up. In that moment, she could have sworn that she beheld the airship. What had she felt then? Oddly, she had felt both horror and lust. Even more peculiar, she had not panicked. As confounded as she had felt, a part of her had almost yearned for a long, plump, phallic Zeppelin to be hovering above.

Herr Wechseljahr tapped her shoulder now. "You were a very bad girl to entice me the way you did that night."

"*I* enticed *you*?"

"Yes."

"Just how do you mean?"

"I mean you wish to fornicate with your long-lost father, and because you cannot do so, you decided to groom *me*."

At once, she felt debased: the subject of her father had always filled her with deepest anguish. When her mother was still alive, she had seldom spoken about him. *What do I even know?*

Apparently, he had once danced the part of the Grenadier Guard in an ice ballet adaptation of the operetta *Iolanthe*. Beyond that, Cäcilia knew nothing.

One of the shapely French girls, a young lady with long, honey-blonde hair, glided over and stopped alongside the boards. She gestured toward Herr Wechseljahr and smiled. "Are you maybe Volga-German?" she asked, her breath hovering in the air as a palpable mist alive with the scent of candied lemon peels.

"I come from Austria," he told the young lady.

"Oh? So, how should it be *you* live *here*? Did you bribe the Home Secretary? *Oui bien sûr.* You have big money. I heard a rumor that soon you'll produce an ice ballet. This winter, you'll flood the Palladium and freeze the water, so that it looks like a big lake up there on the moon."

Herr Wechseljahr nodded. "I intend for it to be the greatest ice ballet ever."

The loudspeakers went quiet for a moment, and then a third elegant recording commenced—what sounded like Erik Satie's *"Chanson Medievale."*

As if excited by the tune, the French girl glided off and proceeded to perform an ambitious catch-foot spiral.

Cäcilia groaned. There could be little doubt that the French girl hoped to take her part as the Moon Princess. The more Cäcilia watched, the worse she felt. Before long, she almost even registered a sensation as of someone strangling her to death. Short of breath, she wrapped her hands around her throat and held them there.

Herr Wechseljahr looked into Cäcilia's eyes. "So, little one, why do you wait for me to chide you? Put on your *schlittschuhe* and take to the ice. Show me something marvelous, your best raindrop spiral or maybe—"

"Something awful has happened." She let go of her throat, and she glanced at her belly before looking up again. "I'm with child."

Instantaneously, the old man's eyes glazed over.

A moment later, he raised a hand—as if to strike her.

Before he could, once again, the honey-blonde glided by.

Herr Wechseljahr regained his composure—or so it seemed. For a time, he did not say a word. Neither did the old man move a muscle, nor did he show any emotion.

Meanwhile, the Satie recording began skipping, as if the stylus had reached a crack in the vinyl and could not continue past the imperfection.

Despite all, the honey-blonde continued skating—as if to prove that nothing could disturb her faculties.

Cäcilia breathed in and looked up past the silvery arches and crossbeams to the grand vault over the rink. By the time she looked back down, she felt dizzy.

The old man took her chin into his hand. "What've you done?"

She pouted. "Maybe we could postpone the ice ballet till . . ."

Over and over, the same note of the Satie recording continued to repeat.

Herr Wechseljahr let go of her chin. "Do you realize the beautiful French girls have come to London to escape all the savagery back in *Frankreich*?"

"Yes, but—"

"*Listen.* If you grow fat with a baby, then—"

"You'll hire a French girl to replace me?"

"Yes, of course," the old man answered coldly. "If you wish to perform in my noble *produktion*, you must destroy the unborn baby."

One last time, the honey-blonde glided by.

No, I *am the Moon Princess.*

CHAPTER TWO

London, 18 October.

On the day of the scheduled abortion, Cäcilia awoke to find a tattered, orange elm leaf lying beside her gas cooker. She took the alluring elm leaf into her hand, and then she sat down upon the Da Vinci bench. Just like that, she revisited a childhood memory—the time her mother had taken her to Anjou.

One day Cäcilia had gone lost in an orchard, and a heap of brittle, fallen apricot leaves had reeled all around her. In no time, they had mesmerized her with their lively dance. After a while, she had come to believe that the fallen leaves intended to share with her some wondrous oracle. From that moment on, she had believed that if she watched fallen leaves tumbling about, a vision would surely ensue—the dance of the leaves having triggered the great revelation to rise from the depths of her unconscious mind. Most crucial of all, the epiphany would pertain to the question of good and evil—and whether to do this or to do that.

Not until her childhood had come to an end had she grown out of her fanciful notions.

A strong, autumn breeze stole through the hotel suite now, and the elm leaf slipped from her hand and proceeded to sail all about.

On and on, she watched it. *How did such a wild thing ever even get in here?*

The other day, when Herr Wechseljahr had stopped by, he must have dragged the tree litter in with him. What a tense visit it had been: the old man had come to tell her that he had located a midwife willing to perform the abortion. With that, he had related the directions to the woman's clandestine workroom.

The breeze continued to blow, and now the elm leaf bounced off the floor mirror and sailed past the antique *bombe commode*.

Cäcilia studied the chest. How had the cabinetmaker ever managed to shape the soft tulipwood so that the face and drawers would balloon out as sensually as they did?

The shape suggested the contours and curves of a pregnant woman's belly.

Another gust of wind sailed through the hotel suite, and the tattered leaf flittered about the northernmost window's sill horn before drifting off through the open sash.

At two o'clock, she slipped into a blouse and a plaid-print, high-rise skirt. In a sulk, she found her way to Soho Square. For a time, she stood beside a dying beech tree and listened to the wedding bells pealing from one of the chapels along Greek Street. The music made her think of a book that she had read years before, a history of the silkworm nurseries of Barbazan.

According to the authoress, the humble workfolk would bring each precious cocoon to the village chapel so that the priest might bless the chrysalis within.

The wedding bells went silent now, and the breeze kicked up—and suddenly, a whole array of brittle leaves rained down from the crown of a cherry tree.

Little by little, vivid, scattered memories of Anjou returned.

Could it be that the cherry leaves hoped to entrance her into calling up some great discovery from her stream of unconscious?

She shook her head, for she was too old to believe in such childish things. Dragging her feet, she continued over to the curbstone.

A horse-drawn governess cart raced by, and the sudden draft kicked up a few more fallen leaves.

When the commotion died down, she made her way across the street.

On the opposite walkway, she did just as Herr Wechseljahr's directions would have her do; after passing by the tall, Regency-period townhouse, she continued past the private fertility clinic.

A few blocks down, a hackney carriage emerged from the alleyway to her left and very nearly trampled her.

Once she had caught her breath, she debated which alley to take. If only she had thought to write the directions down on a slip of paper. Half certain that the alley must be a few blocks up ahead, she continued forward—and as soon as she reached a passageway that felt right, she followed it down to a cobblestone courtyard.

What an austere, desolate expanse: the square proved to be devoid of life. Still, a storm of dead, fallen beech leaves tumbled about in the current.

I think I'm here. She turned toward the door, only to find that the knob shone the color of moonstones. Again, she revisited her childhood excursion to Anjou. Two days after the episode involving the apricot leaves, Mother had taken her to Villers-le-Bel. *And a jeweler sold us a handful of moonstone beads and . . .*

The wind grew strong. Like the bubble and squeak of fried cabbage and potatoes, the current whistled all so playfully.

What might the fallen beech leaves be doing?

Perhaps they're dancing. Twice, she tapped the glassy knob. Then, powerless to resist the temptation, she turned around to have a look.

The beech leaves reeled all about in a perfect circle, as if they longed to share with her some wondrous oracle. Perhaps they hoped to counsel her regarding the entity growing inside her womb.

Just as she had done when she sought to grow out of her childish ways, she told herself to ignore all. Over and over, she told herself that a proper woman does not trouble herself to watch fallen leaves tumbling about in some current. Still, no matter how fervently she sought to ignore the beech leaves, she could not do so. To make matters worse, the more the beech leaves reeled about, the more her left thigh smarted.

Did the beech leaves conspire against her? Perhaps they hoped to dissuade her from honoring the appointment.

The current grew stronger and stronger. Soon enough, the sharp, pungent scent of the autumn breeze betrayed an aroma as of bergamot orange.

She gasped, for Herr Wechseljahr's skin, his aftershave, had exuded that same beguiling scent on the night that she had slept with him—the night that she had *conceived*.

The current died out now—and like fallen soldiers, the beech leaves lay still.

Moments later, an aroma as of plum pudding wafted down from one of the windows overlooking the courtyard.

She staggered back a few steps, until she bumped up against the door. And now she stood still. Had she heard a pair of footsteps approaching from within? If so, might it be some poor girl who had only just aborted *her* baby? Slowly and guardedly, Cäcilia turned around.

The door opened to reveal a tearful, humbled young lady all bundled up in a boiled-wool, plaid trench coat. To some degree, they resembled one another: both looked pale, and each had a narrow chin and wide cheekbones. Still, the strange young lady's almond-shaped eyes appeared almost inhuman—as if fashioned from glass. Did the effect follow from the abortion procedure itself? Perhaps the midwife had administered some kind of sedative.

Cäcilia blinked a few times, but she found herself speechless.

There was not much to say anyway, for each one knew that she shared a deep, *unspoken* bond with the other.

The young lady closed the door behind her and peered deep into Cäcilia eyes. "Do you wish to know whether you ought to continue on inside?"

"I suppose so," Cäcilia answered. "What's it like?"

"What do you think it's like?" the young lady asked.

"What do *I* think? The midwife has a proper hospital chair, I should wonder. With stirrups, I expect. Would that be true?"

The troubled young lady looked to the sky. "Do you regret getting yourself into trouble as much as I regret getting myself into trouble?"

"Oh, yes," Cäcilia answered. "Still, it's a little bit too late for anyone to be preaching the virtue of prudence to a pair of reprobates like us." In sorrow, Cäcilia looked heavenward.

Against the blue and gray of the smoky, midafternoon sky, the moon shone a faint, almost invisible champagne white.

What would it be like to fly there in a marvelous moon ship? Upon touching down, what would it be like to wander outdoors? When the lunar swirls awoke, of course, there would be no fallen leaves to dance about. Still, it did seem quite possible that a field of ice might in fact coat at least some of the craters here and there—perhaps even the Sea of Dreams. *What a neat place to skate that would be.* Even if the lunar waves never froze over, nevertheless, a cheerful moon princess would still hold the power to walk on water—after a fashion. Given the gravitational anomalies, she could caper across some flooded crater not unlike a basilisk lizard.

Little by little now, as she imagined the comical creature darting across the surface of some pond, Cäcilia began to laugh—albeit sadly.

The young lady snapped her fingers. "What's so funny?" she asked. "Let me hear the joke."

Cäcilia looked down from the moon. "Tell me what to do. Given what you've just been through, was it worth it or not?"

"*Please.* Don't ask me that."

"But I insist. Tell me what to do."

"Perhaps you ought to follow your heart."

"*Why?* Does the heart always know what'd be virtuous and what'd be—"

"I know what's got you all so confounded," the young lady interrupted. "You fear going inside because you fear that the Hand of God should punish you. Yes, you fear He'll send you to purgatory. Or you wonder whether you should abort your baby even if purgatory *doesn't* exist."

Up inside one of the little bed-sitters overlooking the courtyard, someone sitting at a pianoforte performed an evocative *cavatina.*

"I know," the young lady continued. "You worry that if you destroy the unborn, you'll look selfish and dull-minded."

As the young lady walked off, Cäcilia clenched her jaw and studied the door—its strong, solid lock rails. *What do I do?* A second time, she looked to the moon and imagined how good it would be to walk across the Sea of Dreams. *Walking on water, walking on . . .*

The ongoing pianoforte melody grew dreamlike and resounded softly—and now the music made Cäcilia think of Christ walking across the Sea of Galilee.

Even if the whole idea were impossible, nevertheless, some ancient mystic had in fact dreamed up the notion—and there must have been a reason *why*, a psychosocial matrix from which the peculiar concept arose.

She thought back to catechism class—the day the instructor had told her the Hebrew name for the Sea of Galilee. Though she could not quite remember the word, she did recall the instructor telling her that it derived from a term for "the Israelitish harp." Evidently, the people had named the body of water thus because both the musical instrument and the body of water shared a similar shape. *Might* that *explain all?* One day, as some clever, Christian girl sat watching the fallen myrtle leaves tumbling about the lakefront, she thought of the way a minstrel's nimble fingers walk across a set of harp strings—at which point her unconscious mind conjured a metaphorical image: the noble, barefoot Savior walking on water. Sometime later, she must have told a few of the evangelists. *Yes.*

Up above, the pianoforte went quiet.

Cäcilia checked her wristwatch. *The hour has come.* She had to decide whether to go inside. Once more, she studied the door. *Oh God, it's now or never.*

CHAPTER THREE

London, 13 November.

On the evening of the first rehearsal, a taxicab brought Cäcilia to the Palladium. No sooner had she exited the vehicle than she felt someone's gaze upon her. For a time, she looked up and down the streets of Soho. *Who's there?*

The taxicab pulled away, and she felt a flutter deep inside her womb—a gentle reminder of the fragile life gestating within her body. Overcome with emotion, she paused to envision the entity inside her; already, the homunculus would have grown into a fetus.

Lost in thought, she walked off down Oxford Street. Three blocks away, she stopped before a nursery shop and baby boutique. There, she studied the articles of clothing in the display window: the petticoats, the bib aprons, and all the hooded cloaks. Unconsciously, she moved her hands—as if she were sewing with a Whitechapel needle, a loving woman darning a virgin-wool coatee for her precious newborn.

When she returned to the Palladium and continued into the changing room, a concoction of odors greeted her—the stench of foot powder and sweaty stockings along with a noisome dish of moldy, banana-yellow doodlebug soup.

Her breath as shallow as could be, she slipped into a shapeless, oversized jumper that reached well below her waist. When she felt ready, she ventured out onto the ice.

By now, the production staff had adorned the makeshift rink with an array of glittery, papier-mâché boulders in order to suggest a dazzling moonscape. What an exotic, enchanting, wintry world. The prop master had even dangled lovely, parchment-paper snowflakes from the rafters. As if all that were not enough, he had also dangled shimmery, blown-glass pendant lights throughout the vault with a view toward suggesting a starry sky.

In the heart of the rink, the futuristic, copper-colored moon ship stood perfectly balanced upon her long, metallic landing legs, a ladder reaching past the finlike rudders and leading up to the control-cabin hatchway. What a splendid acquisition: the very spacecraft that had beguiled the teeming crowds during the Grand Exhibition at Crystal Palace.

To the best of Cäcilia's knowledge, Herr Wechseljahr had paid a great fortune to secure the rights to use the rocket. If the ice ballet were to flop, who could say whether he would ever recoup his losses?

From out of nowhere, the honey-blonde French girl skated out onto the rink.

A while ago, Cäcilia had learned her name: Mademoiselle Céleste. Still, they almost never spoke to one another. Ever since the day Herr Wechseljahr had cast her as handmaiden to the Moon Princess, Cäcilia had despised her.

No matter the subdued light, Mademoiselle Céleste worked up speed—and then the young lady proceeded to perform a series of daring toe-loop jumps.

Cäcilia felt another flutter in her womb. Nervously, she rubbed her belly. How long before an obvious, undeniable protrusion betrayed the baby's presence?

Mademoiselle Céleste skated up to Cäcilia and stopped with expert precision. "So, do you approve of the moon ship?" the French girl asked.

"Yes, everything looks quite remarkable," Cäcilia answered, looking up to admire the wax icicles adorning the nose cone.

Mademoiselle Céleste placed her hand over Cäcilia's belly.

"The old man told me everything, I hope you know. So, did you destroy the little being?"

Cäcilia brushed the French girl's hand away and skated off some.

At last, Cäcilia paused near the moon ship. For the longest time, she held her hand between her legs. *Why didn't I comply with Herr Wechseljahr's instructions?* Now she felt weak in the knees, for she had not merely disobeyed the old man. Even worse, in failing to go through with the scheduled abortion, she had willfully deceived him.

"No, I was never even *with* child," she had told him at one point. "It must've been a simple case of hysterical pregnancy, nothing more."

Mademoiselle Céleste returned to Cäcilia's side now. With a simper, the French girl removed a piece of newfangled bubblegum from her pocket. Then she put the queer confection into her mouth, chewed awhile, and then proceeded to blow a bubblegum bubble—which soon burst with a sharp, pleasing pop. Then she removed her ice skates, and she turned to the moon ship. Boldly, she proceeded to climb the ladder.

Cäcilia put her hands on her hips. "Just what do you think you're doing?"

The French girl did not trouble herself to answer. When she reached the hatchway, she released the latch. "Voilà," she said. Brazenly then, she climbed inside.

Cäcilia sneered and bit her lip. "Come down from there, you."

From up inside the control cabin, the sounds of futuristic devices rang out—as if the presumptuous French girl must be pressing this button and that.

What if she ends up breaking something? Cäcilia removed her skates, and she climbed the ladder. When the French girl refused to come out, Cäcilia continued inside.

The control cabin proved to be warm, stuffy, and much too

cramped. Still, the confined space did contain the most extraordinary, three-dimensional map of the Milky Way—the whole apparatus encased in a glass dome.

She could not help but marvel at the ingenuity of it all. *Oh, to fly away to the moon.*

Mademoiselle Céleste pointed to the Crab Nebula, where it shone a bittersweet pink at the map's far left. "Along the road to Fontenay-sous-Bois, there's an observatory where my countrymen study clouds of gas in outer space. Anyway, that's where I lost *my* virginity."

Cäcilia cringed and thought back to the night Herr Wechseljahr had taken her to bed.

The French girl removed the bubblegum from her mouth. "Yes, what a night. First, the old scholar brought me to the telescope and showed me the Crab Nebula. Then, *doucement*, he did what he did." The French girl returned the bubblegum into her mouth.

By now, Cäcilia felt ill. There could be no avoiding it, for the bubblegum filled the unventilated space with a sickening odor as of spoiled sugar-beet syrup. Three times over, she retched—until the back of her throat burned with the taste of that morning's breakfast, a dish of canned peaches with Devonshire cream.

A moment later, as the back of her throat filled with the taste of warm vomit and stale vanilla, she longed to retreat to her hotel suite. Once there, she would swallow a spoonful of Mother's Cordial. *Oh, how good and comforting that'd be.*

The French girl blew another bubble, and then she eyed Cäcilia's belly. "If that old astronomer had made me pregnant that night, I can't imagine what my papa would've done."

Cäcilia suppressed a violent shudder, and her thoughts turned to her long-lost father.

The silence must have troubled Mademoiselle Céleste, for her expression changed to one of chagrin. "Don't be jealous," the

French girl continued. "I only wish to confide in you and be a good friend."

"No, you wish to dissuade me from skating. Just like some tawdry girl hoping to exact a favor, you hope to take my place as the moon princess."

"Maybe. Any of us French girls would *kill* for the chance to dance a part like the one you've got." One last time, Mademoiselle Céleste made eyes at Cäcilia's belly. "*Adieu*," the young lady whispered. With that, she blew another bubble and exited the control cabin.

Thirty minutes later, the rehearsal unfolded uneventfully enough.

Afterward, as Herr Wechseljahr spoke with the lighting designer, a weary Cäcilia bundled herself up in her autumn coat and departed the Palladium.

Just like before, she felt someone's fixed gaze upon her. For a time, she looked all about, but to no avail. Given how dense the fetid, nighttime fog rolling through the streets of Soho that night, there could be little chance of espying the voyeur.

As the fog thickened, Cäcilia walked back to Oxford Street. All the way there, a sense of violation persisted. *Someone's watching me, yes indeed.* She stopped before the nursery shop and baby boutique. Powerless to focus on anything else, she thought of Mademoiselle Céleste.

Might the ill-natured, duplicitous French girl have hired someone to terrorize her?

As the fog rolled up and down the length of Oxford Street, a never-ending procession of footsteps and silhouettes passed by.

Almost holding her breath, Cäcilia recalled a harrowing incident that had happened to her five years earlier: one night, she had felt someone's eyes all over her—at which point, an elderly woman had emerged from the fog.

What a malevolent, unnerving character. She had called herself

Mrs. Cedric T. Purefoy, and she had claimed to be a member of a conservative ladies' society—the Primrose League.

At any rate, as they had spoken, the old woman had grown quite irate. Apparently, she had mistaken Cäcilia for a member of the Fabian Society or perhaps even some sinister, young anarchist.

As Cäcilia had walked away, the old woman had tackled her. "So, you disfavor our genteel circle?" the old woman had asked her.

"No," she had told the peculiar lady.

"The Primrose League addresses all the paramount issues of the day," the old woman had continued. "It's not all jam and Jerusalem. Just last week, we had a symposium on the suffragette campaigns and all them Gladstonians hoping to stuff the ballot box and—"

Within the nursery shop and baby boutique, all the lights went out.

Up and down Oxford Street, several more establishments went dark.

Cäcilia bolted. Three blocks down, she hailed a taxicab and climbed inside. And now she paused to think. If someone did happen to be following her tonight, it would not do to return to the hotel. She leaned forward. "Take me to Duke-of-York Square," she told the driver.

The destination proved to be dark, foggy, and foreboding. Nevertheless, she paid the fare and climbed out of the cab. For a time, she stood beside a lamppost. *What do I do?* She listened for any sign of the enemy—the rumble of a motorcar's engine.

Sure enough, a D-Type Vauxhall proceeded to drive up and down the streets surrounding the plaza.

Who could it be? Once more, she thought of Mademoiselle Céleste. What if the driver proved to be her mother? Perhaps the Frenchwoman had grown mad with envy, and now she hoped to kill her daughter's rival.

As the motorcar continued around the square, Cäcilia looked

all about for some kind of weapon—an object that she might hurl through the opaque windscreen.

Soon enough, she went lost in another memory of Mrs. Cedric T. Purefoy. *How did that whole row come to an end?*

At some point, Cäcilia had reached into the demented old woman's satchel and had removed a heavy book. Then, with all her might, she had repeatedly struck the woman over the head before running off down the street.

At last, sore, and breathless, she had paused to glance at the volume.

The book had proven to be a first edition of *The Runnymede Letters*, one of Disraeli's finest works—the handsome tome boasting an exquisite, pink-primrose design etched into the frontispiece.

After a while, the maniacal old woman had crawled toward her. "How I miss the olden days," the old woman had muttered then. "Back in days Victorian, the English distinguished themselves as a purposeful, God-fearing people, a nation what knew right from . . ."

Not thirty feet away now, the mysterious D-Type Vauxhall stopped to idle.

Cäcilia sought to deny all her fears. She glanced at a concert theater standing across the street, and she whistled the tune to one of Schubert's *Impromptus*. Only when she heard the motorcar's driver-side door open did she turn back.

A gentleman stood there: dressed like a proper *chauffeur de maître*, he waved and smiled eerily.

She raced off down a dark, winding alleyway—until she tripped and fell headlong into a jumble of whitewashed wood bins.

The night grew darker yet, the fog much thicker.

Deep inside her womb, yet another flutter awoke.

The quickening!

CHAPTER FOUR

London, 18 January.

On the night of the premiere, when Cäcilia arrived at the Palladium, she learned that her rival, Mademoiselle Céleste, had styled her honey-blonde hair the same way that Cäcilia had.

A week earlier, on the eve of Twelfth Night, Cäcilia had asked a hairdresser to give her a fashionable Dutch bob. The stylist had done it masterfully well, too—expertly cropping her blue-black hair at the bottoms of her ears and then sweeping the bob to the side. Moreover, the stylist had even thought to shingle the hair in the back.

Cäcilia followed Mademoiselle Céleste into the changing room now.

As the others slipped into their things, Cäcilia studied her belly bump. How to hide the protrusion? Before, whenever Herr Wechseljahr would schedule a rehearsal, she could always conceal her pregnancy by wearing something with a very big flounce.

Afterward, if he were to accompany her somewhere, she could always drape a big frock coat over her shoulders and then strategically fold her arms over her stomach.

Reluctantly now, she removed the moon-princess gown from the garment bag. With her eye upon the dressing mirror, she hung the costume from a rusty nail in the wall.

Twenty minutes to go before the performance, Herr Wechseljahr made his way into the changing room and greeted everyone. Then he turned to Cäcilia and presented her with a pair of lovely, white, satin *mousquetaire* gloves with gold fringe. "I found these in a little glove shop not two blocks from Coventry Street," he explained. "Most exquisite, yes? I think they'll be ideal for your debut. Only the best for *die Prinzessin*."

"Yes, they'll be perfect," she told him. Playfully, she took the gloves into her hands and stroked one of the buttonhooks at the cuff. "*Danke, meine liebe.*"

As Herr Wechseljahr walked off, she espied a few tattered leaves clinging to his dress coat's hem. Instantaneously, she thought back to December—an evening constitutional during which she had followed some wind-driven leaves past a row of garden flats and onward down a begrimed alleyway.

The narrow passage had opened out onto a desolate court-yard. In all directions, there had loomed a common-brick townhouse—each structure in a state of disrepair. On the eastern flank, a gaping hole within the building's rooftop had revealed a crack running through the plasterboard ceiling.

For the longest time, she had watched some fallen leaves swirling about beneath a rusting fire-escape ladder. Soon enough, from the furthest depths of her unconscious mind, a gruesome vision had presented itself: when the time came for her to go into labor, she would surely bleed to death right there in the birthing room.

Naturally, the stark revelation had left her heartsick. "It's a dreadfully unjust world in which a girl perishes while delivering," she had thought out loud, her voice the very softest of whispers. "I'm only young."

After a while, she had continued over to the opposite side of the courtyard—where someone had discarded a tattered, leather pram. Sobbing, she had kicked at the axle—until her big toe had begun to ache. Then, the tears streaming down her face, she had looked to the sky.

What appeared to be a plume of brightly-colored feathers had only just fallen from the clouds. Slowly and gracefully, guided by this current and that, the glorious tuft had sailed east and west and back again.

No matter the strain to her neck, she could not look down. Greatly intrigued, she had wondered if perhaps the plume had come loose from a kingfisher hen—the winged creature flying south in the hope of reaching the Tyrrhenian Sea by midwinter's halcyon days, when the seabird might fashion a nest to float upon the water's gentle undulations.

After a while, Cäcilia had decided that she had only hallucinated the plume of feathers falling from the clouds. She had looked back down then. "Do I deserve to bleed to death in the moment I give birth?" she had asked the fallen leaves stirring yet in the ongoing eddy.

From the depths of her unconscious mind, the answer to her question had presented itself quickly enough: of course, she deserved to perish—for though she had always known that even the most inappreciable stumble might very well result in a miscarriage, nevertheless, she had selfishly chosen to continue skating and to go through with her ice ballet debut.

The costume designer opened the changing-room door now, and he wished everyone well.

Immediately, her thoughts turned back to the present—and as she stood before the dressing mirror, she sought to compose herself the best that she could.

When the costume designer departed, she checked the clock on the changing-room wall—only ten minutes until showtime. *How to put things off any longer?*

At last, she sucked in her gut and slipped into the snug moon-princess gown. Then she turned to the satin gloves and gasped.

Where they lay upon the bench, they resembled the severed hands and forearms of some dispossessed phantom.

When she finally collected the glistening gloves, she slipped her warm, trembling hands inside. Then she stretched her fingers, until the satin felt like a second skin.

Some ten minutes later, as the various members of the London Symphony Orchestra finished tuning their instruments, she guided the other moon spirits to their places behind the glittery, papier-mâché boulders.

When the last of the violinists quieted down, no sound remained save the rumble of the eager crowd. Then a round of applause erupted, as if the music director had only just assumed his place in the orchestra pit. And now a hush descended over the hall.

Cäcilia gazed upon the Palladium's white-diamond chandelier and awaited the felicitous interplay between the concertmaster's violin and the French horn: the moon spirits' cue.

As soon as the violin and the horn commenced their cheerful march, she guided everyone out into the heart of the rink.

Already, the explorers had climbed down from the moon ship's ladder—and as the young gentlemen laced up, she guided the moon spirits around the spacecraft.

Everything went well—at least until the crucial *scène d'amour*, that part of the tale in which she faces the moon explorers' captain.

The sequence should have commenced ever so cleanly, her movements as fine as a ballet dancer's most whimsical glissade—but as the skater portraying the expedition's commanding officer took Cäcilia by the hand, he would not stop ogling the faint protrusion at her belly.

Try as she might, she could not concentrate. Her stomach muscles contracted, too.

Little by little, from this direction and that, various members of the audience burst out laughing. Did they presume the story to be a farce?

As the two skaters commenced their entrée, a heckler in the

second row stood up. "Hey there, it looks like the moon princess has herself a baby bumper," he shouted. "She can't be no proper moon princess at all. She's a *clergyman's* daughter, that one."

"You there, moon explorer, get on back aboard your bloody ship and push on," yet another heckler cried out. "Some other knave has already hired out that tawdry little moon-princess girl, don't you know? She'd be somebody else's trouble and strife."

Despite the derision, Cäcilia did her very best to complete the waltz.

At that point, the lunar tempest arrived. On and on, the drummer pounded upon the tin-bronze furnace by which the music director intended to portray the peal of thunder. At the same time, a half dozen stagehands worked an array of flashing lamps in order to conjure the illusion of lightning.

Faithful to the choreography, Cäcilia guided all the spirits back to their places behind the glittery boulder.

Mademoiselle Céleste tapped Cäcilia's belly. "I wonder what Herr Wechseljahr should say when the performance ends. He should be mortified. Yes, because the Lord Mayor, he's in attendance. *Quel scandale.*"

Speechless, Cäcilia fussed with her gown's built-in bra cups. *After the show, what* would *the old man say?* In all likelihood, he would not say anything at all. Instead, he would slap her across the face.

The tempest died out, and the violins commenced their soft, tuneful *sérénade*—Cäcilia's cue to come out from behind the boulder.

This should have been the most poignant moment in the production: Cäcilia performing a simple, sensual variation, the dance by which the moon princess pleads with her beloved to bring her with him when he returns to Planet Earth.

As it so happened, both the laughter and the heckling had grown so clamorous that she could barely hear the music.

When the explorer drew her into the grand coda, she followed the gentleman the best that she could. Then, when the choreography called on her to perform a demanding finale, she did her best to execute the sequence.

Alas, from all throughout the Palladium, the ear-splitting cat-calls continued.

As she put on more speed, she realized what a perfect opportunity she had to prove herself to the boorish audience. Growing prideful, she permitted the whole of her weight to fall upon her left ankle—something that she had never attempted before. Then she extended her free leg back behind her, as high as she could raise it.

For a time, she performed the exacting maneuver quite well. Eventually, though, her ankle faltered—and when it did, she dropped upon her backside.

The failure had come during the crucial caesura, the solemn moment in the story when no music plays. To make matters worse, just after she dropped upon her backside, someone in the audience placed his hand beneath his armpit and pumped his arm to simulate the sound of a person passing gas.

Soon enough, a whole chorus joined in from every direction—dozens of depraved, jeering louts producing that same hideous noise.

She picked herself up, and she placed her hand over her belly. As the laughter droned on and on, she considered the possibility of making a hasty retreat. Once outside, perhaps she could hail a taxicab. Then she would ask the driver to take her back to the hotel. *Yes, go on.* No matter how tempting the idea, she could not bring herself to do it; if she raced off now, her undignified departure would only invite that much more mockery.

The tenor trombone commenced the pleasing little air that served to introduce the very last dance.

Keep going.

The skater portraying the moon explorer stood perfectly still. "I think you've had enough," he told Cäcilia. With that, he glided over toward the orchestra pit—as if to tell the music director to forgo the last number.

The music director frowned, but he consented.

No matter the absence of any music and no matter the relentless taunts, Cäcilia refused to surrender. On and on, she danced—for she realized that this might be her last chance to be in the spotlight. And now she went lost in delusion, and she reveled in her exalted station as a glorious moon princess—a triumphal woman with no reason at all to feel bereft of her pride.

CHAPTER FIVE

London, 13 March.

For the first time since the opening-night debacle, Cäcilia decided to go outside. *I've got to get on with my life.* In the park, she read the morning edition of the *Daily Mail*.

The paper contained an interview with Lloyd George and a whole exposé regarding a recent Zeppelin bombardment. The article even featured a grainy photograph of a German spy gondola that had fallen from the sky during the barrage.

"Don't read the *Daily Wail*," a voice whispered in a doleful tone. "What if they've gone and printed another article deriding your premiere?"

She looked across the street to a lovely *maisonette* with Palladian windows. *Did the voice come from inside that house there?*

After a while, she could not shake the uncanny feeling that someone must be standing at her back. When she checked, though, she found no one there.

Later, as she exited the park, the voice manifested itself anew: "Mama, come back," a little girl's voice called out to her.

There could be no doubt as to what had conjured the aural hallucinations: her lingering guilt feelings had created the illusion that her own baby, or rather the mischievous little girl who the baby was to become, must be following her through the city.

For a time, Cäcilia rubbed the protrusion at her belly. *The stress, the heartache, it's got me falling apart.* In a state of nerves, she continued along for three blocks before stopping near a department store.

Even if the effect were nothing more than a product of her bruised psyche, she felt quite certain that the other party must have followed her. Determined to keep calm, she approached the department store's display window and considered the wirework mannequins all decked out in the new spring fashions—a line of ruffled-poplin gowns, and one of them a pale, sickly yellow.

If a portent of her daughter did stand at her back just now, how might the apparition have dressed herself? Perhaps the little girl would be wearing a traditional French raincoat, a pink rain bonnet, too, and a simple gown fashioned from plain-weave linen cloth.

And what would she look like? She would have dark hair tinged with turquoise blue, and she would have a fine diamond shape to her pallid face—perhaps even a black mole to the left of her nose. Best of all, she would have wide, almond-shaped eyes—the irises a rich evergreen.

At last, Cäcilia turned around. Alas, she found herself alone on the walkway. Feeling like a fool, she turned back to the display window and fixed her gaze upon a little mannequin holding a long-stemmed rose.

And what about my daughter? If the illusory little girl held something in *her* hand, what would it be? *A long-stemmed rose?*

Cäcilia nibbled at one of her fingernails.

As she did, the sound of a little girl's laughter resounded. "Do you know my name?" a delicate, otherworldly voice asked her then. "*Eroica.* Deep down, that's what you wish to name me."

Again, Cäcilia turned around—and once more, she found herself alone. Trembling all over, she hailed a taxicab. *Just go.*

At three o'clock, she walked past the ongoing *Palais-de-Danse* construction site and came upon an electric skating palace: Hammersmith Ice Arena.

Intrigued, she walked toward the door. Perhaps a pleasant visit would prove to be the very thing to make her forget the illusory girl.

Inside, the vast, humid ice arena proved to be poorly lit. In addition to the dim light, an all-encompassing quietude dominated the space.

Out on the rink, a lone, little girl skated about. Dressed in a blue jumper and a badly wrinkled, crepe-Georgette skirt, she performed a series of sheep jumps.

Cäcilia rubbed her belly. Only yesterday, or so it seemed, she herself had been a child struggling to master the most elemental maneuvers. With a sigh, she climbed into the terrace.

Near the aisle, someone had left behind an edition of the *Sunday Telegraph*—the one featuring the interview with Mademoiselle Céleste.

The French girl had become celebrated all throughout the city, for her dedication and professionalism had 'saved' Herr Wechseljahr's ice ballet.

Feeling perfectly miserable, Cäcilia reread the article several times over.

Her belly churning, she finally coughed up her breakfast— and the warm, yellowy discharge landed all over the grandstand.

With difficulty, she walked off into the washroom and collected a loo roll.

When she returned to the terrace, she mopped up the mess. Afterward, she still felt unwell. *So, I'll wait five minutes.*

In the interval, a malodorous presence crept into the air.

Her lips and tongue burned. *Might it be an ammonia leak?* For a time, she walked all about in the hope of finding the operations manager's office. Having failed to do so, she walked over to the boards. Frantic, she drummed upon the top plate and called to the lone skater out on the rink.

When the girl stopped, she assumed an oddly inscrutable

expression—as if she were as lifeless as something carved from a block of stone or ice. "What do you want?" she asked.

"Don't you smell that torrent of ammonia?" Cäcilia asked in turn. "I think my daughter, my little Eroica, might be to blame. She's bold as brass, that one. That's why we've got to alert the proprietor before someone takes ill."

With a frown, the girl returned to her skating.

On the wall, meanwhile, the telephone buzzed.

Cäcilia took the receiver into her hand. "Hammersmith Ice Arena," she announced, speaking into the transmitter cup.

The caller remained silent.

No matter how impossible the whole idea, Cäcilia imagined that Eroica herself must be the culprit. With her free hand, Cäcilia fussed with her collar. "You'd better speak up already, because I'll not hold the line."

No one spoke up.

Cäcilia looked to the vault and then down to her feet. "I'm warning you. It's never a good idea to keep the telephone engaged for no reason. Why did you ring? Have you got something to say? If so, come out with it."

The peculiar, unnerving silence prevailed.

All around, meanwhile, the stench of ammonia grew steadily worse.

Short of breath, she placed the back of her hand against her brow. *Am I ill?*

When she finally decided that she did not feel feverish, once more, she looked to the vault. "You rang to taunt me, yes?" she asked.

The other end of the line remained silent.

She laughed nervously. "I know. You rang to remind me of just how ashamed I ought to be feeling these days. You rang to remind me what a disgrace I am."

Out on the ice, the girl from before performed one last sheep jump and then departed the rink. Once she had removed her skates, she placed them in a pressed-cane carry case and then exited the establishment.

Several times over, Cäcilia tapped the transmitter cup. "Tell me something. Do you suppose I ought to leave the Smoke and hide in shame somewhere? What about Yarmouth, or what do you think about Maidstone? Do you think I'd be happy hiding in some chocolate-box village like that? Oh, but why ride post for a pudding? Why not live in a leafy suburb right here, near London? Ah, but what if someone there recognizes me? Don't you suppose the sardonicism should be too cruel for me?"

No voice spoke up.

The odor of ammonia grew even more intense.

Cäcilia wrapped her free hand around the transmitter cup. "I know," she continued, her voice wavering some. "You don't want me to skate anymore. Would that be it? Well, let me tell you, as long as I live, I'll do as I please with my body. As a matter of fact, I think I'll get back to training as early as tomorrow. First, I'll get me some cast-iron weights, maybe even a new set of kettlebells."

In the end, she slammed the receiver down onto the switch-hook and then marched off.

An hour later, she entered Harrods Department Store and paused within the inviolable glare streaming through the skylight. *Where to find the sporting goods?*

Quite a long queue had formed before the information kiosk, so she decided to wander about awhile.

When she came upon the electric stairways, she flipped a coin and took the flight of steps going up. Guided by her unconscious mind, she soon found herself in a big, cluttered showroom housing the garden statuary.

All throughout the maze of display tables, the department-store staff had exhibited a large collection of soapstone fairies and sandstone fauns—several English bulldogs, too, each one of the exquisite creatures made from what looked to be coarse-grained crystalline.

Gradually, she forgot all about the new set of kettlebells. And now she stopped before an alluring statuette of what looked to be pale-rose marble: the likeness of a life-size little girl with intricately sculpted, lifelike hair tumbling past her shoulder.

My stars and garters.

There did not appear to be any imperfection. Even the arches of the little girl's stone feet curved all so delicately, all so naturally. Still, what a heartrending expression on the statuette's face—as if she must be dumb with grief. Perhaps most puzzling of all, the little girl held in her hand a solitary, long-stemmed rose.

Oh yes, a wild China rose.

Cheerfully, a sales lady approached and patted the statuette's scalp. "She's enough to charm the heart of a broomstick, eh?"

Cäcilia brushed away a grain of dust from the statuette's collarbone and then caressed the figure's oddly sensual hips. "One thing puzzles me. Do you know why she'd be holding a long, thorny rose?"

"It's because she's *une rosière*," the sales lady answered. "Every summer, the folks down there in Bordeaux gather in the town square to select the most virtuous Catholic girl in the whole village, and then the good people present her with a rose, and they christen her *la rosière*."

Cäcilia studied the statuette closely. Soon, she felt as if she recognized the little girl's face. *It's my baby all grown up.* Cäcilia clasped her hands together. "So, what does Harrods charge for something like this?"

"Well, she's quite the rarefied piece. Outside of *La Samaritaine*, we'd be the only department store what sells her. Still, I can't imagine anyone paying more than half a bean for it." The sales lady sighed, and she pointed to an almost-imperceptible crack running through the little girl's heart. "It's damaged goods, this pretty little dish here. That's why we shan't charge a shilling over three quid."

Cäcilia knelt to the floor and sought to gather the statuette up into her arms.

The sales lady laughed. "You can't shoulder a piece like this one here. She must weigh five stone. If you want it, we'll have a lorry deliver it wherever you wish."

Very slowly, Cäcilia returned to her feet and brushed off her skirt. "No, I can't purchase this piece."

"*No?* Are you quite sure?"

"Oh, yes. At the moment, I've no place to—"

"But you could always stow her away inside—"

"No, at the moment, I've got no use for a statuette," she insisted. With that, she exited the building and continued along the avenue.

One block east, she paused before a bench jeweler's shop. For a time, she swayed back and forth in the languid, late-winter breeze. Simultaneously, she drummed the tips of her fingers against her thighs.

After a long while, she looked up to read the words printed upon the sign hanging over the bench jeweler's door: *Financial troubles? We'll buy your pearls!*

Again, she felt the uncanny sensation of someone standing at her back. *Oh yes, it's the rose bearer, the long-stemmed rose clenched between her teeth.*

All so gently now, someone tapped upon Cäcilia's sleeve.

Heavens. She turned around, but she found no one there— only a tattered page from yesterday's *Morning Post* tumbling about in the current.

And now the debris blew away on the breeze, so she wandered off in the opposite direction.

CHAPTER SIX

London, 18 April.

Early that morning, Cäcilia awoke to a series of contractions that felt much too tight to be the stuff of false labor.

When the chambermaid stopped by, she removed a linen maternity blouse from the airing cupboard and then paused to study Cäcilia. "*Hello.* You're looking sorely afflicted, if you don't mind my telling you. Shall I bring you a bottle of kola champagne? There's nothing like water from a proper English spring to restore a girl's spirits."

Cäcilia could not bring herself to mutter a response, so the chambermaid proceeded to fold the maternity blouse.

Within the wall, meanwhile, a rattling commenced: the clamor of the dumbwaiter's drive train.

When the chambermaid removed Cäcilia's breakfast from the lift, she placed the tray upon the table and departed.

Cäcilia walked over to the window, and she worked the sash pulley. *Have I gone into premature labor?* If she had, then this would be the fateful day when she must bleed to death while giving birth. *Just as the leaves foretold, last December.*

Midmorning, the contractions grew much more forceful.

At last, she slipped into a wrinkled blouse and plaid, pleated, wool-blend skirt. Then she staggered out into the hallway. When she reached the hotel mezzanine, she took hold of a club chair to keep herself from falling. Then she turned to one of the Victorian silhouettes adorning the wall: Sweeney Todd brandishing a cut-throat razor. *Oh yes, I'm bound to die today.* Very slowly, she staggered down the mezzanine stairway.

A moment or two later, in the desolate lobby, she bumped into the hat tree.

The collision knocked to the floor what looked to be an authentic Mexican *sombrero*, a long, black hummingbird feather protruding from the ribbon around the base of the crown.

Outside, beneath the hotel awning, she turned to the porter. "Flag down a hack," she blurted out. "I beg you."

Ten minutes later, as soon as the taxicab reached Chelsea Royal Hospital, she felt a hot rivulet of blood trail down her leg. "I'm bleeding to death," she yelped.

A pair of orderlies helped her into the birthing bed, at which point the specialist administered a shot of morphine.

The prick of the needle made Cäcilia shake all over. "So, would that be what it feels like when the midwife reaches in with *une curette*?" she asked. When the specialist failed to answer, she lay back.

The state of twilight sleep should have followed. Instead, she espied a series of morphine-induced hallucinations—a fantastical storm of autumn leaves floating all about.

Gradually, a dreamlike apparition materialized over to the side: a Japanese girl with olive skin and chestnut-brown hair. What impossible beauty the alluring, fragile figure—especially the way her pert nipples poked through her coral-pink gown.

Where did you come from?

The illusory figure walked over to the instrument table and collected an illusory bouquet of apple-red daffodils, which metamorphosed into roses.

Yes, wondrous roses.

An illusory breeze shook some of the petals, until they began swirling around in a perfect circle—all through the air.

Meanwhile, the baby's feet found their way into Cäcilia's birth canal.

The specialist turned to the chief nurse. "Looks like our blessed event should be a breech birth."

As she looked down to the baby's dainty little feet kicking this way and that, Cäcilia pushed with all her might. "Come, let me look at you before I die," she cried out, her travails growing ever more severe.

The kicking ceased.

Then, as the baby's toes turned Prussian blue, the lifeless body slipped out into the specialist's hands.

The birth cord had wrapped itself around Eroica's neck, strangling her to death.

The chief nurse stepped back. "A-dearie me." No sooner had she spoken than she dropped the delivery forceps to the floor, where they clattered against the tiles like a set of castanets concluding a flamenco song.

As a profound silence descended upon the birthing room, Cäcilia sat up. Had she ever felt so confounded? Until this moment, she had been laboring under the misapprehension that *she* must be the one to perish this day.

Her mouth turning dry, she held out her arms—until the specialist handed her the stillborn baby.

Eroica felt like a ragdoll stuffed with moonstone beads.

Yes, moonstone beads.

After what felt like a long while, Cäcilia turned to the Japanese girl. "This wasn't what the oracle prophesied."

"A thousand pardons," the dreamlike being spoke up. "Maybe you misread the fallen leaves." With that remark, the Japanese girl retreated a few steps and then stood quietly between the washbasin and the weigh scales.

The chief nurse took the baby back. "I'll place your little one in the ice cabinet next door."

As the nurse walked off with Eroica, the specialist retreated into the corner. All atremble, he fussed with the placenta bucket.

Her left foot having fallen asleep by now, Cäcilia contented herself to watch the imaginary rose petals floating about the room.

They swirled about in erratic patterns, a few of the petals bounding off the walls.

At a loss for words, she lay back down and fell asleep—and before long, the most vivid dream commenced.

On the moon, somewhere beyond the Sea of Dreams, two airy spirits guide Cäcilia into a palace and down the corridor to a brightly-lit hall.

What a beautiful space, the walls adorned with pleasant canvases depicting all the places that a genteel, well-educated French girl might love: Le musée Rodin, La Sorbonne, *and several street scenes, too, including* un jardinet.

Perhaps most sensual of all, a section of the wall boasts a stark, pencil-sketch study of the Paris Morgue.

A peppery aroma suddenly fills the air—the scent of ratatouille niçoise, *fresh eggplant and yellow squash.*

And now the moon princess, Mademoiselle Céleste, enters the hall. Without speaking a word, she sits upon the floor and opens her evening bag. Gracefully, she removes a few pages torn from a Guy-de-Maupassant story. Then she removes a few pages torn from Marcel Proust's Les plaisirs et les Jours, *followed by a few pages torn from what Mademoiselle Céleste claims to be* La Revue Blanche.

Finally, she removes a few pages torn from a collection of Mother-Goose tales.

The lunar breeze blowing steadily through the windows, each one of the torn pages begins swirling about like tree litter.

The moon princess, Mademoiselle Céleste, looks into Cäcilia's eyes then. "I've asked both of my counselors to tell me the answer to my question, and neither one has succeeded. So, you must tell me."

"Well then, what's the question?" Cäcilia asks.

"Would abortion be murder, or could it be justified?"

"Please, how could I ever hope to answer such a question?"

"Call upon your powers," Mademoiselle Céleste tells her. "Look upon these torn pages tumbling all about here like fallen apricot leaves and tell me what vision, what revelation comes to you."

At first, Cäcilia looks up at the two vesper sparrows flittering about the French-crystal chandelier.

Half-heartedly then, she turns to the pages tumbling about in the breeze.

In stages, a litany of ideas emerges from her unconscious mind: the notion that life begins at conception, the contrary notion that life begins with the awakening of the psyche.

Faster and faster, the torn pages swirl about.

She thinks of a governess who slays a little girl. "Of course, that would be murder," she thinks out loud. And now Cäcilia turns to the window, and she considers Planet Earth looming in the sky. "What a crowded, miserable world," she whispers beneath her breath.

The moon princess raises her eyebrows. "No more dawdling. Do as I say and determine the answer already."

Cäcilia turns back. Once more, she stares at the torn pages swirling about. "You wish to know what I'd be thinking?" she asks. "Well then, if you must know, I'm thinking about injustice, the way so many scoundrels never pay for their crimes, the way coerced confessions and the rush to judgment doom so many innocent souls. Yes, and I think of all the courts that never prosecute only because they have no money to do so. And I think of the courts that never convict for fear of reprisal. And I think of a jury forewoman beguiled by rationalizations and allowances, pleas for clemency, excuses, pretenses, recriminations, and convoluted theories. Yes, I think about plea bargains and such, all that injustice and . . ."

With her fists, the moon princess smites the floor. "Tell me the answer I seek," she bellows.

Cäcilia's heart races. "Don't you grasp my argument? It's all so simple. In a world so unjust, how should anyone be wrong? That's why a woman should decide for herself whether it would be a good idea to *terminate a pregnancy. Yes, and if some girl finds herself in a society where the courts consider abortion to be murder, then I suppose she has no alternative but to seek out a knowledgeable midwife. And if the girl bleeds to death in the midwife's unlawful residence, well then, the poor thing must* embrace *her martyrdom."*

And now the lunar breeze dies down very slowly, and . . .

Cäcilia awoke in what looked to be the recovery room.

Already, night had fallen; through the window, the suspension cables of Chelsea Bridge shone silver and blue.

Despite the passage of time, there could be no doubt that the effects of the morphine remained strong—for the exotic Japanese girl stood nearby.

"What's your name?" Cäcilia asked the apparition.

"Call me Kyoko," the illusory figure spoke up.

"You've got a lovely name," Cäcilia told her. "Yes, and I'm thankful you're here. It wouldn't do to be alone just now."

Kyoko only shrugged her shoulders, as if she did not quite understand.

Cäcilia climbed out of bed and approached the sash. For a time, she looked out upon the distant bridge and wharf. When she closed her eyes, she thought back to a book that she had once read—a story about an obscure *geisha* living near Osaka.

Upon aborting her baby, the woman had paid an artisan a thousand yen to sculpt a statuette of what the deceased baby would have looked like as an ideal, little girl.

What a finely-detailed statuette the artisan had fashioned, too: a figure as delicate as porcelain, a little girl dressed in a traditional *kimono* complete with a sash and bow tied at the small of her back.

Later, the grieving woman had placed the idol next to her aborted baby's grave that she might speak with the representation whenever she visited. Before long, the elegiac Shinto rite had helped the woman to grow strong again.

In the end, she had lived a good life. At some point, she had published a much-celebrated treatise on *Japonaiserie*. In her later years, she had even made a pilgrimage to Mount Fuji—in an era when very few unmarried women would have dared to depart their prefecture.

Cäcilia opened her eyes, and she looked to Chelsea Bridge—the tower and backstay.

For her part, Kyoko recited a pleasing Shinto prayer and then danced about the room for a while.

Finally, the apparition grew still. "I must return home."

Now it was Cäcilia's turn to shrug. "Off you go then."

The apparition smiled warmly. "Goodbye for today."

Once the Japanese girl was gone, Cäcilia found herself all alone. Not a little bit overcome by the solitude, she let out a shriek. Afterward, she staggered into the hallway.

Thankfully, Kyoko had left behind a spectral bouquet. Alas, the last vestige of her presence did not endure long: in no time, the illusory roses dissolved into nothingness.

CHAPTER SEVEN

London, 29 May.

Early that morning, Cäcilia revisited Highgate Cemetery. As soon as she reached Eroica's grave, she sat down upon her calves with her toes pointed backward. For a moment, she traced the tips of her fingers over the epitaph. In time, she looked upon *la rosière* standing over to the side. "Hello, you. With heavy heart, I've come back to commune."

What a good idea it had been to buy the piece from Harrods and to place it here. If only the likeness commanded the power of speech, though. How pleasing it would be to hear Eroica's magical voice. *Would it emanate from her lips?*

Perhaps the statuette's otherworldly voice would resound from the ovaries deep within the marble rosebud.

Cäcilia touched the tip of Eroica's chin. "It feels so good to join you here," she continued—just the way a young lady always thinks to keep talking after she has greeted someone who refuses to return any salutation.

A disturbing silence persisted awhile. Then a flying machine, a Sopwith Pup, traversed the sky.

Her thoughts turned to the trenches, and she sat back some. "I think the war ought to end soon. It can't go on forever."

A mistle thrush with unexceptional, battleship-gray feathers along its crest fluttered down to a nearby gravestone and glared at Cäcilia—as if her presence constituted the most deplorable crime.

By way of apology, she waved to the songbird and blew it a kiss. Then she turned back to the little girl. As she feigned a smile, she patted the crown of the statuette's foot. "You would've made a most triumphal ice skater." As she withdrew her hand, she hummed the tune to a Delius concerto.

When she ceased, the all-pervading silence returned.

Frustrated, she could not decide just what to do next. A part of her longed to rattle the statuette, just the way a schoolmistress might assail some unruly child. At the same time, a part of her yearned to embrace the statuette affectionately and then speak to it in the most obnoxious manner—the way sentimental fools talk to puppy dogs and such.

As she continued to sulk, the mistle thrush took flight—and now one of the songbird's gray feathers fluttered down, only to settle atop a little granite obelisk standing three plots to the left.

She stared at the fallen plume, until she felt guilty. There had to be a good reason for the songbird's petulance. Perhaps the mistle thrush had built a nest in one of the nearby tulip trees and had only just laid a clutch of eggs.

The fallen plume drifted off on the breeze, and now a sharp spasm awoke all throughout her legs and ankles.

She stood up, and she endeavored to walk off the soreness. Before she knew it, she had returned onto Egyptian Avenue—the walkway that snaked through the heart of the cemetery.

For a moment, she studied a fine, marble tomb upon which a stonecutter had engraved an opulent frieze. *I can't just leave.* Despite all, she continued along—and as she did, it felt good to be free of the cold, indifferent statuette. *Yes, indeed.*

Just like that, she paused before a big puddle.

The body of water looked fresh and healthful. Moreover, the surface shone darkly enough that the puddle appeared to be as deep as the Indian Ocean—or at least deep enough that a pearl diver might leap in headlong without any trouble.

She turned to those toppled pillars lying beside George Eliot's grave. In all likelihood, the legendary authoress would find it awfully cold-hearted for someone to think to come visit some innocent *rosière* and to then walk away.

Cäcilia glanced back in the direction of the statuette, and as she debated whether she ought to return, the breeze grew very strong.

As graceful as could be, a tattered page from the *Daily Mail* tumbled past her feet.

In the end, she walked around the puddle and continued all the way back to the cemetery gates. The guilt would not let her go on any further, however. She paced awhile and then paused beside a street bollard. For a time, she eyed a flower shop one block east. When she turned back, she gazed upon the gilded, wrought-iron gates and counted the finials.

A moment later, she sat down upon a big, Gothic urn standing inside the gatehouse.

As she sat there brooding, a cloud of damselflies flittered about the remains of the gatekeeper's breakfast—a dish of deviled kidneys and a bottle of port wine.

Sluggishly, ashamedly, sadly, gratingly, an hour or more passed by.

When the gatekeeper finally came along, she apologized for her trespass and then returned to Eroica's grave.

The statuette was gone.

Could this be the wrong place? She knelt before the headstone, read the epitaph, and confirmed that the plot was indeed her daughter's gravesite. When she returned to her feet, she looked in this direction and that. *So, what's become of* la rosière*?* As quickly as she could, she marched back to Egyptian Avenue. With all the strength that she could muster, she called out to a gravedigger just then dragging a weathered Italian casket through the walkway.

"What's happened?" the gravedigger asked. "You look like you just spotted a ghost rising up out of his bloody tomb."

"No, I've just come from my baby's grave, and—"

"It wasn't the ghost of Alfie Dickens, was it? I noticed him only yesterday, I did. He were dancing a jig and reel down by the—"

"*No.* Someone pinched my statuette. Only an hour ago, it was standing right next to my baby's grave, and now the statuette's gone."

The gravedigger let go of the casket and snapped his braces. "Have you got the bill of sale? Because if you haven't got the bill of sale—"

"Please, sir, help me find my statuette."

"Listen, love, it's probably long gone."

"But maybe if we look over by the—"

"No, no," the gravedigger interrupted. "I'd say some beastly band of hooligans went and nicked it."

"Hooligans?"

"Aye, that's right. Them stony-hearted thieves come by all the time, don't they? These days they'll take any manner of trumpery. No, I don't suppose you'll ever find your dolly. Not a cat in hell's chance."

As the gravedigger walked off, Cäcilia felt something trickling down her belly—a steady stream of warm milk dripping from her left nipple, the very last remnant of the solution that her body had begun to produce that she might nurse. Aghast, she seized the neckline of her blouse and sought to shake the linen out a bit—as if to do so might serve to dry the spots where the milk had already soaked through. When all efforts failed, she kicked a nearby grave ledger crowded with an array of half-melted vigil candles.

Having stubbed her right big toe, she dropped onto her bottom.

As the breeze continued to blow, she worked the shoe from her right foot. At that point, she proceeded to disentangle the bloodied toenail from the tip of her stocking. Afterward, she picked herself up and followed the gravedigger all the way over to the pauper's pit.

He looked at her and smirked. "It's your own damn fault the dolly would be gone. You can't leave dear-bought things in a boneyard like this one no more. Aye, even as I speak, there's bound to be any number of thieves fiddling about here and there."

"But even if that's true, they couldn't possibly want—"

"No, no. They'll spirit away any damn thing they find."

"But even so, can't you at least help me look about?"

"*No.* All day long, I'd be digging up this dead bird here. And now they got me casting shroud and all back into God's acre. I'm weary, and I got no time for you."

As another drop of milk dribbled down her belly, Cäcilia studied the casket for a moment and then looked out across the pauper's pit. *What indignity.* She staggered back then, and she very nearly fell onto her bottom yet again.

Seemingly indifferent, the gravedigger stood the casket up on its end. "It's the poor maid's kinfolk," he continued. "They can't afford to keep her in her plot no longer. Haven't got the means, have they?" Without another word, the gravedigger pushed the casket over the edge.

Cäcilia marched back down Egyptian Avenue, and she collected her right shoe and the bloodied stocking, too. Then she made her way back to that big, obtrusive puddle from earlier in the day. And now she dipped her right foot into the water to wash away the blood. Then she walked off around the puddle's edge.

A little girl happened by just then, and what a homely creature. She had greasy hair, a crooked nose, and an array of earth-yellow bruises up and down her arms. Despite all that, she proved to be anything but bashful. Boldly, she pointed to the trail of footprints that Cäcilia's one wet sole had left behind in the walkway. "Hey, look there."

"What's all this?" Cäcilia asked her. "What do you—"

"Don't it look like a water sprite with just one leg must've hopped up out of all that spill?" the little girl asked, her voice full of wonder.

In that moment, Cäcilia felt obliged to answer and to make repartee—so she turned to consider the footprints, and she struggled to think of something to say. Given the events of the day, though, the appropriate witticism eluded her.

Soon, a tattered page from the *Morning Post* tumbled by in the current.

She dried her sole with the remnant of the newspaper, and then she contented herself to continue along.

"Now it looks like the footprints suddenly *vanish*," the little girl cried out. "Like some brute must've snatched the one-legged sprite up into his arms. Oh, my. When her mum learns what's happened, she'll be heartbroken."

Cäcilia paused to imagine a vile, child-snatching scoundrel lurking somewhere in the cemetery. Then, as another drop of milk dribbled from her left nipple, she dropped the shoe and the bloodied stocking and placed her palm over her dampened blouse. *Why should anyone wish to bring life into a world where nothing's sacred?* Breathless, she looked to the sky. *No, no, no, nothing's sacred, not even family.*

Somewhat haltingly, the little girl drew ever closer. "What's wrong?" she asked.

Inconsolable, Cäcilia knelt to the earth and grabbed the girl's arms. "Have you no idea what kind of a world we live in? It's a world where the crime of abduction happens, a terrible world where deviants hold lovely, little girls to ransom, a world where predators exploit your freedom and hunt you down and whisk you off to some—"

The homely little girl broke free and hurried off.

At three o'clock, Cäcilia returned to the hotel. By now, she had resolved to transform herself. *Yes, but how?* She wondered if she might leave London someday. *Yes, I could forget all about the past.* Once the war had ended, perhaps she would secure her travel papers and then sail off to someplace truly exotic. *Why not the Port of Ghent?* She knew just how she would finance her adventure, too. First, she would gather together all the pristinely cultured pearls that she had inherited from her mother. Afterward, why not visit the bench jeweler's shop that stood down the street from Harrods? A breathtaking chorus from *Les pêcheurs de Perles* playing upon the elderly merchant's gramophone, he would examine the gems—and then he would eagerly ring his bank to ask that one of the clerks bring him a cashier's check.

And when I get the money, I'll buy a ticket for . . .

Late that evening, she returned to the cemetery.

The graveyard was already closed for the night.

At her back, the traffic sped by—each motorcar's engine all so cacophonous and all so wrathful, the din of something powerful enough to trample to death any living thing in its path.

Perhaps even a little girl. The very thought had Cäcilia's heart beating like fury, and she rattled the gate. "Eroica! Eroica! Eroica!"

II.

CHAPTER ONE

Paris, 29 September 1919.

Just as Cäcilia ventured out onto the ice late that morning, she felt a sensation as of someone ogling her. Indignant, she looked all about.

The whole expanse appeared to be empty but for a pair of innocent *amoureux* sitting together not far from the skating-palace café. Still, a venue of this size would afford a knave plenty of places to hide. What a massive skating palace, *le Colisée*. Indeed, the architect had designed the structure to be an almost precise duplicate of the Roman Colosseum—the only dissimilarities being the copper crossbeams and the vast, dome-shaped glass vault.

What a lovely place. She resolved to ignore the scoundrel. First, she performed a series of waltz jumps. Then she attempted a layback spin. In quiet ecstasy, she throttled back as far as her spine would permit and then raised her long, graceful arms overhead. No matter how fiercely she sought to concentrate, though, she felt the malfeasant's eyes all over the space between her legs.

No sooner had she stopped skating than a young girl sat down at the pedal harpsichord that stood in the bandstand looking out across the ice. And now the musician broke into a piece that she often played of late: "*Mouvements perpétuels,*" a suite that Francis Poulenc had recently composed in honor of Valentine Hugo.

No matter how felicitous the number, Cäcilia felt no inclination to return to her training just yet. Instead, she glided over toward the boards. Her heart rate jumping up and down, she scanned the elliptical-shaped terrace. *Where could* le voyeur *be?*

Through the glass dome high above, a shaft of light poured past the baccarat-crystal chandeliers and onto the heart of the rink. At the same time, a whole array of pear-shaped beads fell from one of the fixtures and landed upon the ice.

Instantaneously, the crystal pieces scattered all about.

Cäcilia could not help but recoil. For one thing, the debris could be quite perilous for a skater. In addition, having trained here for the last month or so, she knew that the manageress preferred to keep the ice free of even the most inconsequential ripple or imperfection. *I'd better clean up this mess.*

Just by chance, as Cäcilia knelt to collect one of the fallen beads, she espied *le voyeur*.

There he sat in the box where the judges gathered during competitions: a wretched, old man with a long, wild, ragged beard, the most extraordinary anguish etched deep into his glassy, dilated eyes.

The bead fell from her hand, and the back of her throat filled with the taste of last night's supper—*Gâteau de Crabe Pamplemousse*, a dish of less-than-fresh crab cakes that *le service de chambre* had probably prepared a little bit earlier for some other tenant who had then sent the dish back.

The lively Poulenc piece concluded now, and as the French girl proceeded to leaf through her sheet music, the odor of ozone grew stronger all throughout the cool, humid air. By now, too, a thick mist wholly engulfed the rink—almost as if some component within the dehumidification mechanism must have malfunctioned.

I might as well go on back to . . .

The mist continued to suffuse the whole of the skating palace, and now another pear-shaped bead fell onto the ice.

She proceeded through the entry gate, but once she had unlaced her skates, hesitated to continue along on her way.

Once more, she glanced at the dirty old man. *Just look at that awful lout there.*

In the thick, white mist, he resembled *un spectre.* Oddly, too, the ghostlike figure suddenly uttered something. *"Une pure merveille,"* he might have said.

His melodrama incensed her. Having had enough, she climbed to the mezzanine-level concourse that wrapped its way around the circumference of the rink. *Why not confront that goddamn knave?*

When she reached the judges' box, only then did she realize how grave the old man's condition was.

He sat in a wooden wheelchair, his body and limbs having atrophied so severely that his face and skull appeared much too big and heavy for the rest of his person. For all she knew, he could not even move a muscle—from the neck down. Nevertheless, the poor wretch managed a friendly, wistful smile. Afterward, in a thick, unmistakably German accent, the ailing old man introduced himself as Herr Verbannung.

Self-consciously, she smoothed out her skating skirt. *"Je m'appelle Cäcilia."*

At once, Herr Verbannung trembled like a child in transports of delight—as though her name held great meaning for him. *"Enchanté,"* the old man blurted out.

At that point, a woman looking to be his nurse happened along. Without warning, she produced a syringe needle and proceeded to shoot some unknown medicament into his frail, bony arm.

From the direction of the bandstand, meanwhile, the music resounded anew—the French girl having decided to perform the Poulenc piece yet again.

As the melody rang out, Herr Verbannung's breathing slowed down—and now he drooled in the most shameful manner. Then the old man looked into Cäcilia's eyes, and he sought to tell her something. Perhaps he intended to explain just why he had felt such a maniacal compulsion to ogle her. Plainly incapacitated by the shot, though, it was quite plain that he could not speak further. Soon, he slipped into unconsciousness.

And as he did, a serene light fell through the vault—and the nurse looked up into the glow, and she flashed an ambiguous smile.

Cäcilia returned to *le Grand Hotel Français*.

As she sat in the hotel café, she sought to forget the old man. When the hostess brought her the usual, *une croque-madame*, Cäcilia picked at the sandwich.

After a while, she imagined her late daughter as a little girl, *la rosière*, standing at her back—the apparition having stopped by to counsel her. *Oh yes, my little Eroica.*

If the little girl were here, there could be no doubt as to what she might say: "Beloved, precious Mama, all afternoon, I've been thinking of you and the poor old gentleman back at the skating palace. Oh, how his woes do make me recall our own misfortunes. Please do something to help him, won't you?"

"But what in the world could I do for someone like that?" Cäcilia would ask, perhaps taking up the sugar tongs and tapping them against the tabletop.

"Oh, but you're so wise," Eroica might say. "What with all you've been through, you'd be just the kind of virtuous woman who ought to serve the poor, pitiful wretch back there at the skating palace."

Three tables over, a regal gentleman with a lazy eye stumbled noisily into the bussing cart.

At once, Cäcilia's daydream concluded. For a moment, she fussed with some of the tableware. *Should I go back and find the old man?* Anxious, she departed the hotel café and stopped before the establishment's beveled-glass lobby doors. *Yes, go.*

An hour later, when she reached *le Jardin des Tuileries*, she disembarked the train as quickly as possible and raced back into *le Colisée*.

When she introduced herself to the French girl up in the bandstand, the musician introduced herself as Clémentine and agreed to assist her in looking for Herr Verbannung. For thirty minutes or more, Clémentine helped her to search the skating palace. Alas, they could not locate anyone answering to the old man's description.

Perplexed, Cäcilia returned outside. The cool, late-afternoon breeze rippling through the triumphal French tricolor, she paused to consider the festival grounds.

The City of Paris had recently placed a magnificent Ferris wheel there, and the structure loomed some seventy feet high. Most miraculous of all, a profusion of bright, Byzantium-violet wildflowers had sprouted up all along the length of the wheel-support tower.

The old man called out her name, and there he was: over to the side of the Ferris wheel, not far from a lamppost, he sat all alone. And now he closed his eyes. Then, his atrophied body trembling all so wildly, he seemed to focus his energy—as if he intended to levitate from out of his wheelchair and to fly over toward her.

Given his absolute helplessness, she felt guilty. Without hesitation, she walked over—and when he opened his eyes, she bowed.

The invalid trembled, as a person consumed by unwarranted fears. "I have something crucial to ask of you. *Oui en effet.*"

She looked all about and espied the stern-looking nurse just now making her way back from *la place de la Concorde.* Nervously, Cäcilia turned back to the old man. "Well then, what do you require of me?"

"First, take me up into the Ferris wheel," he told her. "Yes, before my attendant returns and fills me with more of the serum, you must take me up into—"

"Could it be that I remind you of someone you once knew? I ask only because it's awfully peculiar the way you stare at me."

"Please, please, please" the old man insisted, his eyes and face all so anguished and desperate. "*Emmenez-moi faire un tour.*"

She looked to the Ferris wheel, and then she turned back.

Already, the old man's face had grown red. "*Quick.* Before my nurse returns, we must find a way to be alone. That's why you must—"

"Very well. *Allons faire un tour.*" Almost holding her breath then, she pushed his wheelchair over toward the amusement ride.

Once she had paid the fare, three young *gendarmes* helped Herr Verbannung into the passenger cabin.

A moment later, as the nurse called out, Cäcilia sat down beside the old man.

The spokes and drive rim all aglow in the afternoon light, the amusement ride carried them heavenward.

Not until the passenger cabin reached the highest place in the wheel's rotation did the old man seem to grow calm. "I never meant to menace you so," he told her then. "I gaze upon you the way I do only because I discern something . . . in your *eyes.*"

"In my *eyes*?" she asked, feeling a little bit embarrassed.

"Yes, you have virtuous eyes," he continued. "You have the eyes of an angel, the best one of all, the angel of *death.*"

She found herself speechless.

As the wheel continued along in its rotation, the silence grew unbearable.

By the time the Ferris wheel had made its descent, only to commence another climb, she had grown so tense that she had unconsciously begun to hum the tune to the piece from earlier in the day—"*Mouvements perpétuels.*"

The old man began whistling the tune to what sounded like "*Die Lorelei.*"

On the third rotation, once the amusement ride had brought the passengers back to the highest point, Cäcilia grew quiet.

The old man did the same. Then, as he gazed off toward *le Palais Bourbon*, an air of solemnity suddenly shone in his eyes— almost as if he longed to address the National Assembly that he might reveal to all some monumental edict.

And now he smiled. "You must be the one to help me terminate my miserable life," he told her. "Would you be willing to grant me the kiss of death? *Please.* I just know you command the power. So, tell me that you'd be willing to perform my mercy killing. Yes, and you'll do it even if it means some tyrant from *la gendarmerie* should arrest you and even if it means the authorities should imprison you somewhere a thousand times more atrocious than *la place de la Bastille.*"

Astonished, she looked off to her right.

When the ride ended, she neither spoke to the nurse nor bade the old man any kind of farewell. Quietly, Cäcilia returned to the skating palace.

In the aftermath of the Great War, she could not have imagined a better skating palace in which to train. Still, a big part of her suddenly yearned to believe that *le Colisée* must be the one true Colosseum—the one looking out over the Eternal City. And true to form, the whole place would be filled with a torrid, palpable cloud of dust—a yellow pall alive with gnats perilous enough to poison her with a strain of some awful disease. *Roman fever.*

CHAPTER TWO

Paris, 18 October.

Late that evening, Cäcilia made her way toward Herr Verbannung's modest flat on the edge of *le Quartier Latin*. She had resolved to befriend the miserable old man. *Might that lift his spirits?* Now she continued up to Herr Verbannung's door, where an array of fallen cherry-laurel leaves reeled around in an eddy. *If only they could teach me a spell, yes, a spell strong enough to inspirit the old man with the will to* live.

Little by little, she felt powerless—and given her sense of futility, she soon thought of all those extraordinary women of myth. *What kind of spell would a young witch employ?* Perhaps a sorceress would bring a bottle of *Bordeaux Rouge* laced with potions—and she would hold the elixir up to the old man's lips. *And then . . .*

From the direction of *le Panthéon*, the strains of Romany music commenced: a minstrel strumming upon a psaltery as someone else kept time with a tambourine.

Cäcilia knocked upon the rotted glazing—and when *le valet de chambre* answered the door, he guided her into a darkened salon.

Over in the corner lay a heap of rags, which proved to be Herr Verbannung himself languishing upon a threadbare mattress.

"*Comment allez-vous?*" she asked him very softly. When he failed to respond, she breathed in; the air reeked of dust, goose giblets, and *purée de pommes de terre*.

As she savored the fine aromas, Herr Verbannung coughed

up a torrent of blood that shone the blush-pink shade of apple-spice tea.

Quickly, she collected a sullied table napkin from the floor and sopped up the mess.

As she did, *le valet* pulled a syringe needle from out of a leather case sitting on the windowsill. Without hesitation, he gave the old man a shot.

In due course, the manservant walked over to the corner and placed the medical supplies atop a game table with cabriole legs. "Watch," he announced. "Always, the old man imagines a genie drifting up from the morphine jar."

"A genie?" she asked, incredulous.

"Yes, he imagines Morpheus, the god of dreams," *le valet* explained. "Ah, but the glorious visitation should never fail to displease Herr Verbannung. For the god of dreams holds no true power. No, only the god of *death* may deliver someone so hopeless."

She placed the table napkin beside the mattress. "I wish there was something I could say or do to make Herr Verbannung wish to *live*. Do you know what I mean?"

Le valet de chambre made no response. Instead, he dusted the worn, mahogany *bergère* chair. Then he collected a tarnished *bouillon* spoon from the floor.

She removed her coat, and she checked her wristwatch. *What would a vile, sensuous, young witch say or do?*

As the manservant walked off, she draped her coat over one of the chairs. Then she smoothed out both her skirt and tiered blouse.

For his part, Herr Verbannung studied the throat of the morphine jar—and now his eyes grew wide. "The god of dreams . . . *ach* . . . he's here."

So convincing was the old man's zeal that she turned to look upon the jar. For a time, she even imagined the airy spirit floating about the room amid a storm of acanthus leaves, one of the god's eyes glowing the color of emerald crystal, the other one shining like gilt bronze.

A few times over, Herr Verbannung yelped. "Please bring me the urn from beside the wardrobe. Let's trap the god of dreams inside. We'll not let the phantasm go free. Not until he calls for the god of death to come grant me a taste of blessed oblivion."

"Don't talk like that. There's nothing more precious than *life*. That's why you—"

"When the god of death arrives, I'll demand that he suffocate me with an old throw pillow," the old man interrupted.

She walked over to the wardrobe, and then she glanced back at him. "If the god of death fails to come, I shall not take his place. No, no."

"But don't you wish to release me from—"

"*Ça suffit.* If I were to dispatch you, then I'd have committed the most unforgivable of sins." When the old man failed to respond, she turned back to the wardrobe and studied the urn.

As a matter of fact, the fine *Carrara*-marble piece did look like the kind of vessel within which someone might imprison a genie: how sensual the urn's lip.

She breathed in, and she realized that the inside smelled of strawberry incense. Almost entranced, her thoughts turned back to the idea of a witch looking to inspirit Herr Verbannung with the will to live. *What would* she *do just now?*

Perhaps the bold, vile, shameless seductress would kick off her shoes and remove her coat to reveal that she had dressed herself in nothing more than a silk *chemise*. Then the witch would perform a twirl. To be sure, a dirty old man would fantasize about a fine, comely girl doing something like that—the young, sensuous enchantress healing him of all sorrow by manipulating him into some perverse act. Cäcilia turned back to Herr Verbannung.

Not unlike a Christian mystic who believes that he commands

the uncanny gift of tongues, the old man began to whisper a litany of passionate invocations.

How to reach someone so maniacal? Determined to appear neither puzzled nor doubtful, she walked over to the window and opened the sash.

In addition to the cool, autumn breeze suddenly free to blow about the room, the music of the psaltery and tambourine from before resounded much more clearly. By now, the two buskers performed a joyful tune—what might have been Claude Debussy's "*Danse Bohémienne.*"

As the wildly sensual melody continued, her thoughts turned back to the idea of a young witch having come to call upon Herr Verbannung. *What would* she *do just now?*

The witch would return to the mattress and straddle the old man. "Doesn't it feel good to be with someone so young?" she would ask him. "Now you've got the chance to cuckold all those in their prime, the ones who, by rights, *ought* to be with me."

"*Allez-Vous en,*" the infuriated old man would cry out then.

"No, don't pass up this opportunity," the young witch would tell him. "Think of all your power. A widow who feels she must remain faithful, incorruptible, she has no power at all to act upon her passions. And even if she does act, once she grows barren, she cannot make babies any longer. In growing old, a woman's womb becomes as worthless as a pig in a poke. Yes, indeed, but an elderly gentleman like you may continue to create life till the day you die, if only you decide to come aloft and—"

"*Allez-Vous en,*" Herr Verbannung would cry out a second time.

"*No,*" the witch would tell him. Then she would lay down against his body, and she would breathe in the savory scent lingering upon his ragged beard.

Perhaps it would smell a bit like dried *potage aux carottes.*

In time, the wicked young witch would kiss his lips. *And what would his breath taste like?* Perhaps it would betray a faint trace of spicy *bouillabaisse*.

Cäcilia studied the old man now. "Let me entertain you. Shall I read to you?"

The room contained no books; moreover, Herr Verbannung remained silent.

A second time, the sheer sense of futility made her think of the mythic. *If a young witch were straddling the old man, what might she do?* All so sensually, she would lift his hand and place two of his fingers into her mouth. *And what would his diseased body taste like?*

If it tasted not unlike cannabis gin, the young witch would gag. Even worse, perhaps his flesh would have an aftertaste— something like bitterweed honey. There could be no doubting any of this, for the old man's medicaments would have surely steeped his flesh in all kinds of potent toxins.

In the end, the young witch would let go of the old man's hand, at which point his two fingers would slide from her lips.

"Why must you misbehave this way?" he would ask her then, as the whole of his arm fell to the side.

"Don't you follow?" the young witch would ask in turn. "I've come to make you wish to *live*. So, we'll make a baby. Then you'll watch it grow into a pretty little girl." Unashamed then, the young witch would grind against him. "Yes, we'll make a beautiful little baby."

"*No*, free me from my anguish. Think of all the good it should do. If you destroy me, then countless physicians may study all my organs, and they'll find some way to repurpose everything and plant all my changeable parts into . . ."

Cäcilia turned back to the window and sought to think of something else. As tense and as overburdened as she felt, though, she could not manage. *How would the witch proceed?*

Without a word, *la violeuse* would remove Herr Verbannung's manhood and hold it lovingly. *And then . . .*

Outside, the minstrels concluded the Debussy piece.

In that moment, the sudden silence felt all so refreshing.

Elated, Cäcilia struggled to remember some of her favorite lines from Rimbaud's "*Proses évangéliques.*"

"Do you know any *poèmes, meditations?*" she asked Herr Verbannung then, over her shoulder.

Before the old man could answer, the musicians broke into yet another tune—a song both mournful and romantic.

The strange melody discomfited her, and her thoughts turned back to the witch. *Just how would she violate her prey?* Insidiously, the Lilith-like being would insert the old man's member into her body—and then she would glide up and down, until she felt certain that he had reached climax.

Oh God. Utterly ashamed, Cäcilia showed herself to the kitchen. There, she downed two tall glasses of metallic-tasting water. Then, without even a word of goodbye, she departed.

Outside in the street, a welter of bright-orange leaves fell from the crown of a little hornbeam tree and rained onto the pavement. And now the fallen leaves danced about in the almost-imperceptible nighttime current.

She continued along for two blocks—until the Romany music ceased, at which point she stopped before a darkened pastry shop and peered into the window.

The display table stood empty but for a bell jar containing a lone, mushy almond *madeleine.* What a miserable little cake, too; it lay upon its side, as if someone had picked it up only to toss it right back.

As the nighttime breeze whistled through a few of the plum trees lining the avenue, she drew closer to the window and studied her reflection.

She looked all wrong; her eyes had never burned with such desperation.

From around the corner, the two buskers appeared: a big,

bearded gentleman holding a psaltery, and a diminutive girl holding a double-row tambourine in one hand and a coin-filled hat in the other.

Cäcilia thought of her finances, her ever-dwindling savings. Soon, she would have to find work. What if she could secure a part in an upcoming ice ballet? According to the rumor mill, it would not be long before *la Compagnie de Danse sur Glace de Paris* commenced auditions for an ice ballet adaptation of *Giselle*. Instinctively, Cäcilia looked to the moon. If she were lucky enough to win the part of the heroine, then she would have the chance to skate an affectionate *pas de deux*—and what a great honor that would be.

The two buskers passed by now, and then they were gone.

In the pit of her stomach, a churning commenced—a nagging cramp. Soon, the awful sensation made her revisit all her tormented thoughts regarding the hypothetical, young witch taking Herr Verbannung by force so as to create life.

At last, Cäcilia gasped. If someone ever committed such a trespass against *her* person, she would despise the fetus as an abomination—and she would obliterate the entity, even if everyone around her considered the killing a crime.

CHAPTER THREE

Paris, 13 November.

Cäcilia awoke that morning, only to find a rash of hives up and down the length of her left thigh. She felt utterly demoralized, for it had only been three days since she had checked out of the safe, clean *Grand Hotel Français*—and she had only just begun feeling at home here in her modest, affordable room at the boarding house.

What's gone wrong? At first, she presumed that the bedclothes must be dirty—but when she examined the linens, she found the material to be perfectly pristine.

After a while, she wondered if the boarding house might be infested with bed bugs—but the whole idea seemed implausible. There was no sign of any insects anywhere.

Suddenly, a cool, harsh breeze pushed open each one of the balcony doors.

She barely noticed. A series of aches and chills convulsing through her body, she felt a sensation as of *mal de mer.* And now a burning presence diffused through her bloodstream, as if someone had poisoned her with an elixir—some potent chemical element.

At length, she revisited that night at Herr Verbannung's flat. Could it be that he had somehow infected her with the malady that had worn away at his body?

She slipped out of her things and examined her legs. *Have I got a case of French pox, or what about bone disease?* Either way, it would not be long before she came to experience the very same kind of palsy that had brought the old man to ruin.

The current grew stronger now, rippling through one of the little pink stockings that she had draped over the footboard.

She climbed out of bed, and as she stood there naked, reached back as far as she could to tap upon her spine. The autumn breeze blowing harder, she closed the balcony doors. As she did, though, she noticed the landlady's garden down below: a killing frost must have come the night before, for the Frenchwoman's morning glories had blackened. *What a pity.*

Cäcilia walked off into the washroom to draw a bath. When she climbed inside the claw-foot tub, she lay back until the cool of the porcelain grew good and warm against her back. At that point, she worked her very last bar of lemon soap up and down her leg— until the waters grew as fragrant as *poulet au citron.*

When she exited the tub, the hives only itched and burned and tickled and prickled that much worse. For a moment, she considered consulting a physician—but to do so would cost money that she did not have.

Once more, the harsh winds blew the balcony doors open.

She closed the doors, and then she looked all about the room. If only she had something to make the rash go away. *What about a bottle of scented water?* She had no such thing. Soon, her thoughts turned to the evening before—when the landlady had so graciously permitted her to place her leftover eggplant Provençal in *le réfrigérateur.* Perhaps if she walked downstairs and rubbed the last bit of *beurre noir* into her skin, that might do the trick.

On the other hand, what if the unconventional, impromptu ointment made her ailment feel even worse?

The hives burning up and down her leg, she opened *l'armoire.* Perhaps she had a tube of rosebud salve or one last bottle of egg oil. Increasingly frantic, she poured out the contents of her cosmetic bag—an array of beaded, artificial lashes, several tins of glittery eye shadow, and a tin of face powder. *No kind of balm, though.*

In the end, she overturned an old shoebox in which she had stored all her best black boot polish. *Nothing.*

A third time, the unforgiving current blew the balcony doors open—and now the winds grew strong enough to blow several postcards from her writing table.

Cold and naked, she sought to collect them all—the view of *les Grands Boulevards*, the view of *le boulevard Odette de Champ-divers*, and the one depicting peasant life in Orly.

The array of images only made her feel that much more confounded and directionless, a woman with nowhere to turn. She turned to the wall, where she had framed and mounted a pair of pencil sketches that she had recently made of Herr Verbannung.

Sooner or later, she would have to demand that the old man tell her just what grave disease he had given her. *What if the malady does prove to be French pox?* If so, there could be little doubt as to how he would have contracted the disease: a streetwalker would have infested him. At once, she nearly swooned. Her whole life long, she had always despised prostitution. On more than one occasion, too, she had espied various ladies of the evening standing about *la place de Clichy*—and each time, she had felt unwell.

Outside her window now, the wind moaned not unlike a fallen woman.

The hives tingled awhile, and then the rash itched and burned even more.

She took hold of her left thigh, and she kneaded the sore flesh. *What do I do?* Before long, she resolved to disbelieve that anything had happened; if she acted accordingly, then the symptoms would surely discontinue. *Go, work, resume training.*

At one o'clock, when she reached *le Jardin des Tuileries*, she learned that a Ferris-wheel tragedy had transpired the night before: mysteriously, the colossal wheel had toppled over—and three virtuous little girls from a nearby Catholic *lycée* had perished in the calamity.

Powerless to process the news, she resolved to deny all.

Five minutes later, inside *le Colisée*, she practiced her candlestick spiral but struggled to maintain her poise. *How to concentrate?* With whatever strength that she could muster, she performed a series of exercises by which to improve her footwork.

Meanwhile, Clémentine, sat down at the pedal harpsichord.

A moment later, she launched into *"Mouvements perpétuels."*

Cäcilia focused on a series of step sequences. At the same time, she permitted herself to go lost in thought and to envision the upcoming auditions for the ice ballet production. From all the newspaper reports that she had read, *Giselle* promised to be a monumental success—a tribute to the mores of Catholic society. In addition, the highly-acclaimed choreographer had pledged to keep the show simple—no bombast, no multiple narratives, nothing overwrought.

Several little girls ventured onto the ice now, and as innocent as they looked, Cäcilia's thoughts turned back to the Ferris-wheel tragedy.

The pedal harpsichord went quiet then.

She felt at the rash through her leotards. And now she gasped—for she realized that she had developed skin welts all over her hands. Moreover, when she departed the ice and removed her skates, she discovered welts dug deep into the soles of her feet.

Confounded, she wandered off into the skating-palace café.

As fate would have it, Herr Verbannung's nurse happened to be sitting at one of the tables.

Straight away, Cäcilia raised the palms of her hands to the woman's eyes. "What do all these ghastly marks mean? What's happened to me? Tell me already. Just what disease afflicts the old man? Where might he be? Yes, I'll ask him myself. Take me to him this instant."

The domineering nurse produced her long, perilous syringe needle. "Already I have administered his afternoon sedative. At present, my lord and master sleeps."

Several times over, Cäcilia scratched at the hives. "Could it be that Herr Verbannung suffers from a syphilitic infection?" No sooner had she asked the question than a violent shudder rattled the whole of her body. She dropped the ice skates to the floor, took a butter knife from the table, and clutched the absurd weapon as tightly as she could. "I never touched the old man, so how did he manage to poison me with a strain of French pox? Please tell me how he—"

"No, the noble *seigneur* does not suffer from syphilis. Furthermore—"

"Are you quite sure?" Cäcilia asked, sobbing uncontrollably by now.

"Yes, of course. Herr Verbannung, he's a fine *boulevardier*, clever with all his moneys, too. Do you know he once attended *le Mondial de l'Automobile de Paris*? There, he invested a great sum in a splendid *Peugeot Bébé*."

The butter knife fell to the floor. And now a house fly came to alight upon the utensil, at which point the winged creature proceeded to scramble up and down the length of the blade.

The nurse glanced at Cäcilia's thigh and glowered. "I'd say you display the symptoms you do only because you *will* it so."

"That's preposterous." For a time, Cäcilia studied the syringe needle. Then she shook the table. "What ails Herr Verbannung anyway?" she asked in a loud whisper. "I demand that you tell me what god-awful malady afflicts him."

"No, that's confidential. I'd never tell *you* such things." Without another word, the nurse returned to her feet and marched off.

Cäcilia gazed upon the café's kitchen door. *Have I got French pox?* Over and over, she smacked her lips. *How long before everything tastes dead in my mouth?* She turned to the café wall, and she studied the watercolor hanging there: an idyllic Bobigny landscape, the splendid frame fashioned from what looked to be hammered nickel.

The triumphal work of art made her feel like a failure, something worthless.

After a long while, she walked off into the terrace. Having found no sign of the old man anywhere, she sat down in the judges' box. In almost no time, she went lost in bitter daydreams and imagined Eroica standing at her back.

"Beloved, precious Mama, please go home," Eroica would say. "Go on. Prepare for the auditions. Learn everything you might learn about Giselle. Maybe then her story should inspire you to help Herr Verbannung to go free from this world. Oh, how that poor gentleman's woes do haunt me so. That's why you must help him. Yes, Mama. Even if it means *la gendarmerie* comes to arrest you and the courts sentence you to a lifetime of hard labor and . . ."

By the time Cäcilia returned to the boarding house, she felt no rash of any kind along her left leg. When she removed her things, she found that her skin appeared immaculate but for the pigmented mole that had always adorned her ankle.

The whole effect only made her feel a thousand times worse—something like the deep presentiment that she had felt as a little girl each time she might discern the hush before a strong autumn storm. As a cold, wintry rain commenced now, she sat down upon her little tapestry rug and leafed through her copy of *Le Nouveau Grand Dictionnaire de la Fable*.

The volume explained how Jules-Henri Vernoy de Saint-Georges and Théophile Gautier had derived the concept for *Giselle* from Heinrich Heine: apparently, the poet had alluded to the idea in an ambitious *feuilleton* on the topic of German Romanticism.

As the rain fell harder, she grew fatigued—so much so that she could not even decide whether she ought to shut the sash.

Several raindrops invaded the room, three icy beads falling onto the nape of her neck and dripping down her back.

She pushed the book to the side and curled up into a ball.

Gradually, the veins in her leg felt oddly warm; Herr Verbannung had tainted her bloodstream with something sinister, but what?

The rain grew stronger, and the pleasing clamor lulled her to sleep—but even so, the fleeting respite of slumber soon conjured brutal dreams, dreams of sickness and death and untold tragedy, dreams of imprisonment.

CHAPTER FOUR

Paris, 18 January.

At midday, a dismayed Cäcilia sat down on a park bench just outside the house that once belonged to Olympe de Gouges—the playwright who the Revolutionary Tribunal had famously executed by guillotine.

Earlier that morning, down at a skating palace opposite *le Théâtre des Variétés*, the auditions for *Giselle* had concluded. Subsequently, both producers had wholeheartedly agreed that a local Parisian girl named Fleurette Leduc would portray the heroine. As for Cäcilia, both producers had encouraged her to return to audition for the villainess. On and on, they had sought to convince her how much fun it would be to guide the male lead in an elaborate *danse macabre* complete with a prolonged death spiral.

She stood up from the park bench now, unbuttoned her trench coat, and checked her left leg. She looked healthful enough. How could she have failed to secure the coveted part?

When she sat back down, she fretted over her ever-dwindling savings. *Why not audition for some other ice ballet?* Only a few days ago, as the Parisians had celebrated *Epiphanie*, she had heard a credible-sounding rumor concerning a team of producers that intended to prepare a rink down at *l'Odéon*. Evidently, they planned to do an ice ballet version of *Coppélia*—to the music of Léo Delibes.

A rugged-looking Frenchman sat down on the other side of the park bench now.

She soon felt certain that he represented a very real threat. For one thing, he had a bit of a swagger about him. Worst of all, his attire seemed all wrong for the city; he wore what looked to be a farmhand's winter coat; moreover, his simple, straw beret appeared to be the kind that a brigand might wear.

A harsh gust of wind kicked up, and the hat sailed off his head and onto Cäcilia's lap.

When he reached over to collect the item, she could not help but notice how woefully inadequate his thinning, flaxen hair—as if the last few strands would almost certainly fall out the very next time that he dragged a comb across his scalp.

Unashamedly, he winked. "I beg your pardon."

She closed her eyes in the hope that the gesture might drive him off.

When she opened her eyes, the pest grinned. "I am Émile Lefebvre," he told her, drawing closer. "I know from the way you hold yourself that you must be English," he continued, plainly untroubled by her silence. "I read about your noble country all the time in *Le Populaire*, that's right, and sometimes *Le Temps*. I'll tell you a secret. I've always *preferred* English girls."

She could not help but shudder. Did he hope to entice her into an affair? At the very least, he would insist that she join him for supper. Then, after dessert, he would run off and leave her with *le chèque*. That kind of thing happened all the time.

The rugged Frenchman tapped her knee. "Tell me something, my love. Didn't we meet at the zoo last December? Yes, we sat together at *La menagerie du Jardin des plantes*."

She pushed his hand away. By now, she could barely control her rage. And now she thought back to the auditions earlier that morning. As overbold as the lout was, he had come to remind her of the youthful ice dancer who had won the part of Giselle's beau. The powerfully built ice dancer, Prométhée de l'Enclos, had come from Nevers, where he had trained with the famed Madame Fifi.

At any rate, given how condescending the ice dancer had acted, could it be that *he* had figured in the decision to cast the local Parisian girl?

Still grinning in his sinister way, the rugged Frenchman sat back. "You look uneasy," he continued, fussing with his beret. "What a pity that you must be such a frail girl. Still, it doesn't have to be that way. If you and I were to keep company, I'd have you feeling good. And before you know it, you'd be ready to name the day."

Powerless to control her rage any longer, she shot to her feet, grabbed the lowlife by his lapels, and shook him violently.

"*Portez-vous bien,*" the pest protested, flailing his arms.

"*Qu'est-ce que c'est?*" she asked in turn, throwing him to the pavement.

"*Mais je rêve,*" he whimpered. "*Tu es fou.*"

"*Tais-toi,*" she cried out, wrapping her hands around his throat. With a hiss, she proceeded to strangle him.

When he finally broke free, the coward raced off.

At that point, she threw up her hands. How long before he returned with a policeman? As quickly as she could, she raced off in the other direction.

A few blocks down, she ducked into the train station and boarded *le Métro.* After two stops, she disembarked and wandered off along *le rue Rabelais.*

Up ahead, an alluring establishment beckoned—an elegant, intimate, erotic cabaret with the words *Fleurs pour Osélie* painted in Caribbean green upon the sign over the lintel.

There could be no doubt that such an establishment would be closed for business at that hour, but even so, someone had left the door ajar.

In need of a place to hide, she continued inside.

How quiet the nightclub, the only sound the soothing winter breeze sailing across the empty dance floor.

As an array of old, fallen gillyflower petals began reeling in a perfect circle, she slipped her hands into her trench coat's pockets. "*Que voulez-vous me dire?*" she asked in a whisper.

No matter how fervently the flower petals danced about in the eddy, no revelation emerged from her stream of unconscious.

Four officers from *la police nationale* strolled into the deserted dance hall, each one of the imposing figures wearing *le-Gardien-de-la-paix* insignia upon his shoulder. What if one or two of them noticed how tense she looked? Even worse, what if the officers demanded that she explain her trespass? Who could say just what they might do? Perhaps they would take her off to the nearest *commissariat de police*.

As two of the officers continued across the dance floor, she resolved to act nonchalant; nevertheless, their presence made her feel guilty—wicked even. Soon enough, the sense of guilt turned to desperation. And now she thought of Eroica. *What if she stood at my back just now?*

Gently, she would pull upon one of the trench coat's belt loops. "Mama, help the old man to exit this cruel world," Eroica would tell her. "If you refuse to help, I swear I'll tell everyone what you did to that poor, innocent fellow back there at—"

"Hush," Cäcilia would say, looking over her shoulder. "Even if I believed in such things as assisted suicide and mercy killings and all that, why should I risk my freedom, the rest of my life, for someone I barely even know?"

"You do believe in mercy killings," Eroica would insist.

"No, I most certainly do not."

"Oh yes, you do. That's why, in this moment, you imagine *me* talking to *you* about the point at issue. So, take action. Put an end to Herr Verbannung's agony. Yes, even if you dread the authorities, yes, even if you fear they might burn you at the stake. Like Joan of Arc."

Feeling uneasy, Cäcilia let the gillyflower petals reel all around her now—and as they did, she closed her eyes and thought back to last summer.

Not two weeks after the Germans had signed the Treaty of Versailles, she had decided to depart England for good.

One day, a fishing vessel had brought her to the Port of Honfleur. There, she had booked passage on a steam yacht that ferried passengers down *la Seine*.

The journey had proven to be mostly uneventful, but late one night, the steam yacht had docked at the Village of Rouen—the site where the Diocese of Beauvais had burned Joan of Arc at the stake. Apparently, one of the passengers had insisted that the captain stop to permit her to come look upon the city's monument to the saint.

When the rest of the landing party had ventured off into the city, Cäcilia had resolved to follow along.

What a wondrous night it had proven to be. In the aftermath of the Great War, the people of the city could not have welcomed the pilgrims in a friendlier way. Most pleasing of all, some of the local girls had danced to a melody from that Tchaikovsky opera, *La Pucelle d'Orléans*.

At first, Cäcilia had delighted in the performance. In time, though, she had begun to wonder if the martyred figure might portend her own downfall.

Before anyone else had departed, Cäcilia had returned to the dock.

Back aboard the vessel, she had bundled up in a counterpane that the captain's mate had provided her earlier in the day.

As she had huddled near the foremast, a surly fellow had stolen onto the vessel—the intruder holding an ornate broadsword. He had sought to sell her the weapon, the swindler describing it as a perfect duplicate of the one that Joan of Arc had once wielded.

Cäcilia had flared her nostrils then. "*Allez-Vous en.*"

Her thick English accent had only made him laugh.

She had glared at him then, and she had pointed toward the dock. "*Débarquez tout de suite,*" she had shouted.

The swindler had refused to go. He had even insisted that Cäcilia take hold of the broadsword's cheaply made hilt. "Look at the four crosses etched into the ricasso above the rain guard," he had told her emphatically. "The crosses prove this piece must be genuine. Still, I offer a good price. For you only. *Oui.* Eighty francs, no more."

In the end, the whole degrading experience had only served to convince her that she would indeed find great misfortune here in France. *Just like Joan of . . .*

The winter breeze died down now, and Cäcilia opened her eyes.

Lifeless, the gillyflower petals lay scattered about at her feet.

She grabbed a broomstick and a dustpan, swept up the mess, and dropped everything into a rubbish bin containing what looked to be a clean, fresh overlay.

At the bar, meanwhile, the four policemen spoke with a woman who looked to be the hostess.

Half certain that the woman would soon protest her presence, Cäcilia walked over to the window at the rear of the establishment.

A mild whiteout presently enveloped much of the back alley—two dozen or more snowflakes swirling about the wreckage of an old barrel organ.

A second time, she imagined Eroica standing at her back—the little girl pulling on the trench coat's right-sleeve loop. "How badly does Herr Verbannung suffer?" Cäcilia would ask her, if in fact the little girl stood there in that moment.

Lovingly, Eroica would press her brow up against Cäcilia's thigh. "He suffers more than you'll ever know," Eroica would say. "So, be bold and strong. Just like Joan of Arc. Release the old man from this wicked world. Let him go *free.*"

Cäcilia moved restlessly. *Oh, to be free.*

CHAPTER FIVE

Paris, 13 March.

No sooner had Cäcilia awoken that morning than the hives returned up and down her left leg. Despite how alarming her condition, she chose to ignore the affliction. *I've got so much to do today.* In fact, she had an appointment with Herr Verbannung; after a good deal of dawdling on his part, they would finally be meeting in order to devise a stratagem for implementing his mercy killing.

When she reached *le musée du Louvre,* the skin up and down her leg itched and burned as never before. Regardless, she made her way through the queue at the ticket office. Quickly then, she continued to the rendezvous point—the museum café.

As it so happened, Herr Verbannung arrived twenty-five minutes late—the nurse pushing his wheelchair through the doorway. "Nourishment," the old man whispered, licking his lips.

The attendant purchased *une profiterole au chocolat,* and when she returned to the table, popped the treat into his mouth. Afterward, as Cäcilia followed along, the nurse wheeled the old man back into the hall and onward through a maze of corridors to that brightly-lit space housing the immortal *Vénus de Milo.*

Almost immediately, Cäcilia noticed a scattering of yellow spots in the deity's vestibule—the erotic space between her breasts.

The discoloration did not trouble Herr Verbannung: plainly awestruck, he ogled the goddess. *"Die Schöne und das . . ."*

Cäcilia's hives itched and burned even more. As discreetly as she could, she retreated to the side of a window overlooking *la place du Palais-Royal*. There, no matter how unladylike it must have appeared, she lifted her skirt and scratched at the rash.

There could only be one explanation for the return of the curious ailment: in agreeing to help him to pass on from this world, her stress levels must have grown severe enough to trigger the symptoms. How to avoid such complications, though? No matter how much she pitied him, nevertheless, she could not bear the thought of the French Republic charging her with murder.

For a time, she hummed a sad refrain—the tune to an old Austrian *romanze*. Then, as overwhelmed as she felt, she made her way over to the old man's side.

In measured language, Herr Verbannung instructed the nurse to depart. Then he turned back to the sculpture. "Do you realize what happens at this hour?" he asked Cäcilia. "Always, a sweet, little girl comes by. Océane, that's her name."

Sure enough, from the direction of *la galerie d'Apollon*, a little girl walked into the hall and dropped a sketchbook and some colored pencils beside the window. Oddly enough, she did not study the sculpture. Rather, she stared at the sculpture's pedestal. And now she knelt to the floor, and she reached out her hand. At once, she gasped—as if her fingers had pierced some precious aura hovering there, some sedate, invisible glow.

Mystified, Cäcilia thought of the little artist girls back at *la place de la Nation*. On more than one occasion, she had watched as a lovely girl from *l'École nationale supérieure des beaux arts*, or an art school like that, had removed her sketchbook from her shoulder bag and had then proceeded to render a study of the bronze monument dominating the square—that angelic being, *l'esprit de l'Hexagone*.

The syringe needle in her hand, the nurse returned now.

When Herr Verbannung demanded that the nurse go away, Cäcilia turned to the domineering woman. "Please leave him alone. No more injections. Not today. Go away and permit us to—"

"*Soyez silencieux,*" Océane spoke up. "*J'essaye de me concentrer.*" Once more, the little girl turned back to the space before the pedestal.

At that point, Herr Verbannung and his nurse began to argue quietly—each one ranting at the other in a heated exchange of whispers.

Up and down her left leg, Cäcilia's hives continued to itch and to burn.

At last, she retreated to the lady's apartment. With all the grit that she could muster, she grabbed a cake of soap and scrubbed up and down her thigh.

The course of action failed to alleviate her condition.

When she exited the washroom, she stopped before a window boasting a view of the distant *Colisée*. Only three days before, as she had practiced a candlestick spiral, a little girl had told her that someday soon *l'équipe olympique* would be training at that very skating palace.

Apparently, the Minister of Commerce and Industry, a gentleman named Lucien Dior, had recently introduced an ambitious scheme for the French Republic to host a future Olympiad in either Grenoble or Chamonix.

Cäcilia hummed the tune to "*Mouvements perpétuels.*" Might she be good enough to make the French ice-dancing team? If not, she would have to find gainful employment—and soon, too. *Why not work as an orderly?* She had heard that *la clinique Notre-Dame* would be hiring at some point.

As a tall, stern-looking girl walked by, Cäcilia looked to her feet and imagined Eroica pulling upon a fold in her skirt.

If the little girl did stand there, she would be pleased with Cäcilia's decision to help the old man to expire.

"I'm glad you're happy," she would tell Eroica. "Still, how do I avoid paying a heavy price? It'd be just awful to have to waste away in some—"

"Maybe we could sail away to someplace safe."

"No, little one. I'd much prefer to remain here."

"No, after you release the wretched old man from this world, you and me should—"

"*No*, I wish to skate for the French Republic in the upcoming Olympiad and maybe—"

"Listen, Mama, please. Let's sail away to the Island of Reunion. And we'll hire *un jardinière* to plant beautiful Bourbon roses in our garden, and maybe someday . . ."

The nurse approached Cäcilia. "Go back to Herr Verbannung. For some reason, he wishes to speak with you. *Alone.*"

Cäcilia made her way back, and she knelt before the wheelchair. "Shall we discuss the delicate matter between us, or would you prefer to—"

"Please, we must speak very quietly," he told her. "Yes, as quietly as possible. The little girl, Océane, she's working now."

Indeed, the little girl no longer knelt before the pedestal. Now she sat beneath the window, the sketchbook in her lap and a colored pencil of Mediterranean blue in her hand.

At first, Cäcilia presumed that the little girl must be drawing a picture of the Venus—yet she never once looked upon the famed sculpture. Cäcilia followed the little girl's eyes, and there could be no doubt that she must be sketching something lying on the floor—something invisible to the naked eye.

"What's she doing?" Cäcilia finally asked, in a whisper.

"She's sketching a ghost. Yes, the little girl must be sick. Delusional. She feels sure that she holds the power to detect the spirit that haunts this hall, the phantom that crouches before the precious *Vénus de Milo*. As a consequence, day by day, the little girl returns here, and she loses herself in fantasy and . . ."

Cäcilia remembered having heard something about the ghost. When he had lived, had he not worked as a poet? In time, though, a deadly microbe had gnawed away at his spine—until his body had almost withered away. Then one day his nurse had wheeled him into the museum that he might admire the incomparable Venus. And then something like a bolt of electricity had shot up and down his spine such that a warm, miraculous sensation suddenly granted him the power to stand—for the first time in years. And then the poet had stood up from his wheelchair, only to stumble to the floor—just there at the pedestal. A moment later, just before he had breathed his last, he had gazed upon the goddess and had spoken his famous last words: "*Dieu me pardonnera. C'est son métier.*"

Over beneath the window, Océane turned her colored pencil sideways and proceeded to shade in her sketch. The task did not take long. Calmly then, the little girl placed the colored pencil to the side.

Herr Verbannung's eyes flashed. "Go look," he told Cäcilia.

The hives burning badly, she took hold of her left thigh and squeezed. Before long, though, she approached the girl and knelt to the floor. "*Montre moi.*"

Looking reluctant, Océane grimaced a bit and then handed her the sketchbook.

What a striking, poignant image: the ghost poet huddled beside the pedestal. To some degree, the figure resembled Herr Verbannung. Each had the same glassy eyes and very nearly the same kind of ragged beard. Even the dimensions of the ghost poet's skull in relation to his withered frame appeared to be identical to that range existing between Herr Verbannung's cranium and *his* contorted, atrophied body.

With the tip of the colored pencil, the little girl poked Cäcilia's arm such that a dot of soft, heavenly Mediterranean blue appeared upon her sleeve. "*Le fantôme, il vous regarde,*" the little girl whispered emphatically.

No matter how ardent Océane's tone, Cäcilia had always disbelieved in ghosts—so she shook her head. "*C'est impossible,*" she insisted.

Now the little girl shrieked, as if the ghost poet must be crawling toward Cäcilia. Plainly beside herself, the whole of Océane's body began to tremble violently.

Cäcilia turned to Herr Verbannung. "What's come over her?"

Softly, Herr Verbannung groaned. "Océane fears that you'll reach out your hand and pierce the ghost's heart. And if you do, just what should happen? I think she fears the ghost's heart must burst. And of course, that's just what the ghost's heart must do, in the same way a teardrop explodes."

Still shaking all over, the little girl raced off—and now Cäcilia stood up and returned to the old man's wheelchair.

Herr Verbannung closed his eyes. "I do hope *la gendarmerie* spares you. If they don't, though, perhaps some of my friends from *la Société Français* might be willing to pay your legal fees. Does that sound amenable?"

She did not trouble herself to answer. Instead, she continued over to the sculpture. And now she envisioned herself pouring a cup of deadly laurel water and holding it up to the deity's lips some lonely, sultry, moonless night. *Drink.*

CHAPTER SIX

Paris, 18 April.

Cäcilia had still not managed to put Herr Verbannung to death.

Time and again, the old man would find some reason to delay the date. Apparently, he had a whole set of issues to resolve with his executrix—an exacting, unhurried woman working out of an office in Munich.

Early morning now, Cäcilia stopped in the heart of a flower market.

The blossoms should have emitted the sweetest scent, but the aroma came off as displeasingly medicinal—even the baby's breath.

Oh, the baby's breath. She suddenly realized that the second anniversary of Eroica's stillbirth had come around, and now she imagined the little girl standing at her back. "Happy birthday," Cäcilia whispered. "Many happy returns of the day." She glanced at her lady's coin watch. *It's eight o'clock.* She had no time to dawdle, so she continued along.

Only two weeks before, she had signed on as an orderly at *la clinique Notre-Dame.* What good fortune, too. Already, she had managed to pilfer more than enough lethal sedatives to send the old man to his reward—all of which saved her from having to deal with drug traffickers.

When she reached the hospital, *l'infirmière en chef* showed her to one of the examination rooms and told her to sweep the floor.

The cramped, windowless space reeked of rubbing alcohol and oversweet, mint-flavored mouthwash. In addition, an array of malodorous glass phials and half-empty specimen bottles littered the washbasin.

When she collected the medical chart that had been lying upon the floor, she found that it belonged to an elderly man suffering from a severe loss of muscle coordination due to a case of *le saturnisme*—lead poisoning. Her breath grew labored. Might a grave case of lead poisoning explain what happened to Herr Verbannung's spine? *Yes, that'd explain it.* Before long, she recalled the metallic-tasting water in his kitchen sink. *Yes, that'd explain* everything.

Upon sweeping the floor, she placed the medical chart up against her bosom and walked off to find the patient in question.

When she located what should have been his room, she discovered an old woman pacing about in a blouse of wrinkled crinoline and a pair of sullied French knickers.

What had become of the old man? Had he succumbed in recent days? Cäcilia sought to forget him, but she could not do so. Soon, she decided to check the isolation rooms at the very end of the corridor.

The first room proved to be occupied by a young Parisian who had recently crashed his racing motorcycle, the accident having left him with a devastating brain injury. Now he sat on the floor, playing a game of solitaire.

The second isolation room was occupied by an Irishman dying of pneumonia. Before she could manage to close the door, he gestured toward her. "Let me ask you something, love."

"What's that, sir?"

"Don't you think society should be much improved if we was to do away with the sickly and the bloodless? Think about it. Don't you suppose society ought to be finding ways to make humanity stronger? Forced sterilization, maybe that's the way to—"

"How should anyone think to talk like that?" she asked him. "Have you no sense of decency?"

"So, I offended you, did I?" the sardonic patient asked. "Well then, please accept my humblest apologies. I forgot that an orderly like you ought to believe in charitable endeavors and all that. Aye, you believe it's better to give than to receive and so on. You ain't the cheeseparing kind. Maybe you wish to help the sick and poor. Aye, a proper almsgiver, you'd be. Anything less would be the stuff of sinful misanthropy, eh?"

She shut the door, and she continued along down the corridor. When she found the third isolation room empty but for a bustle with cotton flounces lying beside a wobbly, wooden chair, she dropped the medical chart to the floor and climbed up into the window frame.

As the April breeze played through her scalp, she thought about the old man. How long until she delivered Herr Verbannung from this world, and how would she escape the authorities' retribution?

In the street below, a band of minstrels performed a tune from what she believed to be the penultimate scene of Massenet's *Cléopâtre*—and as the music played, a pretty girl in a camisole and can-can skirt danced for the passersby.

The exotic music made Cäcilia think of the ice ballet, *Giselle*. By now, it had become a most celebrated triumph. Every week, yet another newspaper printed an article on some aspect of the production. Over and over, she had read rave reviews regarding the choreography—the noble entrée, the heartfelt adagio, the intricate variations sequence, and the jubilant coda. As if all that were not enough, the wardrobe mistress had provided the star with an especially lavish gown—one embroidered with bright moonstones. Determined to enthrall the audience, the woman had very carefully consulted a select *maison de couture* on *la rue du Faubourg Saint-Honoré*—and by all accounts, the various garment makers there had supplied her with material that had once belonged to the last empress herself.

For a moment or two, Cäcilia checked over the simple pinafore overall-dress that the hospital required the orderlies to wear. *How awful.*

Little by little, the April breeze died down.

In the street below, a policeman told the buskers to move along.

The thought of a policeman patrolling the neighborhood had Cäcilia feeling short of breath. What would the authorities do to her if she helped Herr Verbannung to die? In a Catholic society such as this, the punishment would be severe. She wondered if the courts might send her away for two whole decades. *Oh God, that's too much.* The more she brooded about her future, the more she doubted the idea that she would even survive her incarceration. Once the old man was gone, she would have to make a triumphal escape; if nothing else, she could make her way to *Le Champ-de-Mars* and board a vessel bound for Conflans.

Midafternoon, faint traces of cheap, custard-apple perfume began to swirl about on the cool, spring breeze.

Her thoughts turned back to the French girl dancing the part of Giselle. On and on, the bitter, intense, fiery, insidious jealousy gnawed away at Cäcilia's nerves.

Late afternoon, the air filled with the aroma of elephant garlic—the hospital's chef two floors below cooking what might have been onion cakes.

Yes, onion cakes. Again, Cäcilia thought of the French girl. Only yesterday, a newspaper article had mentioned all the luminaries presently inviting her to this lovely soirée and that. According to one rumor, Gertrude Stein had recently invited her to an exclusive engagement at No. 27 *rue de Fleurus*. Another article claimed that Alice B. Toklas had served the French girl two sponge cakes laced with tinctures of opium. *If only she had consumed one too many of the treats such that her heart gave out!*

The spring breeze returned now, and as the air grew cold, Cäcilia felt guilty for having wished her rival harm. *What's wrong with me?* Feeling like a failure, she exited the hospital and then paused beside a heap of fallen leaves—each one a fine shade of Caspian-Sea green. *Where do I go?*

Two fallen laurel leaves tumbled off to the right, and then a few little fragments of bog myrtle blew leftward.

Why not call upon Herr Verbannung? If the old man felt ready, she would remove the deadly pills from her coat pocket and place them between his lips—just like that. To be sure, he would delight in the sensation. With a sad smile, the old man would swallow each one—and by the midnight hour, he would be gone. *What then?* Maybe she would stick her pinky finger into his mouth. Afterward, if she were to place that same finger onto the tip of her tongue, perhaps she would register a metallic taste as of some potent chemical element. *Yes, lead.*

Down the street, she boarded *le Métro*. In no time, the train took her to a stop only six and a half blocks away from Herr Verbannung's flat in *le Quartier Latin*. As she walked along from the busy train station, she decided to take a shortcut by turning down *le rue de la Femme condamnée*. Before long, she found herself hopelessly lost.

When a policeman happened by, she could not bring herself to request his help—and just like that, he was gone.

From out behind a fireplug, a few mice crawled forward and paused to study her.

When they would not move along, she continued over to a four-stall *pissoir*—and what a grievous odor: the stench of the stale urine made her nasal passages burn.

Not far away, the glow of a lamppost shone down upon a copy of the evening paper lying in the walkway.

She walked over and looked down. As fate would have it, the front page featured a photograph of the ice ballet: the French girl pinning a dazzling *boutonnière* upon the dancer portraying the Duke of Silesia.

At that point in the choreography, the two lovesick characters would skate a simple *pas de deux*. Afterward, as the Duke of Silesia held Giselle in his arms, the spectral maiden would throttle back like a broken doll.

By the time she had completed the maneuver, she would be lying upon the ice—the ghost girl gone forever.

Cäcilia imagined herself skating the coveted part. In that moment when her character was to expire, she would hold her breath lest someone in the audience notice it turn to mist. Only after the lights had gone down would she even permit herself to exhale.

A repulsive hacking cough resounded now, and from out of the shadows emerged a disfigured, enfeebled old man.

When she espied the French war cross pinned to his lapel, she wondered if he had served with *la Légion étrangère*. For all she knew, he had participated in the occupation of the Sahara.

Whoever he was, the old soldier continued into the repulsive *pissoir*. And now he began whistling a few simple songs, *mélodies*.

How to avert her gaze? Positively rapt, she stared at the wretch—on and on. *He looks a little bit like Herr Verbannung.*

At last, she removed her lady's coin watch from her wrist. Then she nudged the pin lock through one of the band holes. *Why not give him my ticker?* She clutched the watch tightly and debated whether she ought to go through with the offering. *Yes, come tomorrow morning, he could always pawn it.*

Slowly, he exited the urinal. When he noticed her standing there, he shot her the most damning glare—as if he presumed her to be some tawdry *délinquante* who enjoyed watching gentlemen as they passed water.

Of course, she sought to explain—and she offered him the watch.

The old soldier shuffled his feet, and he refused to come too close.

She flashed a friendly smile. "*Prenez la montre-bracelet. Vous pourriez peut-être le mettre en gage.*"

He only scowled, and then he continued along down the deserted street—and the sound of his terrible cough trailed off into the night.

She followed him for a while, until she realized where she was. At that point, she walked the rest of the way to Herr Verbannung's flat. Then she stood outside the sitting-room window, and she listened as a pair of familiar voices debated the ethics of death sentences.

In hushed tones, Herr Verbannung argued that there would be nothing wrong with sending someone to the scaffold.

For his part, *le valet de chambre* emphasized the necessity for a reprieve in order to give an appellate court time to confirm that the guilty party would indeed be guilty.

In the end, the old man grew wrathful—as if he considered a stay of execution to be a crime far worse than the hanging of a wrongly-convicted person.

She sat down upon the doorstep. For a time, she sought to envision that moment when she released the old man from this world. *And what about the aftermath?* For a moment or two, she thought of the wake and wondered what *le valet de chambre* might serve those who stopped by. *Perhaps he'll prepare a sumptuous mushroom mousse, or maybe . . .*

A policeman approached now, and he nudged her foot. "*Avancer.*"

Her heart pounding, she returned to her feet and continued all the way back to the train station. There, she sat down beside a pair of gaunt, half-dead mice reeking of phosphides—an especially potent kind of rat poison. *Mercy.*

CHAPTER SEVEN

Paris, 29 May.

Early that morning, Cäcilia realized that more than five weeks had gone by since she had terminated Herr Verbannung's life. What a dank, dismal morning it had been, and what a most unsettling aftermath, too—a day of guilt and sorrow and deepest apprehension.

Now she paused to think. Given how much time had passed, might she visit the old man's grave without arousing suspicion?

At nine o'clock, she departed the boarding house. When she reached Montmartre, she paused before the chapel where the funeral services had taken place.

In time, she espied *un gendarme* standing across the street.

There could be no mistaking his fixation with her. Several times over, he gave her a sideways glance. Most sinister of all, he held a box camera beneath his arm. Did he mean to take a photograph of her?

With no better option, she continued inside and sat down in one of the pews—as if she had come for no other reason than to say a prayer. The whole time, though, she gazed upon the altar and sought to picture Herr Verbannung's tulipwood casket.

Inside the box, how would he have looked? Perhaps the priest would have placed bronze coins upon Herr Verbannung's eyelids—the coins shimmering as brightly as buttered *pain aux raisins*. As for the old man's grave clothes, it seemed unlikely that the mortician would have had the power to disguise such a woefully atrophied body. Given that sad fact, the dutiful priest had probably not even permitted anyone to look upon the corpse. In all likelihood, the priest would have kept the lid closed beneath a traditional, muslin shroud.

For a time now, Cäcilia looked about the nave. How many people had even troubled themselves to attend the service? Most likely, a character like Herr Verbannung would have attracted but a paltry number. She looked upon the altar rail and pictured a wilted sympathy bouquet lying there. Soon, she hummed the tune to the Requiem Mass—the solemn, slow-moving *Introitus* that would have commenced the proceedings.

Later, as she whistled the humble *Offertorium*, someone sat down behind her.

Oh God, it's le gendarme. Her left leg all atremble, she hummed a mournful *Benedictus* followed by a silent *Agnes Dei*. Then she paused to think. With regard to forensic evidence, just what did the authorities know? If and when they had examined the old man's corpse, had they traced the poisons back to *la clinique Notre-Dame*?

Eventually, she returned outside. On the walkway, she resisted the temptation to look back at the figure following her. Instead, she continued along in the direction in which she imagined the undertaker's horse-drawn *coupé* would have transported the casket.

The policeman followed her, the echoes of his footfall strong and steady.

Three blocks on, she paused before a column-shaped kiosk to study an advertisement for an upcoming circus boasting '*un charmeur de serpent.*'

Over to the left, from within a grandiose townhouse shining the color of blanched almond, a gramophone crackled to life: the recording proved to be someone playing upon a celesta—a tune that sounded something like *Thème varié* by Camille Saint-Saëns.

The music growing louder, she thought of *le Colisée*. How long had it been since she had frittered away the day there?

Le gendarme belched—and then a blinding light the color of Roman silver suddenly flashed. Had he just photographed her?

Once more, like so many times before, she felt the hives up and down her left leg begin to itch and to burn.

Up above, meanwhile, the gramophone went quiet.

She continued past an abandoned banana-crêpes cart swathed in dust and soot, and then she paused beside a corroded rubbish bin containing a cracked, tin-glaze soap dish.

She turned to her right, and she looked down the length of the adjacent alley.

Strewn with broken footstools and badly-tattered gondola chairs, the narrow passage reeked of oil-based wood stain.

Le gendarme stopped not five feet from her shadow.

Up and down her left leg, the hives itched and burned even more. Despite all, a part of her longed to bolt. If she were lucky, she would lose the lawman. Later, in the summertime, she could visit Herr Verbannung's grave then. If she did, she would bring him an offering—either a basket of Belgian pears or a bag of cashew apples. She drew a deep breath now. *Go, run down the . . .*

As if he held the power to read her thoughts, *le gendarme* walked over in that very direction—and he blocked her escape route.

She feigned indifference and walked as far as a sewage-pumping station, where she paused to listen to the clamor emanating from within—the cacophonous rush of the highly-toxic waters.

Miraculously, on the side of the large, brick structure, a badly-faded mural advertising *l'Olympiad Paris 1900* had survived the passage of time.

She studied the nostalgic landscape, and she quietly debated whether the illustration depicted the French Alps or perhaps *les Pyrénées*. For a moment, she revisited her erstwhile fantasy of someday joining *l'équipe olympique de France*.

At length, she had the most promising epiphany: if she stole inside the sewage-pumping station, she could escape through the endless, labyrinthine tunnels. *Yes.*

Looking as inconspicuous as possible, she drew close to the door.

No sooner had she done so than a band of maintenance technicians emerged, at which point the tall one turned to her. "*Que voulez-vous?*"

"*Pardonnez-moi,*" she told him. Then she shot a glance back toward the officer tailing her. Almost immediately then, she retreated over toward the curbstone. Why not bide her time, until the maintenance men had departed?

One block east, from behind a derelict building, a transport from *la gendarmerie* rolled into the street.

Suddenly, she found herself greatly fatigued. *Why don't I go ahead and surrender?*

A crimson-colored Citroën B Torpedo passed by, and the roar of the powerful engine served to emphasize just how listless she felt.

As she teetered some, a gust of wind tore through the faded *l'Olympiad-Paris-1900* mural—and several paint chips rained onto the walkway.

Five minutes later, when she reached Montmartre Cemetery's *porte de garde,* she paused just as the funeral procession would have done. Then, before *le gendarme* had caught up to her, she continued through the gates and onward down *avenue Principale.*

The groundskeepers had paved the route with faded-gray bricks, but any number of clove-pink wildflowers had sprouted up through the cracks.

For a time, she stood beside a dead carnation and debated whether she ought to advance any further. *Turn back.* If she continued all the way to Herr Verbannung's grave, then perhaps *le gendarme* would take a photograph of her standing there.

In the end, he would arrest her. *And then maybe . . .*

The breeze kicked up, the current reeking of lead-based paint commingled with cabbage and moldy *béchamel.*

Not a little bit sickened and delirious, she imagined Eroica standing at her back.

With the end of a long-stemmed rose, the little girl would tap her thigh. "Go visit the grave," Eroica would tell her. "When Herr Verbannung's ghost arises, you'll reach your hand into his body and pierce his cool, spectral heart and then watch it splinter apart. Won't that be splendid?"

The springtime current kicked up again, and the odor of lead-based paint grew that much stronger.

Cäcilia walked along past a band of bronze-alloy angels presently deteriorating into a disagreeable shade of tart-apple green.

Fifteen minutes later, she located Herr Verbannung's tomb.

The oblong structure could not have appeared more unprepossessing. For one thing, it boasted neither funerary art nor inscriptions of any kind. Beside the door, however, someone had placed a syringe needle. Most likely, the old man's nurse had left behind the odd memento. Who else?

To the side, up in the boughs of a chestnut tree, a lone, seemingly lovesick turtledove commenced a discordant tune.

Not a moment later, *le gendarme* walked forward and stopped to Cäcilia's right.

From behind a large, unkempt evergreen shrub, a mustachioed gentleman advanced over to her left. He just had to be a plainclothes detective.

She endeavored to ignore him. Slowly, she removed a leaf of paper from her skirt's in-seam pocket. *Hello.* In faint characters, she had carefully jotted down her solicitor's telephone exchange: Montmartre 15-55.

The plainclothes detective removed his hat. "We know it was you who poisoned the old man last month."

The fatigue having grown worse, she sat down beside the tomb.

Le gendarme sat down beside her. "*Avouer.*" When she failed to say anything, the policeman grabbed a twig and began tormenting a stag beetle just then crawling past his foot.

As for the plainclothes detective, he turned westward and pointed toward an opulent grave some thirty yards away. "Do you notice the tomb there?" he asked.

"What about it?" she asked in turn.

"That's the tomb where the exiled poet Heinrich Heine rests. I've heard it said that sometimes his creations come to mourn him."

"His creations? What creations?"

"The fantastical personages about whom he wrote. Magical spirits and such. Every now and then, we hear reports. People describe . . . *encounters.*"

All the talk of apparitions brought to life by poetry weighed upon her. The whole notion that the figures might command the power to come visit their creator's grave only made her feel deflated, *defeated*.

The forlorn turtledove concluded its displeasing song, and now the winged creature fell silent.

From the direction of the cemetery gates, several more officers from *la gendarmerie* marched forward. Soon, they would demand that she tell all—and perhaps one of them would even ask that she justify her decision.

She sought to speak up and to explain just why it was right to help an anguished old man exercise his right to die. She could not find the words, though. Still, she felt no guilt. As a matter of fact, she felt as virtuous as *une rosière*. Indeed, she felt resolute. *I've committed no sin.*

The forlorn turtledove took flight, and the creature streaked across the sky.

With spirit now, she hummed the tune to "*Mouvements Perpétuels.*"

book three

The Daughters
of Lilith

I.

CHAPTER ONE

London, 29 September, 1917.

In the dead of the night, Manon returned to her hotel suite and lay down in bed. *Please, no more nightmares.*

At dawn, she had a terrible dream.

A long, plump, phallic, pulsating Zeppelin approaches the city.

Like every other tenant, she exits Chelsea Court Hotel. Alas, as she races past one of the refuge islands rising above the thoroughfare, she trips and falls.

From all directions, meanwhile, various artillery units open fire—and the terrific cacophony of battle roars and blasts and rumbles and bawls.

As the shell-shocked crowds rush down into the neighboring tube station, a lady beggar approaches. "Stay where you are," the wretched woman tells her. "It'd be your destiny to perish during a tribulation such as this."

In time, a fragment of what looks to be the Zeppelin's rudder plummets into the park not thirty feet from the place where Manon stands.

And now she looks up to find that a torrent of flames has engulfed the airship's nose.

As the doomed Zeppelin drifts this way and that, the bitter-sweet-orange blaze spreads down the length of the passenger gondola.

With an awful hiss, the airship's carcass descends toward her and then . . .

She awoke from the dream, quite certain that she must be

tangled up in the gondola's guy-ropes. Blinded by the morning light, she thrashed about.

Ultimately, she fell out of bed. *How to go on living here?*

At one o'clock, when she arrived at the offices of the London Moving-Pictures Company down on Coronation Avenue, she paused before the reeded-glass doors and debated whether she ought to resign her post. *Why not go home to Manchester?*

A dark presence rolled through the sky. Could it be a Zeppelin passing by overhead, the bomb bay slowly opening?

The darkness proved to be nothing more than a large skein of geese, but even so, she felt positively frantic—and now she continued through the door. Hopefully, the hall porter would be willing to tell Mr. Pomeroy that she had decided to back out. If so, she could be on her way before the production manager had even had a chance to protest.

As it so happened, the hall porter was nowhere to be found. Apparently, everyone had gathered in the banquet room at the end of the corridor.

Feeling not a little bit tense, she continued onward through the door.

Inside the banquet room, a hundred or more guests walked about—the ladies dressed in beaded gowns and court shoes.

Most surprising of all, a trio comprised of alto clarinet, violin, and viola, performed a lively *scherzo*.

"What's the occasion?" Manon asked the art-department supervisor.

"Didn't you hear?" he asked in turn. "Pomeroy, he's finally discovered the right girl to star in our upcoming production. Some lovely bird from Swansea. Miss Glynis T. Rhys. That's her name." The art-department supervisor turned away then, and he pointed across the crowded room toward a chaste-looking young lady dressed in a gown with a black-velvet bodice and long, sinuous skirt.

Her hand upon her left breast, Manon considered the actress very carefully and noted every detail: the young lady from Wales had big blue eyes, a cleft in her chin, and ginger hair bound up in a psyche knot. What a sleek figure, too—a fine, lithe body.

At last, Manon's heart skipped a beat—for the very presence of the refined ingénue filled her with an implacable hunger. *God, no.*

The young lady from Wales knelt to the floor, and she collected a carnation-pink cabbage rose that someone must have dropped there.

Once more, Manon's heart fluttered.

Gracefully, the young lady from Wales returned to her feet and arranged the wildflower behind her left ear—and now her ginger hair shone even more radiantly.

All throughout Manon's being, the implacable hunger grew stronger. Had she ever felt so instantaneously lovesick?

To be sure, this Glynis T. Rhys *deserved* nothing less than to be loved—for aside from her beauty, she could not have looked more *fragile*. Indeed, she appeared to be one of those delicate young ladies prone to self-starvation.

Talk to her.

As she drew close, Manon smoothed out her blouse and checked over her modest brocade skirt.

Alas, before Manon could even manage to speak up and to introduce herself, the young lady from Wales turned to one of the producers.

At once, Manon trembled all over—for the back of the young lady's gown plunged all the way down to the base of her spine, where a little brown mole sparkled as sensually as a chocolate diamond.

The producer whispered something into the young lady's ear. Then he tapped a cocktail spoon against his glass. "Listen up, everyone. Our lovely, little Glynnie has agreed to indulge us with a sequence from *Lady Windermere's Fan.*"

As everyone applauded, the waitstaff removed all the dishes and champagne bottles from the buffet table.

Once the assistant director had helped Glynis onto the tabletop, she clasped her hands together and looked out upon the crowd. "I suppose I'll do something from the third act," she announced. "This here's what Lady Windermere says just before she attempts to cuckold her false-hearted husband." At that point, the young lady flashed a girlish smile—as if feigning a touch of bashfulness.

There could be no mistaking her false modesty. How could someone so appealing not feel just right towering over everyone else as she now did? Earlier that day, Glynis must have sulked at her dressing table for an hour or more—the vain young lady hoping and praying that someone might grant her the opportunity to display her skills at this very engagement. Still, given the measure of her beauty, did she not deserve her conceit?

Yet again, Manon's heart skipped a beat. *Best of British, my dear.*

Without any further ado, Glynis delivered the monologue. What an artful, accomplished actress, too—especially the way she might reach for some imagined prop and then pantomime whatever deed the stage direction required.

Manon found herself short of breath. How to watch someone perform so effortlessly? The fact that Glynis possessed such beauty and undeniable talent served to emphasize how miserable was Manon's fate. Like most everyone, she would never be worthy to take to the stage and to bring to life this or that fanciful character.

When the performance concluded, everyone except Manon applauded.

A part of her rather despised Glynis, for Manon had never felt content to watch others perform. There could be no avoiding such feelings of envy. When she had been a little girl, she had devoted herself to her school's time-honored drama club. By graduation, she had performed in several productions. What had any of it mattered, though? The older she had grown, the more despondent and bitter and inward she had become—until her own self-loathing and introversion precluded any meaningful involvement in the business of theater.

In the end, she had no alternative but to accept her obscurity.

The applause died out, and Mr. Townsley, a director on loan from Vitagraph Studios, climbed onto the table and kissed the back of the young lady's hand. Then, before Glynis even had a chance to say anything, he stuck out his tongue and licked her flesh—across the length of her forearm, all the way to her elbow.

Holy kicker, that's harassment.

Now the drunken knave turned to the crowd. "She tastes just like Welsh rabbit."

While everyone else laughed, Manon hunched her shoulders. A bead of sweat trickling down the bridge of her nose, she clenched her fists. How could such a comely, graceful young lady permit anyone, even a film director, to trifle with her in that manner? Jealous, confounded, and incensed, Manon advanced toward the table. As soon as the young lady climbed down to the floor, why not confront her?

Thankfully, when Glynis finally did climb down, Mr. Pomeroy stepped in front of Manon and proceeded to dry the young lady's arm with his neckerchief. Then he stepped back some, and he smiled at her tenderly. "Only yesterday, the set designers promised me that everything should be up to the hub in another fortnight or so. That said, when the time comes, you must permit me to show you about." Quickly then, Mr. Pomeroy turned to Manon. "Why don't *you* come along as well? I'm quite sure you'll marvel at the world we've cobbled together."

Manon should have declined the invitation, for it was the perfect moment to tell him that she intended to move back home. She said nothing, however.

When the production manager turned away, she retreated over to the corner and paused before a floor lamp—its handspun brass shade lying on its side upon the carpet. Already, she realized that her sudden, shallow obsession with Glynis would not permit her to depart the imperiled city. *No.* Overcome with emotion, she studied Glynis anew.

How glorious she looked—her eyes, her face, her perfect skin.

Manon felt sick. Before, whenever she had encountered someone so appealing, she had always been able to *resist* falling prey to infatuation. If nothing else, she might convince herself that the nubile thing could not possibly share the same predilections—so why enter into some frustrating diversion?

Manon trembled all over. In silence, she felt at the contours of her face. Did it not feel a touch too oblong? Self-consciously, she fussed with her misshapen left ear—the one that had no lobe. Now she groaned like a wounded dog. Even if Glynis harbored the same Sapphic passions, why would someone so alluring settle for someone so homely? Increasingly ashamed of her left ear, Manon struggled in vain to conceal the deformity behind a shock of hair.

A plain-looking woman walked by, meanwhile, and flashed a smile at her.

At once, Manon could not help but curse herself. Why did she have to be so vain as to prize only outward beauty? Even regarding cinema, she had only ever prized the quality of any given *image*— the pleasing cinematography that followed from the lens design, the mere *look* of the picture. What did the story matter? Even now, as many as three whole weeks after having signed on as the script girl for the prestigious London Moving-Pictures Company's upcoming feature, she had yet to muster enough curiosity to read the screenplay. How foolish, though: even silent film hinged upon *mythos* and its attendant, unheard dialogue.

From the corner of the room, an ash-gray biscuit beetle crawled forward. Had the creature detected the presence of something sweet?

She knelt to the floor to afford herself a better look, and there it was: a treacle toffee lying at her feet. *Aha.* She marveled at the absurdity of it all: a frail, repugnant, inconsequential pest longing to consume something so grand.

CHAPTER TWO

London, 18 October.

When the day arrived for Mr. Pomeroy to reveal the sets, Manon boarded the morning train to Battersea. *Very well, Glynis, here I come.*

Manon reached the studio complex at eight o'clock. As she looked about, she failed to locate the production manager. Before long, she walked past the prop warehouse and then made her way through a maze of stage wagons. Soon enough, she reached the building in which the production company would be shooting the film.

Would the structure even be big enough? She doubted it. By now, she had read the script twice—and it had proven to be an epic.

The intertitle on the second page introduced nothing less than high adventure:

'The daughters of a primordial dæmoness by the name of Lilith have come to live
in the gardens and orange groves of Tel Aviv. There, the infernal brood seeks to seduce
the otherwise pious women of the quiet, fledgling town.'

As for Glynis, she would play one of the unsuspecting victims: a Greek-Orthodox girl named Philoméla. What an effective inciting incident, too: when the virtuous Philoméla spurns their advances, the daughters of Lilith blame her for a series of thefts perpetrated, in truth, by a magpie.

Manon looked to her feet now. The more she thought about the script, the more discomfited she felt—for the film equated lesbianism with wickedness. *The whole story, it's a product of intolerance.*

As soon as Mr. Pomeroy happened along, a part of Manon yearned to say something brazen. Still, if she were to estrange the production manager, then perhaps he would sack her and hire someone else to take her place. *And then I'll never see Glynis again.*

In time, a chauffeured Atalanta deposited the beautiful actress not far from an office building standing over to the right.

Manon cringed. *Of course, Glynis just had to arrive fashionably late.*

Once Mr. Pomeroy had greeted her and had subsequently accepted her seemingly halfhearted apology, he guided the two young ladies through the studio doorway.

Inside, what a spectacle. The studio stretched out like a football pitch. What a remarkable glow, too, for the vast structure boasted a glass vault in place of a proper rooftop. Because of this, the sun illumined everything in a profusion of natural light perfect for making movies.

As the party walked along a pathway reaching this way and that through an array of absurd, faux-Levantine sets, Manon felt increasingly uneasy.

After a while, she grew so distracted that she walked right into a camera dolly.

A moment or two later, she stopped beside one of the grandiose backdrops—a tapestry depicting an array of purple clouds.

"Everything's all so contrived," she blurted out. "This whole film, it's nothing more than the stuff of caricature and histrionics and prejudice and . . ."

Mr. Pomeroy removed his pince-nez. "No, no," he insisted. "Hear me out. We must take the bold, revolutionary, *Expressionist* route so that we may show just how our heroine would've perceived her surroundings. Realism and such, that's for dullards."

Manon put her hands on her hips. "*Bigotry* and such, *that's* for dullards."

Mr. Pomeroy buffed his lens against his coat sleeve, and then he put the pince-nez back atop his nose. Instantly then, he gestured toward a big, gypsum-plaster fountain standing some twenty feet away. When everyone continued over, he activated a device by which to conjure a thick, foreboding mist. "How's that for some extra flash and footle?" he asked.

Like a little girl, Glynis giggled so. Plainly, the young lady from Wales approved.

Mr. Pomeroy shut down the apparatus. Then, as the smoky mist dissolved in the warm light, he pointed toward an extravagant pool on the opposite side of the building. "Come now, ladies. Let me walk you over to the Port-of-Jaffa set."

Manon hesitated. In addition to her deepening sense of alienation, she had also come to feel greatly overpowered by the stench lingering in the air—a blend of lacquer paint and freshly-laid stucco.

After a while, she felt a tingling sensation in her fingers. And now a violent coughing fit came over her.

When she finally recovered, she stepped back some and turned toward a potted crab-apple tree. Almost immediately, the enchanting prop made her think back to the script.

During one crucial exposition scene, a daughter of Lilith relates a bit of her mother's story—at which point, the intertitle would read:

'On the sixth day of creation, as soon as Lilith awoke in the tedium of the primordial garden, a sensation as of spite welled up all throughout her newfound being.'

A detailed flashback would commence then: a sequence featuring Stella Fithian, the famed actress who the producers had cast as Lilith. What a beautiful actress, too, what with her silvery-black hair, green, tapered eyes, and olive-colored skin. Sensuously, she would look to the sky—and then a second intertitle would appear:

*'As she pridefully marched toward the gates of the earthly
   paradise,
Lilith willfully pronounced the Ineffable Name, and in so
   doing,
blithely forsook the Kingdom of Heaven.'*

The very next shot would show Stella Fithian's Lilith walking along the Red-Sea shore, where she encounters the dæmon Asmodeusz. In the hope that it might vex God Almighty to no end, the evil spirit grants the spiteful woman life everlasting. And from that moment on, Lilith reigns as the most murderous kind of sorceress.

A set of footsteps approached now, and Manon turned from the crab-apple tree.

Glynis had just walked back from the elaborate Port-of-Jaffa set, a splash of water having dampened a strand of her ginger hair such that it shone like *aubergine* satin.

Instantaneously, Manon's chest swelled. A part of her longed to profess her love then and there—perhaps even kiss Glynis upon the alluring, soft, powder-blue vein reaching across her left temple.

Manon did no such thing, for she had no right to so. Besides, how to kiss someone so plainly obtuse regarding the film's obvious illiberalism?

Glynis stopped beside a bundle of gunny cloth and scratched at her scalp. "I'm quite sorry if you consider the sets vulgar."

"It's not just the sets," Manon told her. "As far as I'm concerned, everything about this production feels wrong."

"Wrong?"

"Yes. Haven't you read the script?"

"Of course," Glynis answered. "I didn't—"

"What about all those awful intertitles?"

"What *about* all that?" Glynis asked.

"If you read between the lines, the script makes it clear that society ought to think of goose girls as something ungodly. Like the daughters of Lilith."

Looking perplexed, Glynis remained silent. At the same time, though, her belly rumbled noisily—as if she must be hungry.

"Why do you insist on starving yourself?" Manon asked her.

"Starve myself? I'll have you know that just last night, I had some flaxseed."

"But how long has it been since you treated yourself to a proper repast? Be honest. You haven't had a healthful supper in more than—"

"What do you know? I would've had fish and chips just last night, but then I noticed how the cook scratched at his armpit. And then, with the very same hand, he handled the lovely fillet that I'd selected. As mortified as I felt, of course, I had no choice but to—"

"Would it be Pomeroy? Would *he* be to blame? Maybe on the day he had you sign your contract, he added in a court-approved stipulation what says you can't weigh in at more than a certain weight."

The young lady from Wales shook her head, and she laughed in a malevolent tone.

At that point, Mr. Pomeroy called out from the east end of the studio and insisted that the two of them come meet him over at the nickelodeon set.

Manon followed Glynis through an array of potted Aleppo pines, and when the two young ladies reached the opulent nickelodeon, Manon rejoiced—at least at first.

The set designers had adorned the cinema house with tea-stained glass doors and a notice advertising a French picture show, *Les Aventures de Baron de Munchhausen*. In addition, the set designers had included a bright-red popcorn cart—complete with a finely-polished, state-of-the-art popcorn popper housed within the heart of an oblong, glass oven. How true to life everything appeared: the set designers had even thought to scatter two dozen or so multicolored ticket stubs all about the pavement.

Manon recalled the very first picture show that she had ever attended: *Das Mirakel*, an ambitious German work that related the tale of an ivory Madonna that comes to life and saves a fickle nun from various temptations of the flesh.

Had the filmmaker intended *that* picture to be a thinly-veiled attack on lesbianism?

Manon staggered back a few steps, until she very nearly knocked over a hand-crank camera mounted upon a wooden tripod. Silently, she brooded. If she continued to work on this libelous picture, how could she live with herself?

The relentless glare of the midmorning light grew brighter and brighter—and as the heat pounded upon the nape of her neck, she felt increasingly unsettled.

At her feet, something gleamed all so gloriously.

The object proved to be a putty knife.

She took the implement into her hand. Lost in thought, she placed the point against her throat and nearly drew blood.

For a time, she thought of the screenwriter. Had they ever spoken? She did not think so, but she could not be certain. Now she turned from the nickelodeon, and she sought to envisage the screenwriter wandering through the studio.

How good it would feel to confront him, to chide him.

The putty knife in her hand, she returned to the potted crab-apple and breathed in.

What with all the chemicals swirling about the building, the crab-apple failed to exude any raw, organic aroma. If anything, the leaves reeked of celluloid.

She studied the crown. *How could a tree like this ever manage to bloom?*

The light grew brighter and brighter, until the heat felt positively intense.

At last, she stepped forward—and she took refuge within the shade.

From back toward the nickelodeon, a burst of laughter resounded: Mr. Pomeroy must have shared some glib witticism, and Glynis must have found it terribly amusing.

Manon refocused upon the crab-apple. Feeling sardonic, she imagined it the tree of knowledge of good and evil. *Why not pluck one of the forbidden fruits?*

Even if such an act of disobedience were to bring about her fall from grace, nevertheless, would she not learn something profound in the process? If nothing else, perhaps she would learn just why it must be that so many scoundrels despise her kind. *Yes, yes.* Once she had tasted of the fruit, the epiphany would surely come to her.

On the other hand, perhaps the knowledge of good and evil would simply confirm what she already suspected—that those who despise her kind would feel the way they do only because they fear their own *secret* impulses toward homoeroticism, androgyny, and transvestism.

She plucked one of the fruits, and now she realized why the crab-apple tree happened to be in bloom at this time of year: the prop proved to be wholly *unreal*, the trunk and all fashioned from either Bakelite or some natural rubber.

Blushing, she sought to attach the fruit back to its place upon the fake bough.

From back in the direction of the nickelodeon, Mr. Pomeroy shouted her name.

She cringed. "I'll be right there," she answered. On and on, she struggled to find some way to mend the prop—but the endeavor proved hopeless.

A second time, Mr. Pomeroy called out her name.

Finally, she dropped the fabricated fruit amid the fabricated roots—and then she made her way out from the shade and back into the merciless light.

CHAPTER THREE

London, 13 November.

Late that night, as the cast and crew prepared to view the dailies, Manon stopped before the screening-room door and cursed herself. By now, she felt utterly loathsome and servile for having agreed to participate in the movie. Still, she had not found the strength to quit. Indeed, across the course of the past week, her obsession with Glynis had only intensified.

Manon's heart fluttered now. As she eyed the screening-room door, she placed her hand over her left breast. *How to go free from my heart's only desire?*

On edge, she continued into the crowded, dimly lit screening room and sat down to the right of Glynis.

Moments later, from the direction of the projection box, the soothing rumble of the cinematograph resounded—and now the rushes commenced.

Five rows up ahead, the director lit his long, elegant *fume-cigarette.*

Sensually, the tobacco smoke coiled and danced and drifted all about.

Manon sought to focus on the sequence presently playing— the arc shot depicting the moment when the thieving magpie flutters off with a cheaply made cherry pitter belonging to the daughters of Lilith.

No matter how fervently Manon sought to concentrate, the smoke addled her so.

After a while, she stood up and walked over to the window. Once she had lifted the sash, she looked to the silvery clouds. *How long has it been since a Zeppelin terrorized the city?* She revisited all her terrible dreams—all those visions of dying in some god-awful bombardment.

On the screen, an alternate arc shot commenced—the magpie looking a little bit uncertain about holding the cherry pitter in its bill.

Manon glanced at Glynis—her shadowy silhouette crowned by the reddish, black glow of her ginger hair. Then Manon studied her face. Despite the darkness of the screening room, there could be no mistaking her sunken cheeks. *Why must she starve herself?*

Up in the clouds, a clamor as of an airship's engine rang out. Or had it?

Feeling certain that she had only imagined the disturbance, Manon ignored all.

As a third arc shot played, she returned to her place beside Glynis and leaned in. "You're looking much too thin and fragile," Manon whispered.

The young lady from Wales almost groaned, as if she had heard such criticism a thousand times before.

"Tell me why you insist on fasting," Manon whispered into the young lady's perfectly shaped ear. "*Why?*"

Glynis looked to the hem of Manon's skirt. "I wish to watch the dailies," she said softly yet sternly. "*Enough.*"

Manon turned and looked straight ahead.

By now, the ash at the end of the director's *fume-cigarette* had already built up as much as a whole inch.

Manon turned back. *Shall I give Glynis a kiss?* Unable to harass her in that way, Manon tapped upon the young lady's shoulder instead. "Could it be you've fallen victim to some kind of vanity-driven hysteria?"

The production designer turned back and chided Glynis, as if he believed that *she* had been the one doing all the talking.

Plainly chagrinned, Glynis folded her arms across her bosom.

Kiss her. Like so many times before, Manon's misshapen left ear itched and twitched and burned. As such, she failed to muster the nerve to kiss the delicate beauty. Instead, Manon tapped her shoulder again. "It's all so funny."

"*Funny?* What's so funny?"

"I have so many imperfections, yet I don't feel any impulse to transform my body in some extreme way. On the other hand, even though you're positively perfect, you cannot accept yourself. So, you waste away. Like a hunger artist."

Again, the production designer turned back to chide Glynis— as if she and she alone must be to blame for the ongoing banter.

The severity of the scolding made Manon feel guilty. *A girl like Glynis deserves compassion and understanding, not criticism.* Manon breathed in, and then she exhaled.

Up in the projection box, the reel jammed such that an absolute darkness suddenly enveloped the screening room. In that moment, even the twisting, turning wisps of cigarette smoke disappeared.

As the projectionist fumbled with the reel, one of the cinematograph's sprockets made a noise. Other than that, the screening room remained silent—as if everyone were accustomed to the occasional mishap.

By stages, the darkness intensified. Had a massive billow of clouds only just obscured the moon?

She longed to turn to Glynis and to kiss her. *No, that's far too forward.* Manon turned to look at her. *Maybe a kiss on the temple?* Manon hesitated. *Maybe I ought to whisper something affectionate.*

She never had a chance: as if Glynis had intuited all her lust, the young lady drummed upon her thigh and then returned to her feet.

A moment later, she continued out into the aisle.

At last, she marched off and continued out the door.

Three rows up ahead, one of the set designers lit a cigar.

No matter the cool breeze sailing in from the window, the added smoke soon grew intolerable. Manon stood up, felt her way through the darkness, and continued into the projection box. "Could I help you any?" she asked the operator.

"No, I've almost got it," he answered. "No worries."

"Very well." With that, she drew close to the cinematograph. Without qualms, she placed her right palm up against the red-hot lamp house. As embarrassed as she felt, there could be no avoiding it. *How to escape the night without a token of penance?*

Despite the anguish, she refused to withdraw her hand.

The sharp, hateful, unforgiving heat scorched her skin.

Finally, the operator noticed—and with a gasp, he pushed her away. "What's come over you?"

At first, she sought to explain—but no matter how ardently she moved her lips and tongue, she could not make a sound. Before long, she blushed. Given the whole state of affairs, she had the feeling that in that moment she must have looked like an actress in a silent film—her lips and tongue moving as if to supply a set of lines that only a deaf person accustomed to the art of lip reading would ever be able to discern.

When she exited the projection box, she returned through the door and continued out into the hallway. There, she stopped before the stock-footage room to think.

What if Glynis tells everyone what I am?

The production crew would laugh and say the most insulting things.

In the end, the torment would come to feel something like battle fatigue.

Manon buried her face in her hands and thought back to her school days—a girlfriend who had fallen in love with a sporting lad. When he had spurned her advances, she had become vin-dictive: over the course of the proceeding month, she had told everyone in her congregation that he must be "one of those sodomites."

As a consequence, the poor youth's reputation had suffered greatly.

Manon examined her hand now. Here and there about her scorched palm, the skin had already begun blistering. Demor-alized, she exited the building. Shortly afterward, down by a fingerpost twisted to one side, she hailed a taxicab and asked the driver to take her to an all-night nickelodeon in Soho.

When she reached the cinema house, she found that a pleas-ing picture show had only just begun: *Tarzan of the Apes* starring Elmo Lincoln. The Wurlitzer-organ music resounding from inside, she purchased a ticket and then followed a fussy usherette this way and that through the crowded stalls.

Just as Manon sat down, the movie reached that melancholy scene in which Tarzan ventures into the ruins of Greystoke cabin and espies a dagger shining in the dust.

What a magnificent, deadly blade. As the story turned to a tense chase scene through the jungle, she continued to obsess about the perilous weapon—until her train of thought turned to yesterday's *Daily Mail*, an alarming exposé about a Japanese crime syndicate that had recently sailed from the Port of Hiroshima all the way to Mozambique in order to procure an assortment of elephant tusks. Apparently, the gangsters had aimed to ship the plunder to Tokyo and to sell the precious ivory to various, selfish, sexually inade-quate collectors who had no better way to compensate for their insecurities than to turn the elephant tusks into hilts for their long, phallic, samurai daggers.

Even now, her misshapen, left ear twitched uncontrollably at the thought of all the orphaned elephant calves wandering lonely and distraught through the vast African plains.

On the screen, meanwhile, the story returned to Greystoke cabin—Tarzan preparing to do battle with a big, maniacal ape.

As she sought to refocus, the organ grew frantic—the music the perfect complement to the struggle between Tarzan and the fierce animal.

By the time the young Tarzan finally plunged the dagger's point deep into the beast's throbbing heart, her ongoing twitch had grown so violent that she felt as if the whole of her left ear must soon detach from the rest of her body.

The organ music reached a crescendo, and now she shrieked and tumbled out into the aisle—at which point, a violent seizure ensued.

A portly fellow called for a physician and then knelt beside her.

As panicked as she had become, she inadvertently kicked him in the shins.

And now a large number of people stood up from the stalls and gathered all about. Did they hope to witness some outlandish spectacle?

After a while, even the organist turned to watch.

A sense of shock overcame the whole of Manon's being. Suddenly, everything seemed to transpire slowly. Moreover, she heard nothing—not even the steady hum of the cinematograph up inside the projection box.

The silence did not last long.

Soon, she heard or else hallucinated the trumpeting of an elephant calf—as if the poor creature's grave, plaintive, uncanny cries resounded from thousands of miles away.

The usherette happened along then, and Manon grabbed hold of her ankle. "Can't you hear the baby elephant?"

"What's that?"

"Come with me to the jungles of Africa," Manon pleaded with her. "We've got to thwart the poachers."

"What're you talking about? Listen here, sister. If you don't gather your bloody wits this instant, I'll ring the bobbies and—"

"Don't you realize what's happening? We've got to get to Africa and rescue the baby elephant and—"

The usherette pulled Manon up from the floor and then smacked her across the face.

The blow proved just enough to remedy Manon's hysterics. Overcome with shame, she hurried out into the lobby.

Moments later, when she paused beside the theater cashier's office, the organ music recommenced—and now the Wurlitzer sounded all so *exquisite*.

She listened all the way to the end of the scene, when the chord came to resolve itself in a mystifying way—the last three notes wholly estranged from the rest of the score, a broken chord ringing out from a world of fractured reality, agonized dreams.

CHAPTER FOUR

London, 18 January.

That night, Manon resolved to kill Glynis. *How else to ensure her silence?*

Halfway to dawn, when Manon reached Battersea Park, she paused beside a wrought-iron *banquette* and removed a paper knife from the pocket in her double-breasted winter coat.

Just before Christmas, she had purchased the unlikely weapon at an antiques market not far from Waterloo Station. When the salesgirl had let her hold it, Manon had carefully examined the cheek for any imperfection in the luminous blade. "Would you be willing to whet the edge some?" Manon had asked then.

"Of course," the salesgirl had answered, taking the perilous letter opener back into her hand. "We keep the grindstone in the back room."

Manon had smiled then. "Make the edge as sharp as possible. Sharp enough to . . ."

The blade gleamed softly in the moonlight now, and the pewter hilt felt good and warm in her hand.

With her free hand, Manon ran her fingertip down the length of the paper knife's spine and then nestled the sharp, steely point against the heel of her thumb. Then, as she placed sheath and all back into her coat, she turned toward the studio complex. For a while, she wondered just what scene the director had shot that day. Could it have been another one of the frustrating, time-consuming sequences involving the magpie?

Whatever the scene, it would not be long before Glynis emerged from the endless wreaths of coal smoke.

The foghorn called out, and Manon sat down upon the park bench and eyed the birdbath standing in the nearby glade. For the longest time, she studied the curious, humble-looking caryatid holding up the basin with her impossibly-long fingers.

What fierce indignation in the statuette's eyes—as if the caryatid were a sentient being.

Yes, a sentient being who intuits my murderous scheme. A second time, she removed the letter opener. How brightly the blade gleamed in her hand. A second time, she returned the sleek, immaculate weapon into her coat.

A gentle storm commenced, and a few snowflakes drifted into the birdbath's otherwise empty basin. Could the poor caryatid feel the added burden?

The frozen rain kept falling, and the night grew colder.

Manon looked to the sky. *Oh God, it feels like February.*

A memory awoke: the recollection of an extraordinary incident that had happened some six years earlier, her very last semester of grammar school.

One night, about two weeks before Valentine's Day, a diminutive, redheaded peddler girl all wrapped up in a frock coat reeking of cabbage and pork kidneys had stopped her in the street.

"So, would you care to purchase one of my Valentines?" the little girl had asked her in a thick, Irish brogue.

"No, thanks," Manon had told her then. "I haven't got anyone to—"

"You ain't promised forth to no one? Well, that's no trouble at all because I'd be willing to sell you a *dream* Valentine."

"A *dream* Valentine?"

"That's right," the peddler girl had answered, holding up a heart-shaped card pasted to a paper-lace doily. "You send it to Juliet down there in Verona, Italy. General delivery."

"Ah, so the Valentine ends up in the post office, the dead-letter room most likely. And then, when it's time to discard the rubbish—"

"No, the postman takes everything to Juliet's tomb." At that point, the peddler girl had proceeded to perform the sequence in which Juliet discovers Romeo's body—and not unlike an accomplished actress, the peddler girl had even wielded an imaginary knife while uttering her immortal lines:

"*O happy dagger!*
This is thy sheath; there rust, and let me die."

The peddler girl had plunged the imaginary knife deep into her bosom then, only to collapse into a patch of winter pansies.

Through the darkness now, a pair of footsteps drew close.

A feeling of awe washed over Manon's person. *Could it be Glynis?* When the figure paused to fuss with her coin purse, Manon recognized her as one of the extras.

Manon's thoughts turned back to the fateful encounter with the peddler girl. *How much did she charge?* To the best of Manon's memory, the price for the dream Valentine would have been six shillings. In that moment when Manon had offered the payment, however, the peddler girl had stepped back.

"I've also got a beautiful silk rose," she had cried out then, hopping up and down as if her life depended on making the sale. "It's only a half a quid for the imitation rose, and then you'll slip the blossom in with the card."

"What's this?" Manon had asked then. "A rose?"

"Yes, all around the world, people send Juliet pressed flowers and such," the peddler girl had explained. "Some send love-lies-bleeding or maybe a dozen forget-me-nots, but what could be better than a silk rose? Yeah, that's why goose girls prefer to send the like. Have you ever heard of them goose girls? They only kiss other girls."

"You don't say," Manon had whispered then. "Very well, I

should be quite pleased to purchase one of your dream Valentines, along with . . ."

A noisy Britannia cyclecar sped past Battersea Park now, the clamor resounding like the rumble of a Zeppelin's diesel engine.

Manon sat back some. In the coming weeks, would any goose girls living here in London feel compelled to post dream Valentines to Verona? If so, just what would the lonely, sensuous, young ladies ask of Juliet? Perhaps they would ask for nothing more than her willingness to consider their most heartfelt confessions.

A second pair of footsteps resounded: it proved to be a woman who worked as a seamstress in the movie studio's costume department.

A burning sensation returned all throughout Manon's hand, her flesh still quite tender from the night she had willfully injured herself in the projection box. Now she held out her palm in the hope that she might catch a few snowflakes—anything to soothe her scorched skin.

Thankfully, three soft crystals soon came along. Two melted against her wrist, and another dissolved along her fate line.

A moment or two later, the fourth evanesced at the very tip of her ring finger.

Yet another figure passed by, the stranger seemingly oblivious to Manon's ghostlike presence.

She returned to her feet. Twice, she circled the birdbath. Then she gazed to the clouds and whispered a favorite line from Shakespeare: "*Come, gentle night, come, loving, black-brow'd night.*"

The winter storm grew stronger, each one of the myriad snowflakes shining a dazzling whisper white.

She reached into her coat pocket, wrapped her cold fingers around the letter opener, and then withdrew her hand. *Do I even have what it takes to plunge a sharp, steely blade into some unsuspecting young lady's gut?*

On and on, the snowflakes danced all about. Before long, one of them came to alight upon Manon's bottom lip. *Oh.* The delicate touch of the crystal felt like a stolen kiss and tasted just as sweet.

An elegant, ladylike figure in silhouette approached along the walkway. Due to the distinctive shape of her tall-crowned Welsh hat, there could be no doubt as to her identity.

Nervously, Manon removed the paper knife and pressed her thumb against the heel.

At almost the same time, Glynis stopped beside a postbox. "Who's there?" she asked, her tone of voice all so bold.

Manon said nothing. Instead, she thought of all those sensuous goose girls who post dream Valentines to Verona. If she went through with her scheme, all the London newspapers would print one editorial after the next denouncing her crime of passion. In no time, everyone all throughout the empire would come to equate Sapphic love with the most reprehensible kind of pathology. As a consequence, the goose girls of the world would come to despise her name.

Later, as she rotted away in some filthy jailhouse, countless young ladies would oppress her with letters of condemnation— for in killing Glynis, Manon would have provided any and all illiberal bodies and psychosexually-insecure louts with a fulcrum for their bigotry.

Glynis advanced a few feet now and stopped. "You there, say something."

Manon's guilt grew overwhelming. How could she commit a crime that would only serve to confirm others' prejudice regarding her kind? Did she not have an obligation to preserve the goose girls' collective reputation?

Glynis advanced a few more feet. "Manon, would that be you there? If so, what's this all about? Kindly explain."

Manon retreated some, the small of her back bumping up against the very edge of the birdbath's cold, stone basin. Her thoughts turned to the last month or so. Had she suffered any vilification or derision? She most certainly had not. Which could only mean that Glynis had not actually told anyone. *And perhaps she never will.* Remorseful, a part of Manon felt an urge to cut herself with the paper knife—the way an emotionally delicate girl might cut herself, deliberately profaning her body. She had no time, however. As the young lady from Wales approached ever closer, Manon dropped the weapon into the birdbath. *I'd better run.* With whatever strength that she could muster, she raced the length of the park—until a nagging, merciless cramp began to stab at the abdominal wall on her left side.

In total agony, she finally stopped.

All so swiftly, a pair of footsteps approached: paper knife in hand, Glynis had resolved to give chase.

Despite the stabbing sensation, Manon hurried along. Faster and faster, she ran. *Keep going, willpower.*

CHAPTER FIVE

London, 13 March.

Tense and chastened, Manon returned to the offices on Coronation Avenue early that morning and proceeded into the screening room—a desolate hall with a high ceiling and seven ornately draped windows. A young composer by the name of Peter Warlock would be scoring the film that day, and in need of extra pay, she had agreed to work the cinematograph.

With furrowed brow, she dropped her raincoat over one of the occasional chairs. Then she circled the film projector. There could be no avoiding her sense of anxiety, for Glynis had rung the night before to say that her cousin, Sabine, would be stopping by. What a disquieting exchange: Glynis had renewed communication. Even more dramatic, there could be little doubt that this mysterious Sabine happened to be a goose girl. Furthermore, given the overly gracious way that Glynis had spoken about her, there could be little doubt that Glynis fancied herself a matchmaker.

And she expects me to get together with this Sabine.

From the moment Manon had surmised the scheme, she had felt indignant. Because of this, she had dressed herself in a simple blouse and a drab bustle skirt before leaving the hotel that morning. *Why not make myself look as unappealing as possible?*

For a time now, she looked to the floor. Then she flinched. A part of her rather longed to meet Sabine. *And why not?* Now that Manon had resolved *not* to harm Glynis, there could be no denying the fact that the two women would have to work through their issues.

Could it be that Sabine held the key to some kind of reconciliation?

At nine o'clock, Peter Warlock arrived. The well-dressed gentleman stood quite tall, and he had greased back his thin, flaxen hair with pomade. "Shall we begin?" he asked, sitting down at the concert grand.

Manon bowed. "Yes, sir."

A moment later, a young lady bundled up in a coat with a virgin-wool collar continued through the doorway and sat down beside the cinematograph. "Hello."

The stranger just had to be Sabine, for despite her pixie bob and Roman nose, she vaguely resembled Glynis.

All the time fidgeting, Manon greeted her and then turned away. Quickly, she reached for the first reel.

From what sounded like several blocks to the east, a steam hammer began pounding.

In her misshapen ear, each thud reverberated like an explosion—a volley dropped from a merciless Zeppelin, the very one destined to destroy her. Despite all her nerves, she activated the exciter lamp. Then she paused to consider the last three blisters festering upon her palm. Before long, she whispered a prayer.

Peter Warlock switched on his piano lamp, meanwhile. Then he reached over to the wall-plate and dimmed the ceiling lights.

As Manon arranged the reel onto the feed spool, she felt the weight of someone's eyes all over her body. *Sabine.*

Moments later, as the cinematograph rumbled through the darkness, Peter Warlock commenced the struggle to reconcile his melancholy music to the images flickering upon the screen—specifically, the sequence in which the daughters of Lilith accuse Glynis of purloining the cherry pitter.

The heat of the cinematograph grew intense, and a bead of sweat trailed past Manon's misshapen ear.

Sabine tapped Manon's left thigh. "Do you follow the war reports?" the young lady asked, her voice barely perceptible over the clattering film projector. "I do because I wish to serve as a helpmate to all them nurses working the hospitals down there in Ypres and war-torn places like that."

Manon turned to the creamy glow of the piano lamp shining down upon Peter Warlock's sheet music.

Had the young lady's whispers begun to vex the composer?

Sabine crossed her legs. "Wouldn't it be good fun to enlist?" she asked, her voice loud and clear.

Manon remained quiet. Still, she begrudgingly admired the young lady's idealism. For whatever reason, this Sabine felt a sincere calling to serve. She did not prize fame, nor did she feel any selfish impulse to engage in the merely profitable. Unlike most people, she aspired to help others.

Once more, Sabine tapped Manon's thigh. "Can't you imagine what an honor it'd be to serve king and country?"

Conscience-stricken, Manon nodded. "Yes, of course." The heat of the cinematograph washing over her face and neck, several more beads of sweat trailed past her misshapen ear.

Outside in the distance, meanwhile, the steam hammer continued to pound away.

Sabine turned to the screen, a close-up of Glynis. "Just look at her. So very thin. Do you realize she'll go without grub for days on end? Then, when she finally breaks her fast, she'll not let herself bolt down anything but a dish of egg whites or maybe one little cheese leek or maybe just one roasted hazelnut with black pepper. It's all so dreadfully tragic. Who should ever think to—"

"Maybe you should forget the soldiers," Manon interrupted.

"Tend to Glynis, why don't you? Listen to her. Don't judge her." With that, Manon turned away.

A third time, Sabine tapped Manon's thigh. "Don't you like me?"

Outside, the steam hammer grew a little bit louder—much faster, too.

Sabine let out an exaggerated sigh. "Won't you give me a chance? *Please.*"

By now, a part of Manon despised the young lady. For one thing, her tone of voice sounded so desperate—as if she must be very lonely. How could a person like Sabine ever take the place of a genuine challenge like Glynis?

Looking impatient, Sabine uncrossed her legs. "Shall I do a moody and say something to flatter you?"

"*No.*" At once, Manon could not control her fury. She glared at Sabine. "Don't you realize you must act *disdainful* if you wish to impress? That's what gives a goose girl a certain *mystique.* Which you've got to have going for you if you wish to make friends and play the game of flats."

On the screen, the scene faded to black. At the same time, the end of the film reel began thrashing about the take-up spool.

The piano fell silent, and Peter Warlock jotted down several more measures before looking over his shoulder. "Let's continue to the next clip, shall we?"

Dutifully, Manon leaped to her feet and changed the reel.

Moments later, an especially powerful scene commenced: the moment the falsely-accused heroine contemplates suicide.

There she stood in her bedchamber, a famished-looking Glynis holding a dagger in her hand.

"She looks like a disgraced noblewoman from back in Shogun times, a woman fixing to plunge the point into her belly," Sabine whispered. "Have you ever heard of all those traditions, ceremonial disembowelment, and the like?" By now, Sabine's neck veins bulged—almost as if she herself felt a stabbing sensation in her own gut, a magnificent samurai sword thrust deep into her belly, the point exiting near the base of her spine.

Manon longed to say something, but the right words eluded her.

On the screen, the celluloid Glynis dropped the dagger to the floor.

Sabine exhaled. "Look there," she whispered. "It's as if some fine Shinto god's tender mercies must've saved her."

Outside, the steam hammer pounded so.

Up on the screen, the sequence concluded.

In time, Peter Warlock asked Manon to rewind the reel—and without a word, she returned the film onto the feed spool.

Late afternoon, Peter Warlock stood up from the concert grand. "I think ye fine young ladies have done more than enough for today," the composer announced. "Why don't ye run along now? Go on."

For the next hour, Manon did and said everything she could to dissuade Sabine and to drive her away.

Nothing worked.

At dusk, Sabine practically dragged Manon to Sloane Square. When they arrived, the young lady sought to convince Manon to sit with her beneath a sweet-chestnut tree.

Thankfully, a lone bluebird swooped down upon them and chased them away.

Sometime later, the desperate young lady grabbed Manon's arm and pulled her along to a peculiar looking house of worship: the Church of the Holy Trinity.

The structure shone pumpkin orange—a color wholly unbecoming of a sanctuary. Even worse, two hideous, carnation-pink towers inappropriately streaked with white stripes reached up on either side of the apse window.

Sabine guided Manon over to the side of the church door,

where a National-Service advertisement depicted a lady farmer working a draft horse. Several times over, Sabine tapped upon the caption. Then she read it out loud: "*God speed the plow and the woman who drives it.*"

As the gloaming dimmed a little bit, Manon sat down upon the church steps and closed her eyes. Almost immediately, she thought about the horrors of war. And the more she thought of the bloodshed, the more she revisited all her nightmares— the notion that someday soon she must perish in a Zeppelin bombardment.

From one block away, the steam hammer resounded yet again.

Shivering some, Manon opened her eyes and listened carefully.

Each thud filled the air like an artillery blast—the kind of clamor that surely erupted from the German fire trenches, day and night.

From out of the east, a biplane with a failing engine sputtered across the sky.

Manon shivered even more, and she imagined that the troubled flying machine must be a vengeful Prussian Air-Corps Fokker D. VIII.

Perhaps the enemy had only just descended from the clouds, and now the pilot intended to strafe the whole of Chelsea.

Sabine must have intuited all, so she sat down at Manon's side. "There's no reason to fear death," Sabine told her. "When it's time for *me* to pass from this world, I know I'll face it the way Christ would. Yes, I'll go out as a passion bearer."

Manon laughed, albeit silently. "It's wrong to emulate gods and saviors," she said then, looking deep into Sabine's eyes. "No one requires salvation. Not even you."

The biplane vanished into the western sky, and Sabine wandered off into the church.

Now's my chance. Manon returned to her feet. Then she raced all the way down the street, and she ducked into a little wax museum.

In the night, she returned to the film studio's offices on Coronation Avenue.

Peter Warlock had never left, and by now an array of tattered sheet music lay strewn about the concert grand. In addition, over by the cinematograph, several reels had dropped their cores such that a terrific tangle of film littered the floor.

Most troubling of all, when she checked the cinematograph, she found that the exciter-lamp fuse had blown and that the power-supply socket had very nearly overloaded. "Have no fear," she told the composer.

Not long afterward, once Manon had returned each length of film onto its core and had mended the hardware, Peter Warlock returned to work.

As a torrid love scene played on the screen, Sabine appeared in the doorway.

A sick feeling in the pit of her stomach, Manon walked over. "Go away. Find something to do with yourself. Get yourself a hobby or—"

"Come to my place for a late supper. I know how to grease my gills, I do. And I've got me a good recipe for kidney pie."

Manon returned to the cinematograph.

On the screen, the love scene played out.

The composer slaved away purposefully.

In time, Sabine walked off—and then she was gone.

Feeling embarrassed, if not guilty, Manon yearned to penance herself. With no better option, she turned to a ceramic ashtray sitting upon a chair over to the side. *So, how about the wearing of ashes?* She dumped the debris into her hand, and then she ran her fingers through her dry, brittle hair before digging her filthy fingertips down into her warm, oily scalp.

CHAPTER SIX

London, 18 April.

Midmorning or thereabouts, Manon walked into Battersea Park and discovered a badly mangled woodcock lying dead in the birdbath. Breathless, she backed away and slumped into the wrought-iron *banquette*.

Her thoughts turned to the film's premiere the evening before and the fact that each one of the morning papers had panned the picture.

One critic had objected to the whole premise. He had interpreted the story as an elaborate metaphor for political Zionism—a movement that he equated with the worst kind of iniquity. At that point in his review, he had enumerated the abounding transgressions and many murderous crimes associated with the mythological Lilith.

For a time now, Manon revisited a legend all about how Lilith crept into nurseries at night in order to strangle to death innocent little girls. Almost burning with curiosity, Manon considered the fold of skin between her thumb and first finger. Was it not that very webbing that provided her, indeed anyone, the power to hold fast another person's windpipe?

A few tattered broadsheet newspapers tumbled by in the April breeze, and then the current died down.

Her thoughts turned back to the critics, all the bad notices. Some of the reviews had disparaged Glynis herself. Despite the tension between them, nevertheless, Manon felt bad for the young lady from Wales. Deep down, Manon had always hoped that the critics might greet the young lady's debut with at least some praise.

Manon closed her eyes. *What might Glynis be feeling just now?* Given the malevolent notices, she would probably be feeling as if her heart had burst into flames.

Steadily, a pair of footsteps resounded now.

Manon opened her eyes. *It's Glynis herself.*

Looking pale and greatly disheveled, she continued forward and then stopped some six feet away—between a lamppost and a fogbound evergreen tree. "Have you heard the news?" the young lady from Wales asked, her breath reeking of raisin wine.

"Yes, the critics, they slagged you off something rotten."

"No, not that. It's Sabine."

"*Sabine?* What about her?"

"She's dead."

"She's *dead?*"

"Yes, her flatmate found her in a pool of blood. Sabine killed herself. With a paper knife that I myself gave her."

At once, Manon felt a sharp cramp at her side—an ache just like the one that she had felt that night in January, running from this very park. "A p-p-paper knife?"

"Yes, one with a finely-whetted blade." Trembling all over, Glynis gestured toward the birdbath. "Only a few months ago, I found the damn thing in there."

No matter the cool April breeze, Manon felt warm. For a time, she gazed at her shoes' badly weathered toe caps. "Did the flatmate happen to mention *why* Sabine did what she did?"

"*No.* I hoped the girl would hold the line and tell me more, but the line went dead. That's when I came here. I thought I'd sit by the birdbath and commune with the caryatid holding up the basin. Strange as it seems, I couldn't think of anything better to do."

At midday, Manon accompanied Glynis to Sabine's flat—a

modest two-bedroom not far from Waterloo Pier. At two o'clock, once the detectives had returned to Scotland Yard, both young ladies continued inside.

What a somber place, Sabine's bedchamber. On the otherwise austere north wall, the lovesick, temperamental young lady had mounted a badly weathered photograph depicting a tableau from her favorite ballet—*Roméo et Juliette* by Hector Berlioz.

On the east wall, Sabine had mounted the banner representing the City of London—and what an appropriate flag for Sabine to have had, too. Even now, there could be no doubting her public-spiritedness and patriotic sentiment.

If her ghost stood here at present, perhaps it would point to the crimson knife floating in the flag's top left canton. "Look there," the specter would say. "That's how all us fine Londoners recall the martyrdom of Paulus. Do you know what Nero went and did? One cold, April day, the tyrant beheaded the saint. With a Roman stealth dagger."

Sabine's flatmate walked into the room. "Do either of you know whether or not them detectives mean to return the paper knife?" she asked. "They ought to give it to some family relation because it's got to be more kicks than halfpence, an antique like that."

For a while, Manon paced about the room. When she paused beside the bookshelf, she noted the curios and things that Sabine had collected there: a papercraft tulip bulb, a silver York shilling, a bust of Van Gogh, a few crumpled banknotes, and a little glass Sibyl standing beside a little glass Trojan prince.

Eventually, Manon staggered through the balcony doors to consider the view.

The balcony looked out over a restaurant called Mercutio's Tomato Grill, an Italian-immigrant establishment.

She breathed in the array of scents lingering in the air: spicy eggplant, cherry peppers, and fresh gnocchi.

The flatmate walked out onto the balcony. "Might you be Manon then? If so, I got something for you."

"What's that?"

"Sabine left you a load of letters."

"Letters?"

"Yeah, that's right." As the flatmate picked her nose, she guided Manon back inside and over to Sabine's writing table.

Sure enough, among a jumble of black, silk roses, the troubled young lady had left behind an array of what must have been love-letters. Oddly enough, though, she had blotted out almost every word. On one letter, nothing remained but a solitary line: *'Hope this dispatch finds you well.'*

To the left, inside a cupboard, Manon found three more letters never sent; Sabine had addressed each one to her, but there could be no discerning any of the scratched-out content other than the complimentary close and signature.

The first one concluded:

'Patiently yours, Sabine.'

The second:

'Impatiently yours, Sabine.'

The third:

'IMMEDIATE REPLY PLEASE.'

Consumed with guilt, Manon continued over to the lone window on the far side of the room and held her breath. Only when she could not go on for a moment longer did she permit herself to exhale—at which point her breath suddenly appeared as a soft, fragile, white mist upon the windowpane. Displeased, she bunched up her sleeve and endeavored to erase all evidence of the exhalation. What a foolish thing to do, though: all her efforts only made a smudge far worse than if she had simply left the mist to melt away on its own.

From the direction of the balcony, a scent as of Italian onion soup crept into the room.

Open-mouthed, she sat down upon Sabine's bed and sought to go lost in various other concerns. What about Glynis, the picture, the bad notices? Why not tell her all the reasons why she ought to ignore the critics? Why not point out how much opinions tend to change through the years? Time and again, many of the unsung find fame posthumously—while those who had once enjoyed storied careers later fade into obscurity. *What a fickle public.*

Sabine's flatmate exited the bedchamber, brought up some cleaning supplies from the scullery, and went about mopping up the pool of blood in the washroom down the hall.

The scent in the air grew unbearable—an admixture of onion soup, bleaching detergent, and stale blood.

"Are you troubled by the notices?" Manon finally asked, turning to Glynis.

"No, not at all."

"Are you quite sure?"

"In all honesty, yes."

"How so? Don't you feel at least a little bit—"

"Whether the critics praise the picture or pan it, I know I cannot go back to living a life of vanity. I've got to be *practical.* If there's no egg in it, I'll not waste my time. Perhaps I'll ring my friends at Christie's. Maybe it'd be good to work for an auction house and appraise the worth of things. Who knows?"

The guilt and anguish having grown far too oppressive, Manon exited the flat and continued out onto Waterloo Pier.

No sooner had she reached the wharf than a pair of soldiers came along, the servicemen accompanied by a shapely blonde. And now the two flirtatious soldiers along with their lady friend proceeded to make a spectacle of themselves. Did they believe that their banter might serve to amuse others?

Eventually, one of the soldiers knelt at the blonde's feet. "Won't you give me just one little kiss?" he asked her. "Pray, just one peck."

On and on, the blonde giggled and trifled.

Manon walked over to the edge of the pier. As the embarrassing performance continued, she thought of how vain people tend to be—everyone acting, everyone playing a part. For a time, she thought of the madmen who fear that someone must be watching them and secretly filming their every movement.

The two soldiers together with their lady friend walked over to the edge of the pier—not two feet from the place where Manon stood.

"Do forgive the soldiers," Sabine would whisper into her misshapen ear if she stood here just now. "Even the rather objectionable ones deserve our love and devotion."

"But these soldiers here, they're louts," Manon would counter. "These soldiers here, they're callow and self-absorbed and—"

"No, they're not," Sabine would insist. "A soldier defends his nation, and what could be more heroic than that?"

Manon would embrace Sabine then. "Stay with me forever," Manon would whisper into the young lady's ear.

"No," Sabine would say.

"Am I not good enough for you anymore?" Manon would ask. "What do you want, jam on it?"

"*Please.*" At that point, Sabine would vanish in a puff of smoke reeking of flamed mahogany—for she would be nothing more than a ghost.

CHAPTER SEVEN

London, 29 May.

Late that morning, Manon boarded the omnibus that the army had hired to take the latest volunteers to Dover Beach. She just had to go. What better way to honor Sabine's memory than to serve as a helpmate to the nurses working the field hospitals in France?

The driver placed his key into the ignition, and as the petrol engine wheezed, she sat down in the very back and placed her things to the side.

Soon enough, the crowded transport reached King's Road. Then, at the edge of the city, the driver put on speed—and suddenly the farmlands rolled by, droves of cattle grazing in the windswept fields.

Off we go. As the wind whipped through the length of the vehicle, Manon removed the nurse's headpiece from her scalp. Then she looked to her lap and smoothed out her blue porter's gown.

A Model-T field ambulance sped by in the opposite direction, as if rushing some poor soul to one of the nearby military hospitals.

She could not help but think of all the invalided soldiers who would already be there, everyone writhing about amid the all-encompassing odor of mothballs and medicaments. Guilt-stricken, she smiled at the homely girl sitting on the other side of the aisle. "I'm Manon. What's your name?"

"I'm Tuesday Lennox."

"Tuesday? So, that means you're 'fair of face?'"

"No. The way Mum taught me way back when, 'Tuesday's child ought to be full of *grace*.'"

The omnibus rolled past a field of dahlias.

Manon watched awhile and then turned back. "Doesn't it feel like you've got the weight of the world on your shoulders?" she asked.

"No," Tuesday answered. "It's a bobby's job, what we'll be doing down there. All them stewards should know we don't walk the hospitals back home here. So, what should they ask of us? When someone comes in all bloodied by a crab grenade, it's the gas *wallahs* what put him to sleep. And it'd be the nurse what administrates the ether, and the sawbones himself what darns the bloke back together again. A nurse's helpmate only ever tends to the wee little things. Like scrubbing the bedpans. Or else we mother some poor lad kneading his lung while chanting the devil's paternoster. Yeah, and if a case of gangrene kicks off, we'd be the ones what collect the corpse ticket."

Manon fussed with her mess tin and then looked up again. "Why so sardonic?"

Plainly bemused by the question, Tuesday frowned and said something in what sounded like Scottish Gaelic. Then she remained silent.

In due course, the omnibus passed by the fingerpost pointing the way to Canterbury.

Not five minutes later, once the omnibus had passed by the cathedral city, Manon felt homesick. Then, when another fingerpost announced the distance left for Dover as only five miles, she shivered. *Bloody hell, we're almost there.*

After a while, the omnibus rolled onto Ivy Avenue and passed by a never-too-late-to-mend shop. Then, amid a procession of cadets dressed up in fine regimentals, the transport stopped with a shrill hiss that sounded like the dying gasp of a rusty power loom.

Late that night, Manon arose from her hostelry bed. *Tomorrow, I'll be sailing off into the field of battle. How to sleep?* At first, she contented herself to pace. Quietly then, she slipped into her velveteen walking gown.

When she continued outside, she found Tuesday standing by the door.

The homely young lady still wore her porter's uniform, and she had even donned a blood-pressure gauge. "Where *you* going?" Tuesday asked, suspiciously.

"I thought I'd climb the path to Dover Castle," Manon answered.

"Don't do it. Come tomorrow morn, you'll be knackered. Get on back into the dosshouse, why don't you? Besides, if Captain MacShane notices you walking away, he might think you'd be deserting us, and what if he shoots you in the back?"

For a time, Manon looked out upon the Village of Dover and marveled at how lovely the historic *Maison Dieu* appeared that night: a bronze lantern dangling from a nail in the lintel had left the regal, red-brick manor house all aglow.

At last, Manon continued up the pathway.

Tuesday followed along, and she proved to be fleet of foot, too.

When they reached a patch of willow herbs, Manon paused to rest.

Off in the distance, the castle loomed. How noble, too, the way the Roman lighthouse looked out across the waters.

"Why'd you choose to serve?" Manon asked then.

"I'm doing it for the glory, I am," Tuesday answered, her tone almost inhuman. "As soon as the Kaiser rags out, I'll come home to Ipswich with pogues and ribbons as grand as ninepence right here on my lapel. Perhaps even the Victoria Cross as well. And back at the rescue mission, they'll never rib *me* no more."

No sooner had Tuesday spoken than a Maxim gun's distinctive sounding volley of fire rumbled from somewhere out across the chalk cliffs.

Manon walked over to the cliff's edge, and she looked out across the Port of Dover to the battle cruisers patrolling the channel. "I think the Royal Navy must've spotted some ghost ships from the Spanish Armada, every galleon a-cock."

Tuesday failed to laugh. Even worse, the homely young lady made no attempt to add to the repartee.

A moment later, as Manon turned to the distant lights of Guernsey, a maniacal cormorant with big, webbed feet swooped down onto her scalp and let out a croak resembling the call of a sexually excited bull frog.

Oddly serene, Tuesday removed what looked like a repeating air pistol from her coat pocket and opened fire. "That's one for the bitumen," she announced. With that, Tuesday fired off several more rounds.

The bullets whizzing past her misshapen ear, Manon went into a mild state of shock.

In due time, the winged creature fluttered off—gracelessly, too, as if it had sustained a grave wound.

For her part, Tuesday scratched at her chin and stared at Manon—the same way some sullen voyeur might ogle a lovely girl down on the beach.

Her shock having turned to indignation, Manon marched back from the cliff and grabbed the pistol's barrel. Then she marched back *to* the cliff, and she hurled the weapon over the edge.

With raw, seething hate in her eyes, Tuesday glared at Manon. "That was a damn cheek thing to do," Tuesday said. "I ought to prefer charges." Without another word, the homely girl rushed forward.

A violent altercation ensued, Tuesday clearly endeavoring to throw Manon over the precipice.

Thankfully, the sharp blast of a brass army whistle rang out: Captain MacShane, the tall, mustachioed embarkation medical officer, had arrived upon the scene.

As he held Tuesday back, a clamor awoke somewhere amid the clouds.

Had a scout from the Royal Flying Corps detected the presence of a Zeppelin? All her dreams of doom having returned, Manon fell and rolled off the cliff—and as she dangled there, she thought of all the things that she had yet to accomplish in life.

In time, she revisited a memory of Chelsea Kinematograph Theatre. Late one evening, she had attended a French comedy entitled "*Les Résultats du Féminisme.*" More than anything, she had delighted in the scene in which the young ladies dress up as gentlemen and then force the hapless gentlemen to dress up like ladies.

Might that have been the first time that she had ever acknowledged her inborn, Sapphic predilections? *Yes, I think it was.* And now her hands began to slip. *I can't hold on.* Suddenly, the whole of her life flashed before her eyes.

Just before she fell, Captain MacShane raced over. "There we are," he announced, as he pulled her up.

As she lay upon the earth, she gasped for breath. At the nape of her neck, meanwhile, she felt what proved to be the cocking lever to a flying machine's rotary cannon.

When she finally sat up, she took the debris into her hand and held it tight.

Captain MacShane looked her in the eye then. "Why did you come up this way?" he asked, his tone loving and fatherly. "The jam buns have you feeling all affrighted? Could it be you've got some misgivings? Hell and tommy, you've got no cause for great alarm. It won't be long before our lads bash on through the Hindenburg line. Aye, and then we'll have ourselves a proper armistice. I know it."

She looked out across the channel, and she sought to envision the moment, tomorrow morning, when she and the others would be sailing off to war. Most likely, the Royal Navy would employ a battleship with powerful armaments and turrets to ferry everyone across.

Captain MacShane turned to Tuesday. "Get on back to your billet and kip down."

The homely young lady pointed a finger gun at Manon, fired several times over, and then walked away.

Captain MacShane turned back to Manon then. "You've got nothing to fear. Out beyond the horizon, the hounds of war await you, and yes, that's a terrible proposition. Still, your kind of service must be the best labor a woman could ever hope to perform."

"How do you mean, sir?"

"It comes down to *love*, I don't mind telling you."

"What's all this, sir?"

"I mean that if you truly care for others, nature finds a way to reward you. And love comes your way."

"It does?"

"Yes, and in good time."

"Stuff and nonsense."

"*No.* Love comes your way because it knows you *deserve* affection. Yes, love comes your way because it knows you've *earned* it."

For a moment, Manon thought of Sabine. How good it would feel to sit with her one last time.

Captain MacShane helped Manon to her feet. "Let's go on back to the hostelry," he told her then. "We'll share a glass of warm milk and—"

"You're sure you're not cross with me?"

"Quite sure," he answered. Then he took the cocking lever from her hand, and he hurled it over the cliff.

"All that talk about earning love, that was no fib?" she asked him then.

"Certainly not," he told her. And now Captain MacShane walked back to the rocky footpath. Like a faithful sentry, he stood there patiently.

For her part, she turned back to the waters. Her heartbeat slowing, she promised herself that someday she would meet the love of her life out there on the Continent—perhaps once the war had ended. *Yes, and then* . . .

A peculiar quietude descended across the coastline.

Filled with awe, she looked to the stars—and now she felt the deepest elation, as if she and the majestic sky must enjoy perfect communion.

II.

CHAPTER ONE

Prague, 29 September 1919.

Late that morning, Manon exited the Grand Hotel Europa and proceeded three blocks east to Wenceslas Square. Lonely, she sat down upon the edge of the quartz-sandstone fountain and watched the hopeful, industrious people passing by.

How full of promise the Czech Republic, for the Great War had ended—and in the aftermath, the people of Prague had rededicated themselves to the glory of art.

Ever since Manon had arrived in the resurgent city, she had hoped to secure a post with the National Playhouse and to participate in the impending production of a science-fiction drama entitled *Rossumovi Univerzální Roboti*—an experimental kind of morality play about a hubristic madman who presides over the invention of robots. Only yesterday, though, the producers had politely rejected her application.

So, what do I do now? She listened to the traffic. *Where do I go?*

A three-wheeled Cyklonette approached from the east. Seven times, the young-lady driver circled the square. Then she parked beside the fountain.

After a long while, she walked over. What a sensuous woman: she had deep-green eyes, and her brown kiss curls reached down to her temples. How delicate, too: there could be little doubt that she suffered from a case of jaundice, for her skin shone a touch too yellow.

In a thick, Yiddish accent, she introduced herself as Ms. Inbal

Zilberstein. Then she invited herself to sit down. "What are you doing here?" the young lady asked.

Eager to make a friend, Manon shared an abridged version of her story.

When Manon grew quiet, Inbal looked to the sky. "You know something? Soon, I am auditioning for a big, Yiddish-language stage show. *Der Golem von Prag*, that's the name. Also, it's maybe a little bit famous in Berlin. The authoress, the one and only Scheindel Deutschkron, she lives there."

Manon knew nothing about the work. Still, as Inbal explained the plot, Manon did find the premise rather intriguing: the story followed from the tale of a sorcerer who builds a clay automaton or *golem*—a creature strong enough to protect the Jews from whatever kind of harassment.

At last, Inbal invited Manon to visit her later that day—and the young lady provided detailed directions to the Yiddish Repertory Theatre.

At three o'clock, Manon passed through the ghetto gates. When she located the address, she entered the dimly lit building and made her way into the stalls. Beside the orchestra pit, she closed her eyes. *What a thrill to be inside a playhouse.* She breathed in the odors lingering in the air: greasepaint, spirit gum, and finishing powder. When she opened her eyes, she turned to study some of the flats heaped up to the side. No matter how amateurish everything looked, she could not deny the charm. *What fun it'd be to participate in a community theater like this.*

Inbal walked up alongside her. "Soon, the lighting designer should be coming," Inbal announced. "Maybe he should be checking for the best way to light the backcloth."

For a moment, Manon wondered if she ought to make some small talk. Before she could think of anything to say, though, a figure appeared high above in the balcony.

In time, the house lights came to wield a most beguiling effect:

the way the soft, solitary ray shone down upon Inbal's face, the glow managed to take the shape of a heart just below her left eye.

Rembrandt lighting. No matter how foolish she must have looked, Manon could not turn away. Until that moment, she had not grasped the true measure of Inbal's beauty.

I think I'm in love.

By the time Manon departed the playhouse, the infatuation had only intensified.

Thankfully, several days later, Inbal rang her room at the Grand Hotel Europa and graciously invited her to come for supper. With that, Inbal explained the directions to her attic apartment.

Early afternoon, Manon walked down to the riverbank. Having resolved to bring Inbal a gift, Manon fashioned a crude, little clay depiction of the legendary *golem*.

As catchpenny as the piece looked, she felt certain that the offering would amuse the young lady.

In the evening, Manon returned to the ghetto. *Here we go.*

The clay representation snug in her coat pocket, she knocked upon Inbal's door.

The sitting room proved to be opulent, all the tables and bookshelves filled with precious, *fin de siècle*, Viennese-bronze statuettes. For that matter, Inbal owned a set of bentwood chairs along with a console table boasting lyre-shaped legs—the luxuriant kinds of furnishings that a proper German salon hostess might count among her possessions.

Most extraordinary of all, Inbal had gathered several antiquities inside a glass reliquary standing near the gramophone. The relics included a cruse of oil, a stone lot ornately inscribed with Hebrew characters, and an immaculate *dreidel* carved from what looked to be petrified wood.

The shame felt unbearable. Her misshapen ear twitching, Manon removed her coat but resolved to keep the pitiful, homespun gift where it was.

For her part, Inbal grew very quiet. Had she intuited Manon's discomfort? The nighttime breeze sailing through the dormer window, Inbal walked over to the sill. Oddly, she climbed out onto the roof. "Also, you should come following," the young lady announced then, without even looking back.

Manon glanced at the hem of her evening gown. She had not dressed herself for climbing about on rooftops. Nevertheless, when Inbal failed to return inside, Manon continued over to the sash.

What a warm, perfect, starry night. Tantalizingly, too, the aroma of something like schmaltz herring wafted this way and that on the current.

Against her better judgment, she climbed through the frame. Then, shaking badly, she crouched low to keep from falling.

Inbal laughed in a harsh tone. "Rise up," Inbal implored her. "Have no fear."

At last, Manon forced herself onto her feet—and now she looked all about. What a splendid view across the ghetto roof-tops' jumbled chimney cowls and gable posts. Still, no matter how enthralling the surroundings, the current made her feel perilously light—as if at any moment a gust of wind might send her gliding off across the skyline.

Meanwhile, Inbal made her way down the steep, shingled rooftop. Then, as soon as she reached the rain gutter, she stood perfectly straight—not unlike a distraught woman preparing to hurl herself against the street far below.

Manon could not control her emotions. More than anything, she felt guilty for lusting after someone so *complicated*.

From across the rooftops, the strains of *nachtmusik* com-menced—someone strumming what sounded like a discordant baroque guitar.

Manon gazed upon Inbal's ankles. "Do you wish to get your-self killed? Please, come back from there."

The peculiar young lady did no such thing. She only craned her neck.

The guitar ceased then, as if the musician had finally resolved to tune the peculiar instrument.

A moment later, as the music played anew, Inbal looked out to the furthest reaches of the horizon. Then, as if the vanishing point held her spellbound, she began to sway backward and forward— oh so dangerously, too.

Her misshapen ear twitching and burning, Manon could not bear to look. She turned toward the distant church steeples and chapel domes of the New Town. "Please come stand beside me here," she pleaded. "Hold my hand and . . ."

From the synagogue standing at the end of the darkened street, the music of cantillation commenced.

"Do you hear the rabbis davening?" Inbal asked.

"Listen, I really think we ought to go inside and—"

"Again, the Days of Awe have come upon us."

"Please come back before you slip and—"

"Already, we have welcomed the lunar New Year. Next, everyone must observe the big, solemn Day of Atonement."

At last, Manon willed herself to glance back toward Inbal. Much to Manon's consternation, she found the young lady swaying back and forth yet. "Stop that, I say."

Inbal did not respond. Already, the young lady seemed to have slipped into a trancelike state.

Manon pulled at her misshapen ear. "*Please.* No more."

Plainly oblivious, Inbal began to hum a witchlike incantation.

Manon groaned. "Please come back to me before you fall and . . ."

The baroque guitar ceased to play, and for a time, no sound remained but the rabbis' ritualistic chanting.

Unable to watch Inbal teetering as dangerously as she was, an exasperated Manon looked to the stars and thought back to an

Aramaic-language tale that a Jewish girl had taught her back in their school days.

According to the story, the godless, mischievous daughter of Pharaoh had asked all of her courtiers to place a tarp woven with rhinestones over the oasis where she and King Solomon had come to sleep. In the morning, when the king had awoken, he had presumed the cloth sheet to be the night sky and the rhinestones to be stars. Only much later, when the wise king had registered the mysterious heat of the dawn sunlight beating down upon the tarp's exterior, had he managed to puzzle out the ruse.

The cantillation ceased now.

Should I look? Manon turned back to Inbal.

Nothing had changed: the young lady continued to sway backward and forward.

Manon clenched her fists. How to avoid her fury? She felt certain that Inbal only hoped to taunt her. By now, Manon regretted her decision to come here. Back home, plenty of people had told her how insolent the Jews could be—and the ongoing misbehavior displayed by Inbal seemed to confirm all.

From somewhere across the rooftops, an annoying clamor commenced: the sound of someone operating a treadle sewing machine.

The irksome sound left Manon feeling even more vexed. *How to tolerate such a badly-behaved people?* Once more, she revisited her school days—all those verbose lectures regarding the story of civilization. Soon, she recalled an especially absurd address delivered by a bigoted history instructor:

"When the Egyptians enslaved the Hyksos, perhaps the Egyptians did so only because they found the Semitic migrants much too *rude*," the scholar had posited one day. "To be sure, the Assyrians and the Babylonians and the Greeks and the peoples of Rome and Byzantium must have felt the same way. Moreover, how could anyone have expected them to countenance such a stubborn, self-absorbed, woefully insolent nation maintaining hegemony over all those gainful harbors lying between the Nile delta and Byblos?"

From one of the rooftops only three buildings over, yet another sewing machine stirred to life. And now a *third* one started up.

The noise pollution having grown odious, Manon climbed back down through the dormer window and exited the attic apartment. *I'm going home.*

At eleven o'clock or thereabouts, when she reached the Grand Hotel Europa, she paused before the lobby doors. *Have I forgotten something?*

Haltingly, she walked back to the curbstone and then turned toward the river.

How alluring the Vltava looked in that moment, for a shaft of moonlight presently illumined the powerful waters.

Yes, I remember. Slowly, she removed the little clay *golem* from her coat pocket—and then she crushed the crude likeness and dropped it into the storm drain.

CHAPTER TWO

Prague, 18 October.

From the moment Manon awoke that morning, she felt that she just had to return to the ghetto. The reason was simple: the Yiddish-language theater troupe would be conducting the auditions for the upcoming drama—and having grown fascinated with the whole idea of *der golem*, she longed to know just how the modest company intended to cast the crucial part.

At eight o'clock, she reached the playhouse. Uncertain as to whether Inbal would even welcome her back, Manon walked through the door with her head held low. As such, she did not even notice the fantastical creature—at least not at first. Once she had made it halfway down the aisle, though, her intuition told her to look up.

There it loomed in the heart of the stage: dressed in a long, flowing, purple burnoose, the muscle-bound creature stood ten feet tall and looked to be fashioned from invulnerable, slate-gray stone.

She felt confounded. Impressed by the engineering of it all, she almost even wondered if the crude, colossal automaton might in fact be *real*. The notion did not seem so outside the realm of possibility. As a girl, she had once owned several sophisticated mechanical dolls—including a most adorable tin hoopoe boasting a key-wound clockwork mechanism that enabled the winged creature to strut all about. Later, a favorite uncle had given her an extraordinary nutcracker with a winding knob protruding from its back—and whenever the dashing figure would march across the floor, she would delight in the shrill clamor made by the tension springs and driving wheels resounding inside the toy.

Der golem looked upon her now, and its eyes shone a silvery-white palladium.

Almost mesmerized by the beauty of it all, Manon stepped forward but then took two steps back. She could not decide just what to do or just what to think. If the uncanny being were *not* the actual product of sorcery, how could a modest theater company ever have managed such a fantastical display? What kind of special-effects technician could have contrived such wholly revolutionary machinery? Had he studied the science of electro-metallurgy?

The inscrutable being exhaled, its breath a mist of odorless, alluring flamingo pink streaked with electric lime.

As the creature's breath diffused into the air, Inbal peeked from behind the grand drape.

For a moment or two, she addressed the director—a short, bearded gentleman dressed in wrinkled gray trousers and open-necked, pleated shirtsleeves.

Afterward, Inbal climbed down from the stage and walked over to Manon.

Feeling sheepish after all that time, Manon bowed some. "So, where did you find that monstrous creature?" she asked. "I'd love to examine it and—"

"Get onto the stage," Inbal told her. "Also, *you* should be auditioning while our little *golem* rehearses his part." With that, Inbal pulled upon Manon's arm.

Not a moment later, just as Manon passed by the prompt box, the prop master placed a tattered Hebrew prayer book into her left hand. Then an old woman looking to be the costume mistress placed a copy of the script into her right.

Before she knew it, Manon stood upon the apron of the stage—not two feet from the creature.

A second time, the strange entity's unearthly eyes shone like palladium.

A half dozen times over, she gasped for breath.

From offstage right, Inbal quickly explained some of the stage direction and then raised her hands. "Remember. This simple afterpiece, it's maybe the most poignant display in Yiddish theater. Now your character, the rabbi's good, faithful, loving daughter, she should be weeping as she removes the kabbalistic charm from between the monster's eyes, for you know you'll be watching our friendly *golem* go to sleep. Never to wake up no more."

No sooner had Inbal lowered her hands than the director called out a few commands, at which point the creature lay down along the apron.

Manon shook her head. *What am I doing?*

The auditorium grew darker and darker—until no illumination remained but a solitary spotlight.

Little by little, it felt to Manon as if the whole company must be watching—from the stalls, from the glazed-*rococo* balconies, from the orchestra pit, too.

When the time came, she knelt before the monster. Then, upon opening the tattered prayer book to the dog-eared page, she read a simple benediction.

By the time she had grown quiet, each one of the creature's eyes shone the color of a glistening black moonstone. Far from filling her with dread, they put her to shame. For a time, she almost felt like a distraught farm girl aiming to shoot her beloved, ailing horse. *No, I can't kill my pony.* Now she held her breath. How long before her rather enigmatic inaction served to elicit a round of nervous laughter?

In due time, Inbal walked over. Without any semblance of guilt, the young lady removed the topaz charm from the groove etched into the space between the creature's eyes. "That's how you do it," Inbal explained.

The houselights came up then, and a few of the stagehands applauded.

In tears, Manon grabbed the charm from Inbal and inserted the gemstone back into the groove.

Almost immediately, the creature's eyes flashed—as brightly as the metallic-gold scrolls adorning the proscenium arch.

Yes, you're alive. Manon stood up and staggered back. Then, as the creature returned to its feet, she tapped upon its chest. "Might there be someone inside there?" she asked. "Do show yourself. Remove the mask, the headpiece you're wearing. Prove to me that you're human. Tell me how you operate this mechanical disguise."

Inbal laughed, as if in disbelief. Then she shook her finger in Manon's face. "Even if there was a little actor hiding inside, you shouldn't be speaking with him."

"Why?"

"Why? Because any actor who'd play such a mysterious part as *der golem* would be the kind of actor who dedicated himself to stagecraft, the kind of actor who must *become* the part he would be playing. And perhaps the actor should wish to stay in character, yes, until the very last performance, or maybe—"

"*Would* there be an actor inside? How about a child actor? No, maybe the actor would be an adult of short stature. Yes, a little person or—"

"I'll tell you something," Inbal whispered. "If there was an actor inside the body of the monster, surely this actor should be so dedicated to his part that the whole time he does this show, also he sleeps inside the synagogue attic. Just like the legendary *golem*."

Awkwardly, the creature descended the stage. As the monstrous entity returned through the stalls, Manon followed along. Outside, *der golem* guided her down the street—the creature's footsteps loud and ponderous.

When they reached the synagogue, she paused to consider the house of worship.

What a humble-looking building: it had an everyday Gothic frame, a gable roof lined with carrot-orange shingles, and a dark gable wall rising out of the pit in which the Czech monarchy had instructed the Jews to establish the modest structure's foundations.

When the creature advanced toward the door, she hurried over to block its way. "Won't you tell me if you'd be real or not?" she asked. "I deserve to know. Did some chap cobble you together with parts from another automaton? What about a state-of-the-art *Mensch-Maschine*, that robotic chess-player contraption? Would *that* be it? Have you got gum bands and escape wheels deep down inside you?"

Even if it commanded the power of speech, nevertheless, the entity did not trouble itself to answer. With its left arm, the creature merely brushed her aside and then continued into the synagogue's antechamber.

Determined to resolve the vexing mystery, she followed the colossal figure through the doorway.

Once *der golem* had passed through the prayer hall, the creature paused before the high place at the center of the room.

When she came up from behind and tapped upon its back, the magnificent brute let out a heartrending wail that rattled a few of the candelabra dangling from the ceiling.

As the echoes died down, a powerful beam of light burst through one of the stained-glass clerestory windows such that the synagogue's east wall suddenly shone a bright lion orange.

A second time, she tapped upon the creature's back. "Are you man or machine? And if there's person in there, please reveal your face. Tell me about yourself. Hey, you're not serious about sleeping up in the attic, are you? Do you really think that'd be necessary?"

The mighty creature continued over into the stairwell and commenced to climb, each wooden step creaking below the immense weight.

Weak at the knees, she followed along.

Up in the attic, *der golem* lay down atop a heap of old books and scrolls such that the attic floor sagged and moaned. What if the weight proved to be too much? At any moment, the floorboards would crack—and books and scrolls together with wooden beams and large sheets of gypsum would rain all over the people below.

The uncanny *golem* did not seem to fear any such eventuality. Gracelessly, *der golem* turned upon its side—and given the way the creature suddenly lay still, there could be no doubt that it had fallen asleep.

A dozen times over, she clapped her hands. When the creature failed to respond, she sat down upon the doorsill and imagined an actor inside the extraordinary getup. What would he be dreaming about just now? She thought back to scripture. Most likely, he would be dreaming the same thing that Belshazzar had once envisioned—a dream of a metallic automaton fashioned from silver and gold, the idol's feet fashioned from clay.

She laughed in wonder, for how fascinating that ancient, esoteric narratives might contain within them the phenomenology of robots. *Technologies futuristic.*

In time, she continued back down the stair—albeit reluctantly.

When she returned outside, she paused to stretch her arms and legs.

Across the street, at *das Jüdische Rathaus*, the grand clock tolled the hour. What a marvel the way the Jews had adorned the clock's face with ancient Hebrew characters instead of roman numerals. As such, both the hour and minute hands proceeded along *counter*clockwise—in the same way the Jews read the Holy Writ, from right to left.

The clock concluded its count, and as the ghetto returned to quietude, Manon made her way back to the hotel.

Late that night, she could not sleep. *I must know whether* der golem *would be real*. With no better option, she returned to the playhouse and entered through the stage door. Alas, when she called out, no one answered.

A draft glided through a large crack in one of the auditorium windows. Playfully, the current sailed through a few old playbills littering the paint shop.

With feelings of unease, she continued out onto the stage.

What a melancholy scene: the ghost light illumined the empty hall in a shade of soft tangerine—a sad, nostalgic, mystical, dreamlike color.

She thought back upon the audition. *Shall I take the part?* She wondered if she had enough stage presence to succeed, and now she tapped the tip of her tongue against the roof of her mouth. *If I do take the part, shall I take an exotic stage name?*

From back in the direction of the scenery dock, the cool, autumn current grew stronger and whistled tunefully.

At the same time, she felt a presence of some kind—a pair of eyes regarding her.

The presence proved to be a rat, the vermin standing downstage. And now the rodent's eyes served to reflect the light presently pouring in through the windows.

What a light, too—the lush, resplendent glow of the midnight blue.

CHAPTER THREE

Prague, 13 November.

On the night of the big dress rehearsal, Inbal rang Manon's room at the hotel and told her not to come.

"*Why?*"

"We've got trouble," Inbal answered. "You should find something else to do. Why don't you visit the Rudolfinum? Karel Čapek himself, he'll be delivering a lecture."

When the line went dead, Manon made her way to the ghetto—where she found a large crowd gathered about the playhouse.

The source of the commotion proved to be a bespectacled, redheaded Czech youth dressed in a gray town coat and Palatine-purple top hat. He had arranged a magic lantern atop a stepladder in order to project a series of images onto a section of the playhouse wall—and now he stood atop a soapbox, the agitator delivering a passionate address.

Looking tense, Inbal drew close to Manon. "Go back to the hotel, and please don't come around again."

"What's this all about? Who would that speaker be?"

"Stefan Zwinglius. That's his name. He studies at *Univerzita Karlova*, but he and his friends often come around to make a big noise."

Manon studied the youth's face—his unnerving smirk along with the sadistic shine in his otherwise dull, brown eyes. Discomfited, she turned to the wall upon which the magic lantern presently projected a map depicting the Seven Hills of Rome. "What's he talking about?"

"He says the Jews have no claim to any homeland in Palestine because we proselytized too many Gentile ladies back in the days of the Roman Empire. And because of this, we deserve neither Europa *nor* the Promised Land. He says we don't belong anywhere."

One of the stagehands, a fellow by the name of Lazzaro Steinzig, lunged through the crowd and approached the magic lantern. What a peculiar outfit, too; despite the cold weather, he had dressed himself in a Greco-Roman wrestler's snug-fitting attire.

Looking not a little bit timid, Lazzaro toppled the stepladder— and the magic lantern shattered against the cobblestones.

At once, Stefan Zwinglius hopped down from the soapbox. As if on the verge of tears, the agitator yelped in a combination of Czech and German. Then he turned to the stagehand.

Like a petulant little boy, Lazzaro shoved him so that the youth's Palatine-purple top hat fell beside the magic lantern.

Greatly frenzied, the agitator placed the palm of his hand over Lazzaro's face and pushed it back—as if there could be no better gesture by which to wholly dishonor him.

By now, Manon longed to depart. "Let's go," she whispered into Inbal's ear.

Inbal grabbed hold of Manon's arm. "Always it's the quiet ones like this Lazzaro. What a fool. Now he comes along and makes the trouble even worse. And for no good reason."

Feeling ill, Manon broke free from Inbal's grasp and stepped back some. For a moment, she studied the onlookers themselves.

What an obscene, primitive spectacle: both Gentile and Jew had formed a ring around the combatants, and as the ugly altercation continued, each silent voyeur, even the women, appeared to be as enthralled with the violence as some lout delighting in a coin-operated peep show.

Manon felt ashamed of her own willingness to watch the miserable incident unfold.

And now a big, dumb, flaxen-haired oaf with dull-blue eyes bunched too close together walked up to Lazzaro and berated him with a litany of insults. More than anything, the big bully scoffed at the notion that a diminutive nothing such as the stagehand could even think to defy a sporting fellow of proper station such as the noble, law-abiding Stefan Zwinglius.

As the big, irate oaf continued with the cross-talk, Lazzaro kept silent. His eyes bulging, he only clenched his fists—as if he intended to tear asunder the palms of his hands with his very own fingernails.

Meanwhile, Stefan Zwinglius turned to survey the damage to his magic lantern. When he turned back, he pursed his lips and rushed Lazzaro.

Like a coward, Lazzaro turned the other cheek. Did the stagehand not even know how to fight? Why not move to the side at the last moment, or why not raise his arm to block the punch?

The agitator smote the miserable Lazzaro so hard against his left temple that his knees buckled—and now he fell to the cobblestones, where he writhed about like a flatworm.

When the thin, inept stagehand returned to his feet, he did nothing but stand there.

By now, Stefan Zwinglius must have grasped his adversary's utter incompetence—and the realization plainly filled the agitator with pride. Now he hopped up and down, something like a bowlegged prizefighter.

Finally, a black police van pulled up to the playhouse and stopped not far from Inbal's three-wheeled Cyklonette.

As the agitator mourned the remains of his magic lantern, the flaxen-haired oaf regaled the officers with the whole tale. From what Manon could discern, the indignant bully even told the officers that Lazzaro must be a Bolshevik spy.

As for the Jews in the crowd, not a one spoke up in Lazzaro's defense.

In time, a mustachioed officer with eyes devoid of expression approached Lazzaro to ask after his side of the story.

The stagehand showed himself to be utterly inadequate. Plainly-addled, Lazzaro said nothing at first. Then he mumbled something about the time Stefan Zwinglius once implied a certain unwillingness to acknowledge the history of Cossack pogroms. At that point, Lazzaro murmured something about how university professors and their students tend to diminish the gravity of the Jews' suffering or else blame the victims themselves.

Plainly unimpressed, the authorities placed Lazzaro inside an oblong cage mounted atop the police van's flatbed. Then one of the officers slammed the cage door shut with a dissonant, metallic jangle.

Manon could not bear to stay. She proceeded into the playhouse, where she came upon several stagehands sharing a supper of pickled herring, *kreplach*, and cabbage leaves.

One of them, an elderly gentleman with matted hair and a bumpy nose, attempted to hand her a dish.

Manon politely refused the offering, and then she attempted to tell them all what had happened outside.

Oddly enough, everyone acted obtuse—indifferent even.

At last, one of the younger, religious stagehands tapped her wrist. "*Listen*. Lazzaro, he's not even Jewish. *No.* His mother, she's a Gentile. Yes, she even wears a Maltese cross."

Mortified by the heartlessness of it all, Manon continued into her dressing room and sat down in the window frame. By now, she had begun to detect something of herself in the hapless stagehand: just as *he* had been born into an unpopular, interfaith family, *she* had been born of a most unconventional marriage.

Her own father had always seemed so androgynous. And what about Mother's eccentricities? She had always been forceful and manly, and she had always felt inclined to dominate her husband. There could be no denying any of this, for Manon had spied on her parents from time to time—and on more than one occasion, she had observed their peculiar, fetishistic, role-playing games.

The stage manager stopped at Manon's dressing-room door now. "Are you ready?"

She laughed nervously. "What're you talking about? How could we consider going through with a dress rehearsal on a night like this?"

The stage manager scratched at his scalp. "You have no cause to worry about all the trouble," he promised her.

Fifteen minutes later, when the dress rehearsal commenced, she could not stop thinking about poor Lazzaro. *What's to become of him?*

The performance dragged on, and as the spotlight's scorching-hot glare washed over her body, she repeatedly forgot her lines.

Inbal did no better. As it so happened, the glare of the lights demonstrated that her jaundice had grown much more severe. Several times over, she pounded the right side of her chest—as if she felt something burning deep inside her liver.

Der golem had trouble, too: three times, the creature's eyes flashed a disturbing purple-quartzite color.

In the end, the creature's eyes went dead.

Late that evening, Manon exited the playhouse and returned to the place where all the political intrigue had transpired.

Here and there, little pieces of the magic lantern glistened intermittently.

The flashes of color made her think of the graven images that certain sinful Jews of antiquity had once worshipped—metallic-skinned household gods fashioned from nickel and mercury, fine copper and bronze, or perhaps even platinum streaked with dazzling, rare-earth elements. Whenever some calamity would befall the nation, the prophets would never fail to interpret the catastrophe as punishment for the idolatry. No prophet could have ever argued anything other than the theory of divine retribution, for if the people did in fact maintain an everlasting covenant with God Almighty, then only their own sins and failures could ever explain just why that all-powerful deity would permit them to suffer so much hardship.

The fantastical *golem* exited the playhouse and stopped at Manon's side.

Eventually, the enigmatic creature seemed to study the shape of her nose.

She turned to the section of the wall where the magic lantern had earlier displayed the map of Rome. "Just imagine the thrill the Roman centurions must've felt in that moment they razed the temple. Didn't they patiently wait till that very same day in the lunar calendar when the Jews mourn the time Babylon toppled the original building?"

The wind kicked up, and several newspapers tumbled by.

She thought of home. What did she even know regarding the latest scandals, the news of the day, all the melodrama down at London's Crown Court?

Swiftly, the newspapers tumbled off in the current.

She turned back to *der golem*. "Do you know something? Over the course of the past month or so, I've read all about the Jews. Have you any idea what the politics of replacement theology have wrought? From all the cities of the Sahara, all of Christendom, too, both Catholic and Islamic ghettoization law have kept the Jews in a constant state of absolute subjugation. Yes, and don't forget all the expulsions, for why pay debts when it'd be just as simple a proposition to exile any and all moneylenders?" Manon drew closer to the wall, and she placed her hand upon the place where the magic lantern had projected the map of Rome.

As she went lost in thought, she attempted to analyze her liberalism: while so many others had achieved catharsis by casting aspersions upon either the Jewish faith or the Jews themselves, why had she never done so?

In all likelihood, her tolerant nature followed from her own experience. She had always fathomed the way homophobes compensate for their own queer proclivities by persecuting those like *her*—and she had always recognized how closely that process resembled the practice by which certain intolerant Gentiles might project their sins and shortcomings onto the Jews.

Whether a homophobe or a self-appointed critic of all things Judaic, each scoundrel did what he did only because it afforded that illiberal a fulcrum for stress relief.

The ghetto lights dimmed now, and as *der golem* made its way back toward the darkened synagogue, an autumn rain commenced.

A puddle formed at her feet, and now the pool of water assumed the shape of a prickly pear—the miserable kind that only ever grows in lonely, sun-scorched, inhospitable deserts.

The next day, she fashioned a sackcloth ball. Then she made a fist, and for an hour or more, held the ball tight—and as she did, she imagined the handmade instrument of torture a prickly pear from deep in the heart of the Negev. *Penance.*

CHAPTER FOUR

Prague, 18 January.

On the night of the premiere, not ten minutes before the curtain-raiser, Manon learned from the ticket-services manager that the jailed stagehand, Lazzaro Steinzig, had threatened to go on a hunger strike.

Later, when Manon stopped before the callboard to check over her cues, she could not focus. Might the stagehand be miserable enough to starve himself to death? She looked to the ceiling. *I wouldn't be surprised if he did.*

The curtain-raiser concluded, and the audience applauded politely. At any moment, the overture to the incidental music would begin.

Near the prompt corner, she paced back and forth. *Am I ready?*

From the crowded stalls, the rumble of voices grew louder. By the sound of it, the performance must have sold out.

A series of powerful, godlike footsteps approached the playhouse, and the casing began to rattle—so badly that the sash weights smacked against one another.

She walked back toward the stage door, and she looked through the window to the narrow ghetto lane. "*Der golem.*"

As the creature made its way into the playhouse, the incidental music's evocative, klezmer-style overture commenced.

Manon took her place on the stage, at which point everyone appearing in the first scene wished each other well.

Inbal studied her. "What's the trouble?" the young lady asked. "Are you feeling a touch of stage fright?"

Before Manon could answer, the grand drape went up—and how blindingly bright the spotlight.

The first act unfolded uneventfully, and the second act proceeded along well, too. Soon enough, the tumultuous third act turned to that part of the story in which *der golem* battles the mob and triumphally defends the ghetto.

Backstage, Manon fussed with an old cue sheet. Still brooding over Lazzaro's fate, she inadvertently knocked over a bottle of nose putty. Her misshapen ear twitching on and on, she sat down in the corner and proceeded to sulk like a little girl.

"What's wrong?" a stagehand asked her. "Maybe you fear the critics? Do you fear bad reviews?"

"No, it's nothing like that," she answered. "I fear for Lazzaro, that's all. Do you think he might be capable of killing himself?"

The stagehand made a face. "*Oy*, maybe. Steinzig, he's a very strange one."

As the stagehand walked off, she returned to her feet and readied herself for the upcoming scene.

When the time arrived, she persevered the best that she could. Before she knew it, the lengthy third act had concluded—and the grand drape went down.

The time had come to prepare for the afterpiece. Quickly, the stagehands arranged four muslin flats depicting a bone-white wall adorned with cobwebs, the backdrop representing the synagogue's attic storeroom—the place where the monster would sleep its eternal slumber amid a heap of tattered Torah scrolls wrapped in soft, fleecy mantles.

When the stagehands completed their task, she donned her headscarf and collected the prayer book. Thoughts of Lazzaro weighing upon her yet, she assumed her place between the recumbent *golem* and the actor portraying the wise, old sorcerer.

The grand drape went up, and each one of the players recited his or her lines in the properly solemn tone.

How beautiful every dramaturgical detail, especially the way the creature's breath dissolved into the palpable mist conjured by the footlights.

Twice, the sorcerer stroked his long, gray beard. Then he knelt at the monster's feet.

The floorboards sagging beneath the creature's ponderous weight, Manon looked to the catwalks high above. What if the stage were to give way and everyone were to fall into the trap room? She looked down, and she opened the ornate prayer book. The time had come for her to read the benediction, after which she would reach down and remove the charm from between the monster's eyes. *And then* . . .

A series of thunderous footsteps resounded from the lobby. As the audience stirred all throughout the darkened stalls, a second *golem* crashed through the house doors and marched forward. The intruder must have stood at least twelve feet tall, the brute decked out in silvery plate armor with fluting. Most disturbing of all, the monster's maniacal eyes reeled around like sprocket flywheels.

Just look at that thing. She gasped, but she could not move a muscle.

As the audience raced for the exits, the intruder shrieked opprobrium and then continued toward the stage.

Her hands and fingers numb and tingling in the most peculiar way, she dropped the prayer book. "Who the hell are *you*? What're you doing here?"

The second *golem* failed to answer. Instead, it grabbed the proper *golem* by the ankle and pulled the creature down into the orchestra pit. Then, as all the musicians scrambled this way and that, the two foes flailed away so wildly that they soon managed to topple every chair and music stand in their midst.

The other actors raced backstage, meanwhile, but Manon stood firm. "Go away," she shouted at the intruder.

Plainly oblivious, the second *golem* lifted the proper one and rolled back. With a cacophonous crash then, the impact wholly obliterated the orchestra-pit floor—and both colossal figures fell some forty feet or more into the cellar.

In fear and trembling, she advanced onto the apron of the stage. Bathed in the limelight, she peered down into the gaping hole.

How terribly sinister: in the darkness below, the intruder's eyes popped and sparkled like overloaded electrical circuits.

As everyone else in the company continued to huddle back toward the loading dock, she made her way downstairs. There, she paused beside the first *golem*.

The fall had put a terrific dent in its backbone. Even more alarming, *der golem* had lost the lifegiving gemstone that ought to reside within the groove between its eyes.

As the second one sat up, she approached some and then paused to study the creature.

Much like the art of down lighting, the glow from the gaping hole above fell onto the intruder in such a way as to illumine nothing more than the being's scalp and shoulders.

She shook her head in wonder. "What's the meaning of this?" she asked. "Where did you come from?" Wary of what the creature might do, she approached just a little bit more and then stopped beside a heap of wooden crates. "Did you take the gemstone?"

The intruder opened its palm to reveal the topaz charm. Then the creature spoke a few words—in perfect Yiddish, too.

"I don't speak the tongue," she announced.

"No? So, what would a good Gentile girl like you be doing in a place like this?" the creature asked her then.

"Never mind what I'd be doing here. Just give me the charm and go away."

"Are you English?" the intruder asked. Gently, he placed the gemstone upon the cellar floor and moved the precious object this way and that—as if it were a hand-blown glass marble and he would be a little boy playing a game of Chinese checkers.

She pointed at the charm. "Give me the goods and be gone."

The intruder began whistling the tune to an old Hebrew song. When he stopped, she lunged forward and grabbed the talisman.

Not two seconds later, the armored figure's chest plate opened. Inside stood a little person who had apparently been operating the second *golem* with a series of levers.

She placed her free hand against her chest. "What the devil? Who are *you*?"

The little person snickered, and he pointed at the topaz charm. "Return the plunder to me, won't you? After all, I earned it."

By now, she felt short of breath. "What's your name? Are you a jewel thief?"

Grinning all the while, the little person remained silent—and now he climbed down onto the cellar floor.

"Tell me something. Are you a Jew?"

"Yes, I'd be a Jew," he answered. "I'm a very wicked one, though. With me, it's one crime after the next. Like a snake in the grass."

For a time, she studied the peculiar fellow. "What's wrong with you? Haven't you got a conscience?"

"No, not at all. I'd be an evil genius. And that's the trouble. While my kind produces great thinkers in science and commerce and criticism, we also produce heartless *mamzerim* just like me. Within *every* nation, there's bound to be both good and bad. Regrettably."

Now she held the topaz piece very tight. "You ought to be ashamed of yourself for doing the kinds of things you do."

"Maybe so, but I'm not." At that point, the little person must have noticed the measure of her grief because he laughed all so insidiously.

Greatly sickened, she dropped the topaz at her feet.

Almost immediately, he collected the priceless talisman. Then, a crooked smile on his face, he held the gemstone up to her eyes. "Look into this fine piece," he told her. "Peer deep, deep inside."

She did as he told her, and for the very first time, noticed the Hebrew characters hovering *within* the gemstone. "What's all that?" she asked him.

"The letters signify the Tetragrammaton, the Ineffable Name. That's what grants any *golem* the power of life. At least that's what the Jews once believed. How foolish, no?"

She turned to a nest of affrighted mice darting about over to the side, and then she turned back. "How should it be that you despise your own people?"

"Don't take it personal. I despise everything."

"Oh? You must be the most decadent kind of—"

"I'm no worse than the prophets of Israel."

"The prophets? What're you talking about?"

"What am I talking about? Don't you know why they authored all those rhapsodical visions in which angels and messianic figures appear as living, breathing entities all fashioned from precious metals?"

"Give me back the charm and—"

"The prophets did it to conjure *fear*, yes, the kind of fear that promises propaganda value."

"That's absurd."

"No. They hoped to intimidate the people and to convince everyone how much stronger the so-called *living* God must be next to lifeless, immobile, forged-bronze idols."

By now, she had grown weary of all the talk. "Give me back the gemstone and—"

The thief placed the charm into his coat pocket. Then, as she reached for his lapels, he pushed her hand away and darted off.

She chased him up the stairway, and then she pursued him all throughout the stalls and out into the lobby.

When she tripped and hit her head, he paused at one of the lobby doors to look back at her and to laugh in his artful way.

Without a second thought, she shook her fist. Then she removed one of her shoes, and she hurled it at him.

Laughing yet, the mischievous thief continued outside.

Twice, she called out and demanded that he return.

When he failed to do so, she stood up and continued through the door and out into the winter night.

There was no sign of him anywhere.

She ran half a block and then, overwhelmed, stopped in her tracks. Her intuition told her that he must have continued through the passageway to the left—but now she realized that to do so would have been impossible, for the passageway proved to be a blind arch in the wall. *The evil genius, he's vanished into thin air.*

CHAPTER FIVE

Prague, 13 March.

That morning, Manon learned from Inbal that the play had officially closed.

Over and above the disturbance on opening night, a backlash against the production had been growing ever since one of the city's influential newspapers had published an open letter in which a glib, anonymous malcontent had protested the idea of a drama that lionized the Jews at a time when the League of Nations schemed to bring about the rebirth of Israel—an eventuality, which the nameless author considered a great affront to public morals.

Manon sat down on the edge of her bed. *What kind of coward hires the papers to print an anonymous letter?* She returned to her feet. *Don't the Jews enjoy a right to know their accuser's name? How else should the Jews ever hope to consider the source?* The more she thought about the letter, the more incensed she felt. *If the Jews haven't a right to know their accuser, then how should they make recriminations?* She donned her coat and walked off to Wenceslas Square.

As she sat beside the fountain, she thought of Stefan Zwinglius—the chap who had presented the magic-lantern presentation. *Did* he *author the letter?*

Desperate for answers, she finally returned to the ghetto.

As she passed through the gates, a voice called out and greeted her in a snide tone.

The speaker proved to be a venture capitalist from New York City, a financier who had recently invested heavily in the Yiddish Repertory Theatre.

Though she did not know him well, Manon had always regarded him as a touch too condescending.

Now he sat down upon an empty pickle barrel standing in the walkway. "So, do you plan to attend Lazzaro's court appearance?"

"Lazzaro? He's going before the judge today?" Already, she felt guilty—for she should have known. As the businessman snickered, she looked to her feet. "What do you care what I do or where I go?" she asked him. "For all you know . . ."

The self-satisfied American crossed his legs. "Have you the money to post bail? Even if you did, what would it matter? The judge, he'll revoke bail because what kind of sucker would think to stand surety for Lazzaro? He's the village idiot, that *schnook*. Besides, the whole case, it's already resolved. They've served the suspect the papers, and they've obtained any and all statements the judge might require. He'll not even pen a jury summons because your hapless friend doesn't even *merit* a trial by jury. Why should anyone have to offer testimony when everyone knows what the dunce went and did?"

She felt ill. For one thing, she must have been sensitive to the American's oak-moss cologne. Much worse than that, though, the gentleman's tone of voice served to remind her of a smug head-mistress who had once lectured her on "how confused a young lady would have to be to consider her Sapphic predilections some-thing natural or inborn."

The American shook his head now. "Your friend ought to serve time. What else might the courts do to him? Garnish his wages? Ah, but your friend has nothing to collect. Even though his granduncle did quite well in the garment industry, Lazzaro himself never earned one damn penny."

"Pardon me, but—"

"Lazzaro got what he deserved. He's simply got to learn to be more patient with other people's *opinions*."

She continued along on her way, but then she stopped beside the bakery. *Might Lazzaro make good on his threat to starve himself to death?* Before he did, why not befriend the wretch and encourage him to live? She turned to the bakery's window. *Perhaps I'll bring him a crust of bread.* Uncertain as to Lazzaro's preferences, she walked inside and procured a loaf of almond bread, a loaf of braided-egg sabbath bread, and a loaf of sourdough rye, too.

At one o'clock, she reached the Hall of Justice. Once inside the crowded courtroom, she chose a place at the back. Before long, she glanced at her timepiece.

Hopefully, the jailhouse guards would bring Lazzaro along sooner rather than later.

A newspaperman with a mischievous smirk sauntered into the courtroom and took a place in the press box.

She recognized him as a self-righteous crime reporter for the English-language edition of *die Prager Zeitung*.

The newspaperman had recently penned a most unfriendly exposé on the whole petty affair. In reference to Lazzaro's imprudence, the newspaperman had included a whole litany of platitudes regarding the merits of "*free speech.*" At the end of the column, the newspaperman had concluded the piece with a cheap-shot insult posing as a question: "*Why are Jews so paranoid?*"

Along the opposite wall, the door opened—and now a guard walked into the courtroom, followed by a solicitor.

A moment later, Lazzaro followed along—the captive in shackles, a crimson boil upon the tip of his nose.

Amusingly, when he assumed his place in the prisoner's box, a shaft of sunlight streamed in through the window and made the boil glow even more brightly.

As quickly as she could, she grabbed the bread and drew close.

"I've brought you something from the bakery," she whispered, sitting in a chair just behind him.

Plainly ashamed and despondent, he would not even acknowledge her.

The door to the judge's chambers opened, meanwhile, and a thin, angry man in full gowns proceeded toward the magistrate's bench.

When the deputy bailiff turned to the crowded courtroom and ordered everyone to stand, her pride would not permit her to comply. How to resist the chance to show her contempt for the whole proceeding?

The judge took his place, at which point the deputy bailiff asked everyone to sit.

As everyone else did, she almost laughed to herself. Then she fussed with the bag of bread for no other reason than to make noise. What better way to demonstrate her disdain?

The judge scrunched over to read through the bill of indictment, and then he looked up and called Lazzaro's solicitor to the bench.

When the solicitor walked back to the prisoner's box, he promptly whispered something into Lazzaro's ear—and now the servile fool nodded in the most beggarly manner.

She leaned forward and tapped upon his shoulder. "What's happened? Have you decided to plead guilty? Don't do it. Argue the notion that the agitator would be responsible. Here's what you should say. 'The whole affair, it was nothing more than the age-old sport of Jew-baiting.'"

Lazzaro ignored her, as did his solicitor.

Just like that, every muscle in her body grew rigid. "Don't surrender. Demand that the judge dismiss the charges."

No sooner had she grown quiet than the judge delivered the verdict, announced the one-year sentence, and then struck the sounding block with his gavel.

Miserable, she dropped the bread into the rubbish bin and returned outside.

Three blocks away, she sat down beside a toppled lamppost and wept.

Hours later, as the darkness of dusk invaded the day, a gentleman came by pushing a sausage cart.

The air having filled with the aroma of pork and charcoal, she resolved to follow along.

When the sausage vendor reached Wenceslas Square, he arranged a dogwood-rose canopy over the cart and then proceeded to sell his *bratwurst*.

She sat down beside the fountain, closed her eyes, and went lost in fantasy.

Already, she has helped Lazzaro to escape the jailhouse. And now they take a little steam train from Prague to Budapest, where they board the Orient Express.

After the cabin steward engages them in a bit of repartee, she guides Lazzaro into the club car that they might celebrate his freedom.

What a feast, too—veal cordon bleu, Hungarian mushroom soup, and for dessert, sultana raisins and Turkish delight.

When the Orient Express reaches Bucharest, Lazzaro turns to her. "Where are we going?" he asks.

She smiles then. "It's a secret," she tells him.

Sometime later, when they reach Istanbul, she takes him to a bathhouse. Afterward, feeling refreshed, they dress in robes and silky babouche slippers.

And now she draws close. "From here, we'll walk overland to Palestine. Honest, it's not so far. When we grow sleepy, we'll sleep in meadows of warm, fresh asphodel. And as soon as we reach the Promised Land, we'll go into business together. We'll open a bakery and make bread and cookies and . . ."

Wenceslas Square grew noisy, and she opened her eyes. Feeling directionless and deflated, she returned to the ghetto. When she stopped by Inbal's place, she found the young lady looking as unhealthful as ever. "Why don't you consult a physician?" Manon asked her.

"It's not necessary," Inbal insisted. "My jaundice, it's nothing. Just bile pigments floating in my blood, nothing more."

As Inbal spoke, Manon realized that she had packed all her belongings into an array of paperboard boxes and steamer trunks. "Going somewhere?"

Inbal sat down upon one of the steamer trunks. "I'm sailing to New York City. And do you know what I'll do when I get there? Maybe I'll audition for the Ziegfeld Follies."

Manon's leg shook violently. "Don't go. You and me and Lazzaro ought to stay together and travel off to Palestine. Won't that be an adventure?" When Inbal failed to respond, Manon climbed out the dormer window—and now it was her turn to descend to the eaves and to stand with her toes extending over the edge.

Inbal followed along. "What are you doing out here?"

Manon refused to even answer. Feeling giddy, she teetered backward and forward. *What if I fall? Would I let out a shriek?*

Inbal let out an exaggerated sigh. "You should not be feeling cross. I must go. The fortune teller, Madame de Thèbes, she tells me to sail for *Amerika*, yes, each time I visit her shop down on Golden Lane." As a hard rain commenced, Inbal drew closer. "Are you trying to get yourself killed? Listen, you must not mimic what I do."

"Why not? Anything you can do I can do better."

"*No.* I've got the power to commune with the emanations that brought about the creation of the world."

Manon laughed very quietly. "Why must you be so theatrical?" she asked then. "You have no power to—"

"*Listen.* If I were to step forward, I wouldn't fall. No, I'd instantaneously traverse the length of the creation, and my foot would touch down at the edge of the cosmos. *Honest.* So, please. Come back inside."

With bared teeth, Manon fixed her gaze upon the horizon. *Oh, the vanishing point.* She envisioned some glorious prize awaiting her there, something that she might take into her hand and hold all so tight. *Yes, a sharp, pitiless, prickly pear.*

CHAPTER SIX

Prague, 18 April.

Early that morning, Manon resolved to call upon Lazzaro. Considering that he had been starving himself these past four weeks, she just had to get through to him. *Before it's too late.*

At eight o'clock, when she reached the jailhouse, the corrections deputy ushered her into the visiting room.

A diminutive guard with mousy hair sat down beside her. On and on, the little fellow whistled the tune to a sacred Hebrew melody. Did he mean to mock her? Perhaps he assumed her to be Lazzaro's sister.

As a matter of fact, she did rather feel like a relation. At least in *her* mind, a bond had always existed between them. As such, no matter how sinister the whistling, she acted as if she had not even recognized the tune. *Why give the awful louse the satisfaction?* Calmly, she stood up and walked over to the window. *Patience.*

Soon enough, Lazzaro would knock on the door—and then the guard would lift the crossbar to let him inside.

Twenty minutes passed by.

Where could he be? She walked over to the door marked *Damentoilette.* Then she turned around and caught a glimpse of the guard walking over to the door marked *Herrentoilette.*

Finally, she continued into the ladies' washroom.

The chamber proved to be very dark, and the whole place smelled like spirit of turpentine.

As she paced back and forth, she could hear the guard whistling through the washroom wall—the sly fellow acting as if nothing could be more natural than to be performing a sacred Hebrew melody while standing at a disgusting, malodorous urinal.

She kicked loose a green-slate tile, and then she returned through the door.

When the guard returned into the visiting room, he grew very quiet.

Nervous, she looked over her shoulder. "So, what was that song you were whistling a moment ago? Might that have been Louis Saladin's '*Canticum hebraicum*?'"

Twice, the guard belched. Then he recommenced with the ironic serenade.

She stood up as straight as possible. "Let me out into the enclosure," she told him. "*Lass mich meinen freund finden.*" When he refused, she turned to the guard standing in the opposite corner.

What a big, heartless bully.

Feeling submissive, she flashed a servile smile.

The big bully rolled his hate-filled eyes, as if her inappropriate display had served to burden the whole of his being.

She marched over to the door, and she lifted the crossbar. *Just go.* To that end, she continued outside.

The jailhouse yard proved to be quite vast. There was no grass, though. If anything, the earth resembled a field of glacial dust. As for the indomitable walls, they rose in every direction at least forty feet—the claystone a deep, sickly gray presently bleeding into a shade of Egyptian blue.

At first, the yard seemed to be empty. Then she espied what looked like a heap of rags lying on the ground some eighty yards away. *Might* that *be Lazzaro?*

The clouds shifted, and in the same way that a key light floods the stage, the sun illumined the mysterious jumble.

Yes, that's Lazzaro lying there.

She shot a glance back at the door, and then she drew close to the miserable penitent.

Badly emaciated, Lazzaro lay beside a puddle of oil glistening with an array of rainbow-like colors.

She knelt beside him. "*Aufwachen. Setzen sie sich auf.*"

His frail body shifted some, and the young man glanced at her with something like repulsion in his eyes.

As unpleasant as his expression was, it made her think of a birthday party that she had attended when she was a little girl. Just as she had looked at her dish, she had espied a lengthy, grotesque hair tangled about the dollop of otherwise immaculate ice cream. With the tips of her fingers, she had collected the silky strand and had dropped it onto the floor. Still, the knowledge of the hair's erstwhile presence had proven more than enough to sustain her disgust. As a result, she had continued to study the faint, serpentine groove, where the unsightly thread had lain only a moment before—and like a beloved saint bound to resist all temptation, she had found herself powerless to consume even one spoonful.

His empty belly rumbling, Lazzaro turned to the godly, linen-white zenith.

As he did, she returned to her feet. "I can't let you starve yourself. Perhaps I'll tell the jailer to force-feed you."

Neither did Lazzaro answer, nor did he turn to look at her.

Gently, she nudged him with her foot. "If you keep yourself alive, do you know what we'll do? Once you get out of here, we'll sail away to Palestine."

He flashed a sad smile. "I'm a *half*-Jew," he whispered. "I belong in Palestine the way poor Ishmael did. Perhaps I ought to wander off across the desert and find my way to—"

"No, listen. Out along a stretch of dunes, the Jews have gone and built a quaint, little hamlet they call Tel Aviv. Have you heard of the place? It's my understanding the Jews went and named the town after an ancient, mythical place of refuge somewhere in Mesopotamia. Anyway, we'll live there. Like the daughters of Lilith."

"The daughters of Lilith? They live in Tel Aviv, do they?"

"Yes, haven't you ever attended that British picture show? The one all about how the daughters of Lilith come to live amid the orange groves. The film was a big flop, but I myself served on the crew and—"

"No, you didn't."

"Yes, I did. That's how come I know all about the daughters of Lilith. The dæmoness, she conceives each one of her babies by flying through the night and enticing those gentlemen who come to her attention. So, the daughters of Lilith, they'd be *half* sisters, each and every misbegotten one of them. Just like you'd be a misbegotten *half* Jew."

For a time, Lazzaro closed his eyes—almost as if he heard some faint lullaby ringing in his ears.

In the hope that it might regain Lazzaro's attention, Manon whistled the same sacred tune that the sadistic guard had been whistling.

At last, Lazzaro opened his eyes.

She smiled then. "I know. When we reach Palestine, we'll live somewhere amid the rolling dunes and scrub. And do you know what we'll do to make a living? We'll open up a bakeshop and, we'll make fresh bread and—"

"Yes, we'll build the bakery on a stretch of beach," Lazzaro whispered. "A stretch of beach as desolate as the Isle of the Hesperides."

"Oh, but not *too* desolate," Manon insisted. "As soon as we get there, we'll be sure to plant bellflowers with heart-shaped leaves and . . ."

Lazzaro laughed very quietly. Then he muttered something about a travel sketch that he had once read—a volume in which the Orientalist authoress had described a grove of Judas trees standing on the outskirts of Jerusalem.

Judas trees. For the longest time, Manon remained silent. *How to get through to someone so sardonic?*

The whole of the yard grew deathly quiet, and the feeling all so solemn.

Lazzaro's eyes grew wide then, as if he espied something miraculous hovering in the zenith. With his frail, trembling arm, he reached up. "Look at the sky," he whispered. "Won't it be good to depart this life and fly far away?"

"Don't talk like that," Manon told him.

"What do you suppose should happen when I'm gone?" he asked, his arm falling back to earth. "Do you think the people back in the ghetto should drape linen shrouds over the mirrors in remembrance of me?" As if he knew that no one would, Lazzaro laughed a second time—so hard that he passed a bit of gas. Fatigued as he was by his hunger strike, he did not look to be the least bit ashamed.

When he turned back onto his side, his left trouser cuff rode up his shin just enough to reveal how remarkably thin his leg had become—all of it sallow skin and brittle bone. "Do you want to hear something funny?" he asked now. "When my father married a Gentile woman, his family performed a mock funeral on his behalf." With that, Lazzaro lay dead.

Bereft of speech, Manon marveled at how serene his expression.

The door leading into the cellblock opened, and the jailers permitted some other penitent, a raggedy old man, to come outside. He drew close to Manon and coughed noisily—just the way some playgoer always seems to make noise during one of those crucial interludes when both the director and the company would have preferred absolute silence.

She returned to the visiting-room door, and she knocked twice.

When the malevolent little guard finally let her pass through, she proceeded outside into the street.

Two blocks east, a sleek, black Mercedes Simplex very nearly ran her down.

Then, as the motorcar sped away, a little blue party balloon came darting about at her knees.

Could it be Lazzaro's soul?

The toy balloon sailed higher and higher, until it vanished into a cloud shaped like a patch of wild blue stonecrops.

Goodbye, Lazzaro.

In the evening, she returned to the ghetto.

A frigid, springtime breeze blew steadily through the winding streets, and the air reeked of sewer gas commingled with kosher plum brandy.

With nowhere better to go, she strolled over to the synagogue.

As she entered the building, an aged scholar looking like the lawgiver himself began to chant a prayer piece.

She imagined that it must be Kaddish, but now she felt embarrassed. After all, the notion that the piece might be the prayer for the dead would be too perfect—too poetic.

The aged scholar concluded the prayer, wheezed a few times, and then grew quiet.

Softly, hauntingly, the vaulted ceiling creaked.

She opened the door to the stairway leading to the storeroom above. Though half certain that someone would come along at any moment to protest her trespass, she made her way up to the attic's doorsill.

Without pause, the nighttime breeze blew through the rafter vents and baffles.

For a time, she lay down beside the books stacked up alongside the very westernmost baseboard. When she felt something sharp against her right hip, she reached down to discover a cracked ram's horn stuffed with sabbath candles. Once she had removed all the tapers, she lifted the ram's horn up in the hope that the current might begin to play through the crude instrument's mouthpiece. When nothing happened, she tossed the horn to the side.

If only the actor who had been portraying *der golem* had stowed away his costume in this very place. As numb as she felt, she longed to crawl inside the disguise and to imagine herself something nonexistent—just another defunct, lifeless god.

CHAPTER SEVEN

Somewhere Amid the Gulf of Venice, 29 May.

Not long after the SS *Exilarch* had put out to sea, Manon approached the ship's railing and looked back upon the lights of Trieste. *I'm sailing away.*

Already, the crowded passenger ship had traveled as many as three nautical miles from the bustling seaport. In no time, the hills and vales of the Dalmatian coast would be passing by on her port side. And soon, the vessel would reach the Port of Jaffa.

Manon just had to go. In the same way that she had dedicated her service as a nurse's helpmate to Sabine, so Manon would establish a little bakery in Palestine and name it something meaningful: Lazzaro's Place.

A white squall descended upon the ship. At once, a clamor awoke from the direction of the galley: falling pots and pans, clattering tea skillets and steam kettles. Meanwhile, a cracked lifeboat hanging parallel to the bulwark rattled uncontrollably.

The violent interlude made her think back to earlier in the day—the rumor that some mad bomber intended to sink the ship.

For several hours, the ship's captain and all his crewmen had searched both the cargo hold and steerage, too.

Had a saboteur planted an explosive device?

The waters grew calm now, and a tranquil mist of ghost-white steam poured from the galley chimney.

She smoothed out her skirt, and she dusted off her jumper. *There.* Despite the return to calm weather, she did not feel any better. The frenzied beat of her heart pulsating yet, she placed her right hand over her left breast and squeezed as hard as she could. What if an explosive charge did in fact detonate at some point in the night? Great pandemonium would be sure to follow, the ship's bell ringing and everyone shrieking.

From the direction of the officers' promenade, a crewman with a handlebar mustache walked by.

"Did you feel the windstorm a moment ago?" she asked him. "What if it happens again but the ship can't hold together?"

"Don't you fear for nothing," he answered in a thick, Italian accent. "This ship here, she's unsinkable. *Il migliore di sempre.*" With a grin, the crewman removed a Catholic tractate from his coat pocket and placed the little booklet in her hand. "You take this, please. For good luck, yes?"

As the crewman walked away, she placed the tractate in the same skirt pocket in which she had placed her travel papers. Then she turned back to the railing, and she looked out to sea.

The moonlight broke through the clouds and shone upon the waters—and now the waves acquired a fine shade of cadet blue.

In the newfound light, there could be no mistaking a large school of frenzied sea snakes darting about off to starboard. Had they only just traveled all this way from their spawning reef in the Sargasso Sea? If so, they would be eager to find the mouth to some promising, bountiful river.

She thought back to her school days and recalled a natural-science lecture. According to the instructor, once the water snakes had lived out their lives, the curious creatures would return into the gulf—and then they would swim back through the Pillars of Hercules. Later, when they reached the Sargasso Sea, each one would procreate. *And afterward, the breeders must vanish into the abyss.*

The sea breeze having died out, a strong land breeze blew across the ship's deck. And now several tattered nautical charts sailed by.

After a while, she no longer felt alone. *Someone's coming.*

From within the long, crooked shadow of the galley chimney, a figure with a greatly curved back emerged: an old man all bundled up in a somber cloak. He also wore a traditional *shtreiml*, the peculiar hat comprised of some thirteen sable foxtails.

Very slowly, the old man passed by the mast—and then he continued all the way back to the vessel's stern.

As if enthralled by the ship's wake, he stood there for almost thirty minutes.

Intrigued by the old man's prominent brow and disfigured spine, she could not help but stare. *My but he looks familiar. Maybe he's the reincarnation of Moses Mendelssohn.*

When the old man turned forward, he walked up to the place where she stood. Before long, he spoke up to say something in what sounded like French—but he did so with a distinct, incomprehensible, Portuguese accent. Even more irksome, his breath reeked of boiled beer and onion bread.

Manon's parched throat filled with the very same odors. Despite all, she managed a quick smile. "Do you speak any English?" she asked him.

At first, the old man did not answer. Instead, he reached into his coat and removed an ear trumpet.

She repeated the question.

The old man smirked. "Yes, I speak the King's English." And now he paused for a moment, as if debating whether he ought to introduce himself. Gently then, he poked her with the end of the ear trumpet. "I am Benny Moskowitz alias Gideon T. Ostrovsky alias, the one and only Jonah Lipschitz. But you no call me any of these names. Maybe it'd be best if you call me only Reuben P. Levinsky. No, no. Reuben P. *Liebling*." Again, the old man thought for a time before shaking his head. "No, think of me as Josiah C. Hollander. Yes, that'd be a convincing name for a hunchback. Who could ever doubt it?"

She did not introduce herself, for she believed the old man to be a swindler—the kind who cheated someone and then blamed the mark for being foolish enough to let the raw deal happen in the first place.

The old man must have noticed the expression of mistrust in her face, for he smirked yet again. "Are you not feeling well? So, maybe you'll be feeding the fishes soon?"

With a shrug, she turned back to the railing and looked out upon the waters.

Once more, the old man poked her—this time in her shoulder blade. "Why are you sailing to Palestine? You'd be a Jewess, maybe? Yes, you must think the covenant everlasting between the Lord and the blessed patriarchs should oblige you to live there. Yes, you think the authorities ought to let you settle there, yes, for you'd command an immemorial, common-law claim."

She removed the sackcloth ball from her coat pocket, and as she turned her gaze back to the waters, held the torture device as tightly as she could.

The old man tugged at his beard, meanwhile. "I've got an idea," he whispered. "Given all the animosity brewing here and there, you'll tell the Brits that it's a matter of life and death that you find safe haven. Yes, you'll sell yourself as a *refugee*."

She resolved to ignore the old man, and she fixed her gaze upon the faint lights of a distant fishing village.

Soon, not one nautical mile away, a fine old sloop passed by— an elegant moonsail flying atop her mast.

Again, the old man poked Manon in the back. "You should know something. Where you'd be going, it's a place of never-ending war. And like the Mameluke Empire, and for that matter the Sultanate, no one's bound to welcome you. Not unless you've got enough to pay for a dunam of land and the property taxes, too."

She tightened her grip on the ship's railing.

Again, the old man poked her. *"Listen.* I know how you'll convince the English to let you stay in Palestine for as long as you please. When you disembark, you should tell the fellow in the customs house that you wish to come work for the Palestine Exploration Society. Just like all the other Jews do, the rats and vermin, too, you mean to crawl through the tunnels and chambers that house the ruins of the *ancient* cities. Yes, tell the English you'd be looking for—"

"When I get to Palestine, I mean to found a profitable, little bakeshop," she told the old man, over her shoulder. "I'll bake lovely things, too. Olive-oil bread and wedding cakes and cheese bread and muffin loaves and . . ."

"Do you want me to invest? Well, I won't do it because it's only a matter of time before war destroys the Mandate. So, don't talk to me about the blessings of peace. Such prating might be good for business, but that's all."

"Honestly, you must be the most cynical, depraved lout who ever—"

"Let me tell you something. Where you're going, the combatants compare one another to the worst, most murderous of fiends. And when one side laments its losses, do you realize what the rival says about the others' dead? 'But they weren't even human,' he says. Yes, because in this world, a partisan only ever indulges him-*self* in the pride of victimhood." With that, the old man turned south. "All across the world, so many tense peoples long to release their stress and heal the wounds of the past and remedy all fears of the future," he continued. "Yes, that's why they'll welcome the rebirth of Israel, for they require a scapegoat to despise. And who wouldn't want some kind of refuse heap upon which to dump his darkest emotions? And just what could make for a better heap than *der Judenstaat?"*

She grew very ill, and as she vomited over the railing, her throat filled with the taste of horseradish. And now she staggered over to the side, and she slammed her shoulder against the life-boat's forward thwart.

For his part, the old man muttered something unintelligible and then sauntered off.

The masthead light blew out then, and now the steady, power-ful, *basso profundo* rumble of the ship's engines seemed to resound much more deeply. Most alarming of all, the ominous-sounding engines made the whole of the weather deck rattle.

She thought of all the magnificent steamships lost at sea—the HMS *Utopia*, so many others, too. Whenever a vessel like that would find herself on the verge of sinking, of course, a distress signal would go out. And as the boiler room flooded and all the sea waters deluged the coal bunkers, the first mate would fire off a flare—the sudden burst of marshmallow-white light shining as bright as a thousand or more skyrockets on Bonfire Night.

The SS *Exilarch* reduced speed, and her engines grew quiet.

Up in the wheelhouse, the door opened—and now the ship's captain appeared. As the officer smoked his tobacco pipe, he looked to the stars.

For a time, she herself contemplated some of the breathtaking constellations. Then she closed her eyes and sought to picture her bakery—the tables and chairs, the big rack oven, the workbench. And now she imagined Lazzaro's ghost visiting her one day, the specter perhaps materializing right there in the kitchen.

"Stop punishing yourself," he would tell her. "No more self-hatred. No more self-flagellation. No more prickly pears. *Live.*"

From across the waters, a dull thump resounded.

Something's out there. She opened her eyes. *Could it be someone working a rudder?* She clasped her hands together. *What if a band of terrorists draws close?* As the mysterious noise grew louder, she began to pant. *Do they intend to affix a bomb to the ship's plating?*

At last, she cleared her throat and gripped the railing tight. "Who's out there?" she asked in a whisper.

Off to port, a capsized fishing vessel with a badly damaged starboard bow floated by.

It was nothing at all. She dropped the sackcloth ball over the railing, and the object slipped beneath the rippling waves.

A moment later, the waters turned to a pleasing shade of pine green streaked with celestial blue.

ACKNOWLEDGMENTS

A thank you to Brooke Warner, Samantha Strom, and everyone else at SparkPress.

And a thank you to Erica Martin, Simone Jung, Elysse Wagner, and everyone else at Books Forward.

ABOUT THE AUTHOR

Photo credit: Jeannette Palsa

M. Laszlo is a reclusive author from Ohio. *The Phantom Glare of Day* is his first book and follows from an unpublished diary of travel sketches that he made while living in London. He lives in Bath, OH.

SELECTED TITLES FROM SPARKPRESS

SparkPress is an independent boutique publisher delivering high-quality, entertaining, and engaging content that enhances readers' lives, with a special focus on female-driven work. www.gosparkpress.com

The Takeaway Men: A Novel, Meryl Ain, $16.95, 978-1-68463-047-9. Twin sisters Bronka and JoJo Lubinski are brought to America from Germany by their Polish refugee parents after World War II—but in "idyllic" America, political, cultural, and family turmoil awaits them. As the girls grow older, they eventually begin to ask questions of and demand the truth from their parents.

Child Bride: A Novel, Jennifer Smith Turner, $16.95, 978-1-68463-038-7. The coming-of-age journey of a young girl from the South who joins the African American great migration to the North—and finds her way through challenges and unforeseen obstacles to womanhood.

Seventh Flag: A Novel, Sid Balman, Jr. $16.95, 978-1-68463-014-1. A sweeping work of historical fiction, *Seventh Flag* is a Micheneresque parable that traces the arc of radicalization in modern Western Civilization—reaffirming what it means to be an American in a dangerously divided nation.

Girl with a Gun: An Annie Oakley Mystery, Kari Bovée, $16.95, 978-1-943006-60-1. When a series of crimes take place soon after fifteen-year-old Annie Oakley joins Buffalo Bill's Wild West Show, including the mysterious death of her Indian assistant, Annie fears someone is out to get her. With the help of a sassy, blue-blooded reporter, Annie sets out to solve the crimes that threaten her good name.

Peccadillo at the Palace: An Annie Oakley Mystery, Kari Bovée. $16.95, 978-1-943006-90-8. In this second book in the Annie Oakley Mystery series, Annie and Buffalo Bill's Wild West Show are invited to Queen Victoria's Jubilee celebration in England, but when a murder and a suspicious illness lead Annie to suspect an assassination attempt on the queen, she sets out to discover the truth.

Trouble the Water: A Novel, Jacqueline Friedland. $16.95, 978-1-943006-54-0. When a young woman travels from a British factory town to South Carolina in the 1840s, she becomes involved with a vigilante abolitionist and the Underground Railroad while trying to navigate the complexities of Charleston high society and falling in love.